Dale Mayer

Rare Find

Book 6

Psychic Visions

RARE FIND
Dale Mayer
Valley Publishing
Copyright © 2014

ISBN: 1927461782
ISBN-13: 978-1927461785

DEDICATION

This book is dedicated to my four children who always believed in me and my storytelling abilities.

Thank you!

ACKNOWLEDGMENTS

Rare Find wouldn't have been possible without the support of my friends and family. Many hands helped with proofreading, editing, and beta reading to make this book come together.

I thank you all.

Chapter 1

Saturday early afternoon

"I hate to leave you right now," Ronin murmured against her hair. "You shouldn't be alone today, of all days."

Tabitha Stoddard tilted her head and sniffled back the tears. She managed a watery smile. "There's no quick fix for this. I just need time. I'll reminisce about my grandfather today and that will help. Go to the station and speak with your detectives. You need to deal with the phone call." She took a deep bracing breath and added, "I'm fine."

And she would be fine. It just might take awhile.

He looked at her, doubt forcing his gaze to narrow and his lips to twist. She reached up and kissed him lightly. "Go."

"I'll check in with you when I'm done."

She nodded and watched as he walked back to his truck and drove out of Exotic Landscape's parking lot. She was grateful he'd been there for her grandfather's funeral that morning. His presence had made everything so much easier.

Smiling, she turned and walked into the center. Her three-legged bull mastiff greeted her joyously. Even missing his back lower leg, he was one heck of a watch dog.

Just like Ronin who was a protector, a cop, a strong man with strong morals and ethics. A good man. A man's man. And one she'd fallen in love with.

Not that he knew it. They hadn't gotten to that stage yet. She'd planned to stay over at his place this weekend, but her grandfather's death had changed all that.

With tears burning her eyes, Tabitha stared at the picture of her standing beside her grandfather that hung behind his desk. He'd been the mainstay of her life. He'd raised her, shared his passion with her, and although there had been little softness in him, he'd been there for her every step of the way.

Unlike her father who was only there when it was convenient for him.

She snatched up yet another tissue off the desk and blew her nose. How could there still be tears? She'd done nothing but cry bucketfuls for days. Heart hurting, she wandered into his old office. He'd lived sixty-seven years and should have had another twenty to go. The doctors said it was his heart.

She didn't have a hard time believing that. As much as she loved her grandfather, she had no illusions that others would feel the same way. He'd had little heart for anyone else. He was hard. Cold. Unyielding, and unless you walked on four feet or were his granddaughter, he wouldn't give you the time of day. And that included his son and his brother, her uncle who had died when she was just a kid.

But, despite his faults, she'd loved her grandfather.

And the hole in her heart seemed too vast to ever heal.

Tripod nudged her hip with his muzzle. She reached down and laid a comforting hand on his head. He'd been by her side since she'd found him in a back alley on one of her and her grandfather's rare trips into Seattle. Her grandfather had abhorred the city and the minions that scurried around in it. She, on the other hand, had craved it while she was a teen, but after spending time at a girlfriend's place, dead center in the chaos, she'd been only too grateful to return to her wooded acres…and her animals.

She had lots of friends – of the female kind. And although she'd given it a good try, until Ronin she'd found little to commend two-legged males and risking deeper human relationships.

She admired women like her friend, Shay Lassiter. Shay combined her daily work, a partner and her psychic abilities into something that worked for her.

In Tabitha's case, she could do the work, no problem. The partner issue had so far escaped her best attempts, although she had high hopes with Ronin. That detective made her want all sorts of things in life that had eluded her. Like marriage. A family. It was fresh right now. Special. Just the thought of him made her toes wiggle and her heart sigh with happiness – and they hadn't even made it to bed yet.

Her grandfather's old desk caught her gaze – scarred, with broken drawers and bolts for handles, it was decrepit. As she stared she realized that somewhere along the way the desk had lost its leg and he'd propped it up with whatever was handy – in this case, several bricks. Typical. He'd insisted on keeping it, saying that as long as he could keep using it, it wasn't really broken – was it?

Unfortunately, the rest of his office was full of the same and most of it would need to go to the dump after she'd gone through it.

She randomly opened drawers, wondering at the collection of aged papers inside. Dennis – her mostly absent father – had already gone through the desk looking for documents he'd need to settle her grandfather's estate. He even took her grandfather's old ornate box – the one she'd seen many times over the years, but had never looked inside.

Grandfather had told her it contained private papers, hence her father taking it. He'd likely hand it over to Eric, his assistant, or his partner Germaine, instead of dealing with it himself. Tabitha was fine with that. Easier on her.

She cast a final glance around the messy room.

Her grandfather's true legacy lay outside the main buildings in the acres long ago turned into an animal reserve. And though it was expensive to run, her grandfather never shortchanged the animals' needs. He'd go without a meal rather than see his beloved pets do the same.

She'd learned that lesson well. As she stared down at the ripped jeans she'd changed into after the funeral, she realized she might have learned it a little too well. There was money, but only enough to cover the necessities. There were always more animals in need than resources at hand.

In spite of the poor relationship her grandfather had with his son, Exotic Landscape wouldn't have achieved this size or capacity without her father's donations. Guilt money. Then Shay's Foundation money had taken the place to the next level.

Sniffling, she wiped her eyes and turned too fast. Her head pounded and the room swayed around her.

Damn. When would the hurting stop?

She lost time as she sat in the office and let the pain roll.

Her phone rang. She sniffled, until call display showed it was Ronin. Her flagging energy lifted. He always did that to her.

"Hey." She walked over to the window to stare out into the late afternoon sun as she spoke into the phone. "How did it go? Are you done?"

"Yeah, it was probably a waste of time," he said humorlessly. "But I had to check it out. Sorry about having to leave."

"Not an issue," she said tiredly. "It's the job."

"It is," he agreed, "but it's still difficult when being a cop interferes with my personal life. Especially at times like this."

Traffic noises from his phone blocked out everything else for a few seconds. Abruptly, he added, "I'll still be a few hours. Do you want me to stop by afterwards?"

Her heart screamed *yes*, but...she could also use some time alone. She hated feeling so raw. Vulnerable. But grief did that to her. "I'll be fine." She rubbed her eyes again. "The next couple of days will be tough, but I will get through them."

"That doesn't mean you have to get through them alone. And those headaches are nothing to ignore," he said brusquely. "I'll stop by when I'm done here. Gotta go."

Tabitha stared down at her phone. That was the story of her life. The men all had to go – one way or the other. And yet Ronin kept coming back.

As if in response to her mood, her headache started dancing a rumba on her brain. It had to be stress as well as grief. Yeah, that was so possible. She didn't have to look far to find places where her world was off-kilter.

Besides her grandfather's death, there had been a rash of destructive incidents at Exotic Landscape. They had been irritating, costly and left her feeling as if she was under attack. She had no idea by whom. Or why. Or if any of the events were even related. They were mostly little things, like bags of dog food missing and some of the grain walking off. Break-ins at the clinic side of the main offices. Rocks through the window. Her grandfather had ignored a lot of it, but then he'd been in a whole different space this last year.

She had nothing anyone could want, and not enough of what the animals needed. She didn't need to be throwing money away fixing doors and windows and replacing stolen property.

Plus her budget had been shot with the new staff she'd been forced to hire. Not that the break-ins were the impetus behind those new hires; the real reason had been her long slow recovery in hospital after a psychic attack over a month ago. Her friend Shay had been the target. Tabitha was just a casualty. But that episode had changed her life. These incidents at the center had just helped to cement the decision to bring on more staff to ease her load.

On top of that, keeping her off balance, was the fact that nothing had been quite *right* since she'd been a victim of a psychic attack. She felt as if people looked at her differently. She could certainly not explain to her employees what had happened to her. She had a few friends that understood, but as for everyone else, she could hardly tell them she left her body and hid in the ethers to save herself from the attack, now could she?

Without warning, familiar pain slammed into her head, followed by a ripping sensation crawling through her brain. She bent over, grabbing the edge of the desk for support.

Several painful gasps later, she managed to take an easier breath. *Christ.* The attacks were getting worse. Another long moment later she managed a tiny step. When that worked, she took a second. As a test, she straightened, and when that was fine, she tossed her long braid back. Good, her head no longer felt like it was splitting in half. Whatever had been there – it was gone.

A ripple of relief slid down her spine.

Stefan Kronos, her scarily skilled psychic friend and mentor, spoke to her telepathically. *The headaches are troubling.*

And yet what am I to do, she answered just as softly, her heart warming at Stefan's caring voice inside her head. His visits were always a surprise, and always welcome. They also came from his heart. He cared and that was special. *I can hardly ask a doctor.*

He changed topic. *How are the nightmares?*

Better. Still the same nameless faceless boogie man, but the nightmares come less often. I sleep deeply once I get there, but I wake up troubled.

Hmmm. With that, he left her mind without warning. He was good at that.

Out of habit, she sent out a wide sweeping wave of healing energy throughout the building as she turned to leave. Instantly a sense of loss, of grief, bounced back at her along with a sense of finality. Energies from the staff, the animals, maybe even the building itself seemed to be adjusting to the loss of her grandfather.

It would take a long time before the energy changed to a loving reminiscence without the pain of loss.

She was reaching for her purse and keys she'd dropped on her grandfather's desk when something brutal stabbed into her head again. Her knees buckled and a scream ripped through her mind. The sound carried so much rage ...and fear...and pain...

It wasn't her pain or fear.

But it felt like it was hers.

She groaned, trying not to collapse under the encroaching blanket of emotional darkness. She bent over and gasped for air.

Another bolt of pain ripped through her, forcing her to the floor. She cried out and arched her back as the next slicing pain whipped along her spine.

Then it was gone.

As in completely gone. Just like that.

She slowly sat back on her heels and clasped her arms around her ribs, gasping for air. She didn't know what the hell was happening, but Christ...it was bad.

And this had to stop. She couldn't deal with it. The pain was too much.

Tripod whined at her side. He dropped his massive head on her shoulders, his hot breath washing across her cheek.

"I'm okay, boy."

A slight film coated her skin and she shivered more from shock that anything else. Her t-shirt stuck to her and a chill walked over her back, raising the hairs on her arm. Standing was not an option. She was scared another bolt of pain would drop her. After a long moment, she slowly struggled to her feet, steadying herself against Tripod's huge body. A clammy chill and an overriding fatigue rushed though her.

She wanted a hot shower and a hot drink. The place was empty at this hour. She had night staff and security guards, but they wouldn't likely see her right now. She was so grateful that she didn't have far to walk, that her house was only five minutes through the trees.

Walking as gently as if she were recovering from a back injury, she made it down the short path without incident. After unlocking her front door, she entered her sanctuary. Tango's voice rumbled at her from the back. Her baby tiger was no longer a baby anything. In fact, he was an old man. But he was still her baby – or maybe it was the other way around as he'd adopted her decades ago. He hated it whenever she left. But it was hard to run a business with a tiger interrupting your world. She also didn't want the public in on Tango's rather dominant presence in her life. It was better to work from home much of the time.

Being scolded by a tiger was wearying but she'd miss it when his time came. He'd been depressed since her grandfather's passing. She hoped Tango stayed around for months so that she could grieve for one of the dearest males in her life, her grandfather, before having to grieve for another.

Tripod walked over to sit at the entrance to the kitchen. Almost as big as Tango physically, she'd never seen any dog, especially a three-legged one, eat like he did.

She could almost hear his voice saying, *Wouldn't have to scarf my food if you fed me more.*

She'd had Tripod since he was a pup, falling in love with him before she'd realized he'd grow bigger and heavier than her. Of course his size was a definite plus when he played with Tango. And the two old friends were inseparable.

Good thing Tango couldn't speak human. However she understood dog somewhat – so his message didn't go unnoticed.

Dropping her purse on the kitchen table, she smiled down at Tripod. She'd learned to communicate directly with some animals over the years because Tripod and Tango had insisted she learn. Not with words like people. And communication was different with each of them. With Tango, she often saw his emotions in colors while Tripod seemed more human than canine. He sent her both images and emotions although they could be hard to decipher. What wasn't hard to understand was when he told her off for being late.

Or when he was hungry.

Or when he was lonely.

She stopped and bent to hug him. He whined and then almost growled. She stared down at him. "What's the matter, boy?"

He nudged her waist. She bent and hugged him again. Waves of worry emanated from him. He missed her grandfather. She studied his energy waves. They rippled. Some higher, some tighter and still others were lackluster and almost flat. There was a buzz or a hum to them.

She'd spent years trying to decipher those waves, but she hadn't been able to figure all of them out. The buzz happened when they were communicating and she was not listening. With so many animals on the reserve talking to her, she'd been forced to learn to turn it on and off at will.

While most of the time it was a pleasant, almost comforting background hum, sometimes it hit an irritating crescendo and she was forced to shut it off.

Tripod nudged her again with a whimper deep in his throat. Something was wrong but Tabitha didn't know what. She did know Tripod was worried about her.

Then she felt a stab of hunger emanate from him and realized he'd switched from worry about her to worry about his food.

She smiled. Now that was normal.

"Come on, boy. Let's feed you."

By the time she was done feeding the animals in the house and herself, Tabitha was running on empty for energy. She needed a shower and a nap. Since her grandfather's death, her emotions had worn her down. She would love twelve hours of sleep and would be lucky to get four and she had no idea why sleep seemed so elusive these days. She'd tried everything but drugs. Drugs and psychic abilities were so not good together. They left her groggy and disoriented. Herbs were fine and natural and didn't mess up her system. Only she was now out of those and had to go shopping to get more.

There was so much they didn't know about energy work and the world was in desperate need of energy workers. Dr. Maddy was the best she knew, but there were others like Tabitha who had similar abilities. Tabitha's abilities and connections worked best on animals.

Some of the people she knew were seriously talented. They could all communicate telepathically with their partners, and often with other people. Unlike her. Most seemed to have mastered something she could only dream about.

Liar. Stefan Kronos's warm teasing voice rolled through her mind.

She snickered. *Except with you, and no one has said you're human. If not human, what am I?*

His dry voice was so deadpan she had to giggle. *A god, according to most women.*

Oh, please don't get started. My feet are made of clay and I am as far away as possible from being anything heaven sent.

She gave a small tired laugh at that. *Okay, how about you're just a good friend?*

I can work with that.

Did you have a reason for being here? she asked as she headed to her bedroom. She changed out of her clothes and into a housecoat. Sometimes, it took several showers to wash away the animal odors. Tripod sat at her doorway watching intently. He always got an intense look on his face when she communicated with Stefan and this time was no exception.

He's probably listening in.

She grinned. Thank heavens for Stefan and that relationship of acceptance and understanding. *So few people would be able to understand this conversation.*

More than you think. And many more becoming aware that 'this' exists.

True. She stepped into the bathroom and groaned at her appearance. *Crap. Stefan, I look like I've been hit by a truck. You should see the circles under my eyes.*

Lack of sleep? Overwork? Stress?

All of the above, I suppose.

You've just lost your grandfather. And what else...? That knowing voice was calm and understanding. But...

She stilled. And asked cautiously, *What do you mean: What else?*

Do you think I don't hear you every time you cry out in pain?

She winced. *Oh, that.*

He waited, stoic and steadfast but unyielding.

It's not more blackouts, she rushed to reassure him.

Good.

I don't know what they are, she answered honestly. *Stabs of black pain. As if something was ripping into my skull. Then it stops. Comes on suddenly and stops suddenly. I can't figure out the triggers...*

He was silent for a long moment.

Psychic attacks? he asked cautiously.

I don't think so, but I don't know for sure. I can tell you that I've never felt anything like this before. She didn't add that she hoped to never experience it again. He'd know that.

Are the headaches getting worse?

The last few have been. And there have been a few more than usual. Weird ones. They come on suddenly and then just disappear. Like the pain. Then today, there's been a bizarre sense of waiting for something to happen. Then the sensation eases off again and I can almost forget about it.

When did they start?

She sighed. *A couple of weeks ago, maybe longer. But today was bad.*

Silence.

As in they happened before you spent a week in hospital and disappeared into the ethers – or after?

Tabitha hated to be reminded of that week.

And is that also when you started having trouble sleeping?

Yes, but honestly I think it's just a residual problem from being in the hospital. You know how hard it is to come back to physical reality after a long stay out of body.

Hmmm.

She winced, not sure she liked that thoughtful pause.

What are the chances that someone is trying to contact you and you aren't hearing them? Someone might have caught your signature while you were in the ethers and think you are still there.

Her gaze widened in surprise. She hadn't considered that. *Like who? And why wouldn't they be able to communicate with me? When I'm working with the animals, I'm always open.*

Again that irritating pause.

Curious, she asked, *What are you thinking?*

Just considering the information.

I'm sure I'll be fine, she said. *A good night's sleep and I'll be much better.* At least she wanted that to solve everything.

I hope so. I'll say good-bye then. But let me know if anything changes.

Stefan drifted out of her mind. Sometimes he snapped out and other times it was similar to a good-bye hug. She loved the latter.

She stepped under the hot spray of the shower and scrubbed the smell of animals off her skin. The heat washed over her in comforting waves. She bowed her head and let the day and fatigue drain away.

Then it started again.

Pain ripped through her head.

She cried out and clutched the glass doors of the shower. Agony screamed through her nerves and her knees threatened to buckle.

What was going on?

Images slammed through her, but they were woven with emotions that twisted the pictures into sensations. Pain.

Rage.

Panic.

Fear.

The rage was bad, but the fear was crippling.

Tabitha sank to her knees in the shower and could do nothing but ride out the storm. So far the attacks had never lasted long. Water sluiced down her back. The waves of agony wouldn't stop. She had no anchor to hold her safe. She had no protection from this. Her shields were up, but it didn't matter. This energy had stormed right through them and grabbed on tight.

While her mind raced to understand, she felt something so horrific she couldn't understand what was happening. It was as if someone had reached into her head and grabbed her energetic body from inside her skull...as if they were trying to rip her soul from her body.

Noooo! She screamed and tried to fight whatever demonic energy had so much power that made such a thing possible. She was caught in a struggle to stay grounded. To stay attached to her body.

She curled into a ball and tried to focus. Tried to center herself. She mentally kept her silver cord tucked up inside, but it was hard.

The pain was so strong. The sense of being yanked out of her body...intense. She felt stretched so finite she cried out in terror.

And each wave of pain and violation was stronger than the last.

There was a sense of desperation to this energy. She could feel the need of this thing pulling at her. Its panic. Its terror along with her own.

Somehow it had hooked onto her and she knew it needed her – or something she *had*.

She struggled to hold on, struggled to find the strength to be stronger than it was.

This...thing was desperate.

But then so was she.

Stefan! Help!

The next wave could be the big one. When it came, the pull was shockingly aggressive and too powerful to stand against. Her grasp slipped.

Once that bit of weakening started, she lost the advantage of being the one in possession of her body. An advantage she desperately needed.

And she started to slide.

One more tug and half of her was lifted upwards. She stared down at her bent-over body, as if she were twins joined at the hip. Her physical twin was bent over her legs, her etheric twin was sitting up. She screamed in panic and tried to lean over, tried to return to her body.

But this entity had a formidable hold. A panicked hold. And its panic had become hers.

His rage streamed through her blood.

His fear turned her emotions to icy panic.

Suddenly she was no longer alone. Stefan's powerful energy wrapped around her, supporting her, strengthening her. Keeping her safe.

Remember to love. Fear is the tool of failure. Love is the tool of success.

She struggled with his words. Struggled to grasp his meaning. And she struggled to find her center. That part of her that knew all energy was good. It was the emotions people poured into the energy that made it other than good. Her attacker was afraid. And angry. If she could help it by easing his pain...

Yes. Do it.

Her attacker gave one more tug. But Tabitha's energy had warmed and thinned, heating up more as she tried to send out the right thoughts to help her attacker. Thoughts to calm herself.

With a roar of rage and pain and loss, the link snapped.

Tabitha recoiled from the force with a final cry before she blacked out. Her last vision was that of her empty-shell of a body folded in half in the shower, the hot steamy water slowly cooling as it beat down on her back.

Then she knew no more.

Chapter 2

Saturday, mid-afternoon

Stefan Kronos bolted upright in his bed. His heart screamed at him to run. His body refused to move. His bedroom had disappeared into the foggy dreamscape of a different reality. Waves of energy wrapped around a tornado of emotion. A cry ripped through the air.

Stefan!

Someone was in trouble. Only it was more than trouble. A scream echoed loud enough that he clapped his hands over his ears and tried to block it – but there was no way he could. Finally the volume ebbed enough and he recognized the voice. *Tabitha.*

He'd just been talking to her. Even as he emptied his mind and called for her, he double checked the energy signature, hoping he was wrong.

Of course it was her. She'd been on his warning system for weeks now. Ever since her hospital stay. He called out to her again.

No response.

He closed his eyes and sent his consciousness to her house. Not knowing what he'd find, he didn't want to leave his body. He'd met too many strange individuals who would attempt a takeover in a heartbeat if he gave them an opening. That was the problem with being a strong psychic – he knew what existed in the shadow world.

Remembering Tabitha's earlier words about headaches and blackouts, he slipped over to her bedroom and found a pile of clothes on the floor. There was no sign of her. A weird faint roaring sound filled the air waves. From Tabitha or the house or something else?

Tripod howled at the edge of the bathroom, a loud physical mourning that poured ice into Stefan's non-existent veins. What the hell had happened here? In the background, that roaring sound grew louder and louder. If he'd had a body, the sounds and vibrations would have overwhelmed him, sending him to the floor. In this energetic form, he did the best he could and pushed clouds of energy between him and it, trying desperately to distance himself so he could think.

As the roar faded slightly, he sensed a cadence to it. It was animal. Shit. That had to be Tango. The tiger's voice was deep and raspy, as if he'd been screaming.

Stefan shuddered. Something bad had happened. He moved into the bathroom but could barely see for the steam and condensation. The shower door was closed. The rest of the bathroom empty.

Dreading what he'd find, Stefan shifted to the other side of the shower wall.

Shit.

What the hell was happening to her? He hovered over her. Her cord lay hidden protectively in the circle of her body. He could see the rise and fall of her chest as air slipped out of her body with each breath.

This was bad. Like seriously bad.

He backed up slightly and searched her etheric energy, looking for other entities in the small room, trying to get a read on what had happened. The kicked-up emotional cloud of fear and panic said she'd feared for her life. Fought for her life. His only conclusion was that she'd been attacked but won...this time.

But the cost of winning had been devastating to her.

There was no sign of an attacker. No foreign energy that he could see. Unfortunately, her aura was swollen with so much else. Grief for her grandfather, anger that he had left her, a sense of loss as she looked to her future – and then there were the animal energies. So many. Each and every one of them lived in her heart.

Her capacity for caring was huge.

And left it difficult for him to make sense of what should be there and what shouldn't. Adding to the effect, and in response to Tabitha's state, the animals had all responded with their own pain and rage.

What a mess.

And for all he knew, she was still in trouble psychically as well as physically.

Swooping lower, he could see the blue cast over her skin. If she caught hypothermia, that alone would kill her. Her body functioned at the absolute edge of survival level. Her biological system was on rapid shutdown.

Holy hell.

She was under siege from the inside.

And she needed help. Now.

***

Ronin had spent all afternoon working and gotten nowhere. Chasing down leads on a trafficking case that had led to zero progress. Carmichael, another detective in the office, had stopped by to discuss a different case and now Ronin was way behind.

His damn desk was overloaded with his active cases and what had appeared to be a quick stop into the police station had turned out to be anything but. He stared at the stack of files in front of him. Too many files. Again. Always.

He glanced at his watch. He should be able to head out in a few minutes. For Tabitha's sake, he didn't dare stay too late. She needed him.

Now getting her to see that was a different issue altogether.

She was smart and sassy and distrustful of men...

Figures. He sure could pick them. Not that he'd had much choice. Attraction had smacked him up side the head when he'd first met her. Green-eyed leggy brunettes had never been his type. But this one... He'd had to move slowly given her trust issues. He'd made huge steps before her grandfather had passed away. He'd been there for her every day since.

If only he understood what *this* was.

He hated the pain she was in, wanted to help her, but wasn't sure how. Still he'd keep trying. He wanted what his brother Roman had. His brother was unbelievably happy. Grounded. Whatever the hell that meant. He was half of a whole, with Shay, his girlfriend, being the other half.

Ronin had heard about such relationships but hadn't really believed in the possibility. Figured they all turned sour, eventually. Ronin's marriage had as had several long-term relationships. He'd blamed his job. So had they. In truth, the job was an excuse and an escape from whatever bad relationships they had at the time.

What the hell Tabitha was to him, he didn't know.

And the relationship was so new and green it felt fresh. But was he walking down this garden path alone?

Because that would suck.

A young cop walked toward him. Geoff Tollman. After a quick glance around, he pulled a picture out of a large envelope and dropped them both on Ronin's desk.

Frowning, Ronin raised his gaze to Geoff's. "Why did you come to me?"

The young man swallowed and lowered his voice. "I didn't know who else to take it to."

That the two of them had a history played a big part in Geoff bringing the pictures to him. Ronin was pretty sure of that. The kid was his neighbor's son, and he'd helped him get into the force and through the tough years following. He'd been a troubled teen a long time ago, but he'd straightened out and become a hell of detective. They worked in the same department now. Part of the same team and that felt good.

Ronin stared down at the odd photo in front of him. "Where did you get this?"

"It was in the mail."

"Your personal mail?"

"No. Here in the office, along with the other stuff. I saw it on the pile, opened it and brought it here."

Ronin pulled out the rest of the pictures. His old buddy and co-worker, Detective Jacob Harkman, stared back at him. In the background, highlighted by gloomy lights, was an open back end of a truck. Full of cages. Nothing suspicious in itself, but...he glanced up at Geoff. "The pictures don't show anything illegal."

"I know." Geoff shrugged his shoulder. "But why send them?"

"Good question." Ronin stuffed the pictures back into the envelope and spun it in his hand. No postage. No return address. Just Geoff's first name. Spelled correctly. There wasn't anyone else in this office with that same spelling. He dropped the envelope on the side of his desk. "I'll look into it. If you get anything else, bring it to me."

"Sounds good." As Geoff sauntered toward his own desk, he called back, "It's probably nothing."

Ronin hoped Geoff was right. He'd known Jacob a long time. Being a detective took them to all kinds of places, at all kinds of hours. He studied the photos again. What the hell was Jacob up to and why had the photo been sent?

Before he had time to consider the options, his phone rang. Damn.

Pinching the bridge of his nose, he clicked his cell phone and growled, "What?"

Static whispered through his phone, but something about it was straight-out creepy.

He straightened. "Hello? Who's there?"

Help! Taaaa...!

"Hello. Who is this?"

No answer.

He snatched up a pen and jotted the number down. Then stopped. It was his number. His phone was calling his phone.

Goosebumps broke out over his skin.

Shit. He enjoyed a good horror movie the same as any other guy, but this was stepping over the creepy line. But then so had a lot of things in his life this last year – ever since he'd stepped in to help Shay after her fiancé tried to kill her.

The phone was dead in his hand. He swallowed hard and dropped it down on the desk to stare at it, his eyes narrowing at the thought. It wasn't even Halloween. So who the hell was this prankster and how did he do this?

The phone rang again.

He stared at it, loath to answer.

It rang again. He picked it up and checked the number. This call was from Stefan. But that last one...

"Hello?"

"Is this easier for you?"

He frowned. God, this man was cryptic. "What?"

"Never mind. I don't have time. I need you to send an ambulance to Tabitha's house on the Exotic Landscape property. You might need Shay's help. Tabitha is in a bad way."

"Wha—?"

Stefan rolled right over him. "Get Dr. Marsden in. He's a specialist for this kind of thing. Although this time there may not be anything he can do."

"Wait, what are you talking about?"

"Tabitha has been attacked."

And Stefan was gone.

***

"There is a lot of money riding on this deal," the boss growled. "Fuck up and you're done."

Fez, and Roberts, his partner, nodded in unison.

This was a huge payday for them. Fez knew he had an awesome gig here. So far the work had been easy and lucrative. So good, he'd postponed his plans to move back East and start a new life. In the last five months he'd made a lot of serious money. And had spent even more.

Roberts had brought him in. He had the skills, the know how. Fez was the muscle.

And the boss? He was scary but damn powerful and a hell of businessman. He didn't take shit from anyone.

Make for a lot of fast, good deals for all of them.

Still it never did to get too comfortable. When the boss locked that gaze on him, Fez kept nodding. Obedience was paramount. He tugged at the neck of his old sweatshirt, which was stupid because the damn thing gaped halfway down his chest. Old habits died hard, especially when he was stressed.

"Are you even listening to me?"

Fez rushed to say, "Sure, boss. We'll go down to the docks now. The package has already been cleared so it should be loaded and on the road in no time."

The black, icy glare narrowed at him. Roberts stood up and headed for the door. Fez swallowed hard, stood up and muttered, "We'll take care of it now."

"You do that. And make sure that cargo is safe. It was too damn long in transit as it is. Haven't I paid enough to make this go smoothly?"

"Absolutely. No problem." Fez walked to the door. "I'll call you when the truck is loaded."

"You'll call me when you get there. Make sure you get it on the road fast. I want the truck unloaded in the warehouse tonight. Got it?"

The warning in his voice made Fez's stomach clamp down tight. He pulled out a roll of antacids from his pocket as soon as the door shut behind him. He popped two into his mouth.

Roberts snorted when he saw what he was doing. "Those damn things will kill you one of these days."

"They help. Can hardly keep any food down these days," Fez muttered, walking down the stairs beside his partner. He should go see a doc, but what the hell was he going to tell him that Fez didn't already know? And if it was bad news like cancer or something, he would just as soon not know.

He'd take keeling over on the streets to a slow painful end any day.

"Time to quit if the job is doing that to you."

"It's a good job," Fez said. "Hell, you're the one that brought me in."

"Yeah, well, you never know. I just might be the one that leaves if you don't."

Fez turned in shock. There was just something a little too serious in Roberts's tone of voice. "You wouldn't do that. Look at the money we've made."

Roberts nodded but stuffed his fists in his pockets. "And when is enough enough? I've got a bad feeling about this job." He shook his head. "A real bad feeling.

"Don't do this man. We're a team."

"Maybe not for much longer."

After that he fell silent, leaving Fez to worry in silence.

Chapter 3

Saturday, afternoon

Tabitha wandered through the gentle clouds, comforted by the familiarity of her surroundings. She didn't know why she was in the ethers again. But it was such a nice place to be. There were no worries here. No stresses. No money shortfalls to make up or difficult people to answer to. She could still mentally reach out and check on her animals – offer a hug, a stroke, or just a loving pat.

She was happy.

Like she'd been before.

That made her pause, made her consciousness kick in.

She wasn't supposed to be back here.

She'd liked it here a little too well last time. It had been hard to leave.

So why was she here now?

For...safety.

Memories flooded over her. She'd been attacked. In fact, her energy had been damn near ripped out of her body.

She shuddered and sank deeper into the protection of the shadows.

***

Ronin pulled his truck to a ripping stop outside of Tabitha's mausoleum of a house. Surrounded by large trees with little natural light filtering through, the place had a gothic haunted-mansion vibe going on.

There was also a weird deafening silence.

He'd been this far before, but had never been invited in. Her grandfather had been the original reason; apparently she hadn't wanted to introduce the two of them, given her grandfather's health and his disposition. She'd always met Ronin outside the house or at the office.

She ran a reserve where big cats were a major part of the population…and if there was one thing he had a love-hate relationship with…it was cats. He was so not good with cats – not allergic, although that would have given him an excuse for his over-the-top reactions like a nauseous stomach, a closed up throat and headaches with shortness of breath.

And no, he hadn't gone to see a specialist. He never would.

But Tabitha didn't need to know that. At least not yet.

Now Tabitha's grandfather was gone. Would that make it easier for Tabitha to let a male into her inner world? She'd once been engaged for six months so he knew she'd opened that door once before. What would it take for her to open it again, for him?

Just how controlling had her grandfather been? Did he have something to do with her broken relationship? Had he understood she had psychic abilities? Not that she'd mentioned them to him, but he'd overheard Shay and his brother talking one night about how Tabitha was better with the animals than Shay was. He could have gotten the impression that she had abilities beyond the ordinary.

Maybe she'd gotten those abilities *from* her grandfather.

Ronin exited the truck and approached the front door. A large, imposing front facade with no welcoming porch or deck, just a single stair up to a double door. His first impression? Dark. Formidable. Dilapidated.

If her grandfather had any money, he hadn't wasted it on the house, unlike his own grandfather, Pappy, who had the golden touch when it came to big business and kept his personal place immaculate.

Ronin knocked on the huge door before reaching for the doorknob. It turned under his hand but the door did not budge. Inside a howl went up that shook him to the core. Tripod? She'd told him about the monster-sized dog, but Jesus…

The door was locked. He gave it a strong shake and saw the security system, installed by his brother, winking at him from above. He pulled out his cell phone.

"Roman, I need to get into Tabitha's house. Shut off the security system."

"Why? What's wrong?" His brother's voice sounded distracted. He was probably painting, considering it was late on a Saturday afternoon.

"She's been attacked. Stefan sent me here to help her but the house is locked up tight."

"Damn." Now his voice sharpened. "How bad was the attack?"

"I don't know. I'm trying to get in to find that out," he snapped. "The dog is howling. I can barely hear you." He paused. "Is it done?"

As he asked, he looked up at the blinking red light to find it gone. "Thanks."

"Let me know if you need a hand." There were sounds of a muted conversation. "Skip that. We're on our way."

Ronin pushed the door open and stepped inside. "I'm in."

"No wait, Shay sa—"

But he never heard the rest as something as big as a bear, crossed with a pony, raced toward him – howling.

"Jesus H. Christ!" The dog had a huge set of bared teeth. Instinctively, Ronin unsnapped the cover over his gun.

The dog came to a screeching halt, skittering forward on the wooden floor and growling so loud there should have been a half dozen dogs facing him.

In the distance, he heard his brother's voice screaming through the phone. "The dog's name is Tripod."

Because he had only three legs. Yeah, he got it. Only the damn thing looked ready to take off one of *Ronin's* legs.

"Easy, Tripod. Take it easy boy. I'm here to help."

The dog raised his head and howled again. Then it turned its head and pinned him in place with an all-too-human gaze.

Shit. He tried to remember he was a dog person. And that *most* dogs loved him.

The look in this one's gaze made him doubt that was ever going to happen.

His brother's voice reached him again. He lifted his cell phone. "Stop screaming. I'm here."

"Look, Tripod is a big baby but he knows something has happened to Tabitha."

"Understood." He ran his fingers through his hair. "But I still have to get past him to get to her."

Then his brother's next words reached through the phone and grabbed him by the throat. "Easy. If Tripod doesn't calm down, it will get bad."

Ronin stared down at his phone in disbelief. "What did you say?"

"Tripod is the guard dog. But Tango is going to be more difficult. If you can calm Tripod, then Tango will follow his lead." Roman took a deep breath. "*Maybe* it will follow his lead."

"What the hell?" Ronin muttered, keeping a wary eye on the dog as he stepped inside. She had a second one she hadn't mentioned? Why? "I don't have time for this."

"Yes. I know. But a mistake at this stage could be fatal."

At the word 'fatal,' Ronin's hand instinctively went to the gun at the small of his back.

The dog erupted into a growl that had Ronin bolting backwards. "Damn it."

"What did you do?" Roman yelled. "Ronin?"

"I reached for the gun. Apparently he didn't like that." Talk about an understatement.

"Shay's here. She says you have to put the gun away. He'll attack if you try to use it."

God! Ronin briefly closed his eyes to consider the problem, then said helplessly. "You don't understand. I have to help Tabitha."

"Ronin? This is Shay here," her worried voice came on the phone. "I do understand. But you also have to understand something else. This house, these animals are her support system. They are the guardians of Tabitha's soul, possibly in ways she doesn't even understand."

"That's just crazy." Frustration and anger hurtled through him. "Why did Stefan call me to help her? How the hell am I going to do that if I can't get in there?"

"He called you because you are part of Tabitha's support system," Shay explained, "and she needs all of us right now."

"Support system?" What the hell did that mean? Whatever. "Get me inside."

"You have to convince Tripod to let you inside."

Right. "This isn't a damn dog; this thing is the size of a young grizzly bear." In the distance he could make out vehicles but not the sound of sirens yet. "And the ambulance should be almost here. I need to do something." As he studied the dog, he added. "Maybe that's why Stefan told me to come. I can call animal welfare—"

No. Stefan's' objection ripped though Ronin's mind. *You can't. Tripod and Tango keep Tabitha grounded...connected. If you knock either into unconsciousness or, worse, kill them, we risk her losing that connection. Lose that and we could lose her.*

"Shit. This is crazy." He stared around helplessly. "So what do I do?"

Make friends with Tripod. You need to show him your energy in a calm way, Stefan continued. *The dog doesn't care so much about the gun at your back but about the shift in your energy when you reached for your gun.*

Ronin groaned and let his hand fall away. He stepped quietly forward to stand in front of the dog, then crouched slightly until he was eye level with the massive head.

"If this thing bites my head off..."

We'll bury you with all the pomp and ceremony you deserve... said Stefan drily.

"Ass," Ronin muttered half-heartedly. He'd already turned his focus on the dog.

The gaze that stared back at him was almost more than human. There was no artifice there. Only fear. And anger. Someone he loved was hurt. And that Ronin could understand. The dog wanted its owner to stand up. To have its life back to normal.

And he wanted it in a bad way.

Close your eyes and talk to him. When your eyes are open, your conscious mind interferes with what's possible. I know you calmed several irate animals over your career.

Ronin was often able to soothe a dog that had been hurt or was angry or injured. But not always. "Yeah, normally dogs respond well to me."

And animals respond to the capable, calm, almost soothing nature of your energy. But right now, you're worried and the dog is worried. So you're rubbing up against each other's fear, increasing it, instead of easing it. Tabitha talks to Tripod all the time. That's what he's looking for from you.

Shit. Tripod. I'm here to help. Ronin closed his eyes and spoke to the dog mentally. *Tabitha is in trouble and I need to get to her. She's hurting in a bad way.*

A rumble washed over him. Ronin frowned and repeated his statement. The rumble deepened. Ronin swore he could see the dog's features as clearly as he would if his eyes were open.

Only they weren't. Ronin's eyes were definitely closed.

It's a vision skill. Keep seeing the dog in your mind and stroke him in your mind. See him accept you. See him liking the attention.

Ronin struggled to follow through. He eased into the vision of the dog's face, soothing him as he spoke to him about helping him. Helping Tabitha. He reached out and felt a warming of the energy around him and the fear easing.

Then a huge tongue caught him by the chin and stroked upwards across his face.

The smell was gross, but his heart leapt. He opened his eyes to see the dog gazing into his eyes. A plea for help deep inside. "That look can't be real."

It is. Once a connection is made... Stefan's voice trailed off.

Ronin stood, gently patted the dog then squeezed between the dog and the doorway. The dog trailed behind, whining deep in his throat.

Ronin stopped to take stock. And was hit with waves of nausea and a horrible buzzing in his head. He shuddered. His whole system went into lockdown. He could hardly breathe.

Damn. A cat was here. Somewhere close by.

But Tabitha needed him. His hand at his throat, struggling to hold back the panic, he tried to study the rooms in front of him. Instead of a nice clean layout, the house appeared to be a maze. "Where is she, Tripod? Show me Tabitha."

The dog cocked his head to one side, as if understanding him, then bounded upstairs. Ronin followed, barely seeing where he was going until he dashed into a bedroom.

"Stefan said she's in the shower," he said, and felt like an idiot for talking to the dog. His chest eased slightly, making it easier to focus. He raced for the small room off to the side. Clothes lay crumpled on the floor. Otherwise, the room appeared empty.

He pulled back the shower door to find Tabitha nude, in a ball, with a bluish gray cast to her skin. Icy water beat down on her back. He turned off the water. His hands went to Tabitha's neck. He could barely find a pulse under her clammy skin.

Crap. He raced back to Tabitha's bedroom, tugging something white and pillowy off her bed. Back at the shower, he bundled it around Tabitha and scooped her up in a cocoon. As he turned toward the bedroom, a tall blonde stood in the doorway. Shay.

He didn't slow down.

"Good, you've got her." Shay was already leading the way back outside. "The ambulance is coming up the drive. Roman is waiting for them."

Ronin brushed past her, and carrying a still-wrapped Tabitha, carefully made his way down the stairs to the front door. He'd cleared the front porch when the ambulance came to a quick stop. He took his first clean deep breath. The men raced out and opened the back doors.

"She's in a bad way."

He laid his precious bundle down and stepped back as the men went to work. Before he knew it, she'd been loaded into the ambulance, one man still working on her as they ripped down the driveway.

He stood and stared down the empty road. Tripod howled, then abruptly walked over to sit beside Ronin.

Ronin stared at the huge dog who gazed solemnly back at him as if he were telling Ronin to fix this.

***

"What the hell is going on?" Fez said to the empty night. They should have been here by now. That they weren't, was a huge problem. These goods had to be moved to the next destination. And fast.

Fez paced the long rows of docks. What was the hold up? He should be out of here by now. He'd called the boss once... He checked his phone again. At least his boss hadn't called back. But if Fez didn't check in with him soon, there'd be hell to pay.

Especially since Roberts had taken off to do something and hadn't come back yet. Fez glanced around. He couldn't shake the feeling that the boss was going to show up any second. The man came and went like a damn ghost.

Shit. Where the hell was his package?

Even more important, were the contents still alive?

Chapter 4

Saturday, late afternoon

Stefan stood at Tabitha's bedside, his medical specialist, Dr. Marsden, at his side. He studied the pale face on the white pillows. Tabitha's beauty shone in an unearthly way. Her skin appeared luminescent. He asked, "So there's nothing physically wrong with her?"

Dr. Marsden shook his head. "Nothing that is showing up on any tests. I think she's terrified...and has gone into hiding."

"Originally..." Stefan rubbed his temple and tried to marshal his thoughts. "When I heard her screaming for help, I caught scattered bits of her thoughts. She *believed* she was going to die. When I found her, she'd curled tightly around her cord as if protecting it."

The doctor nodded. "Sensible. What I can't be sure of is whether her previous attack had something to do with this one, or...if that attack left her open to this one and possibly others yet to come."

"They weren't the same attacker. I know that for sure." The words barely out of his mouth, Stefan winced. There were no sureties in this world, but as far as he knew, the woman who'd attacked Tabitha a month ago was dead. Along with her murderous brothers. "But she's spent a lot of time in the ethers leaving her body unprotected. For all we know, someone in the ethers picked up on that and was planning to take over her body."

"It's possible, but why wait until now?" Dr. Marsden walked to the end of Tabitha's bed.

"We all sleep and dream walk, and there are many other people to target. So why Tabitha? Her energy? Her abilities?"

That caught Stefan's attention. "Her abilities," he asked cautiously. "Why would her abilities make a difference?"

Dr. Marsden glanced his way. "Many people would be mentally damaged by the experience, yet Tabitha obviously has an ability to stay in the ethers."

That prodded something in Stefan's memory. The last time Tabitha had been in the ethers for a prolonged stay, she'd hidden out there until it was safe. "You think she's *choosing* to hide in the ethers?"

"Exactly. Most people, even psychics, won't do that. Can't do that. It takes a special ability to walk in the space between life and death. I've heard of that space, the In-Between."

"Hmm. Isn't that backwards? She hides there when she feels under attack...yet by leaving her body open like this, she's actually putting herself in a more vulnerable position."

Dr. Marsden laughed. "You'd have thought so, but take a closer look."

Startled, Stefan glanced back at Tabitha's long and lean frame. He shifted through the layers of energy, but it was hard because the energy was compressed, lying tight and hard against her body.

"I can barely see her aura as it is!" Stefan exclaimed.

"Exactly. It's some kind of defense system. Her energy is locked down in protective mode that stops anyone from accessing her body from the outside. Even her cord is hidden."

Stefan had never seen a case like this. Or an energy system like Tabitha's. He searched the ethers looking for her cord – the so important connection to her physical body that kept her alive...and couldn't find it.

Yet she was lying there breathing naturally. Normally, as if in a deep sleep.

"See what I mean?" The note of wonder in the doctor's voice had Stefan walking closer to study Tabitha. "Her cord is actually dispersed all around the room. If you look closely you'll see signs of it. Just not how it connects to her."

"So once again, something new." Stefan snorted at that. "Does she need anything from us?" The two men stared down at the comatose woman.

"Not from me." Dr. Marsden turned to study him, one eyebrow raised in question. "Maybe from you."

Stefan nodded his head. "Could be. I'll check." He looked around the small private room. Should he try contacting her here or from home? Here he'd have to deal with so many other interfering energies.

"Do you want to try now, while you're here?"

Stefan shook his head. "Want to? No. Should I? Yes."

Dr. Marsden turned in a slow circle to study the sparse room. "It's hardly the best place for a session, is it?"

"Depends on the number of spirit entities hanging around. Considering it's a hospital, there're likely to be more disembodied souls here than living people."

Stefan hated being in crowds to begin with, and although he was comfortable with the dead and walked the ethers as easily as Tabitha, dealing with angry, frustrated, or needy disembodied souls was not fun. If he could slip past that to the ethers, he'd be fine. But if not...

"I'll do it here. At least long enough to make sure she's fine." He spied the chair in the far corner. He pulled it up to her bedside and walked to position himself back in the corner where he sat cross-legged on the floor.

Ignoring the doctor, Stefan settled his back against the wall and took a deep breath. He released the old stale air from his lungs and consciously brought in fresh, life-giving air.

His energy shifted slowly, then faster and faster as he drew on his years of practice to make his exit from his body that much smoother.

He opened his eyes. And found himself in the In-Between. A light-colored fog filled the room that no longer existed. He swept away the fog, preferring clear openness to the muted look of clouds. Here the energy responded to thoughts and he could make it look as he wished. The practical side of him said not to bother, he wouldn't be here long enough to arrange the setting to his personal style or artistic sensibilities.

He zipped through the ethers. In his mind's eye, he focused on Tabitha's cord. On finding it healthy and happy.

And there it was. He smiled. The cord shimmered a deep lavender, almost as if it were covered by glitter paint. It was fun to see this side of her because in the physical world, she was down to earth and practical. No glitter to be found.

His journey was fast and easy as he moved through the vast space. He traveled faster and faster, navigating with his senses as he headed to her side.

Hey. Tabitha's laughter told him he'd reached her.

He grinned and opened his eyes to find her standing there smiling in front of him.

Damn. You look good.

Thanks. I'm feeling quite a bit better actually.

He studied her features, seeing what she wasn't saying out loud. She might be feeling better, but her energy didn't glow like it should. There were dark hollows, dents in her energy as if she worried and was trying to hide it. Like she'd hidden out here.

With a gentle shake of his head, he said, *No, you're not. For you, this is a safety zone. But I want to know what happened to bring you here and why you felt you needed to retreat here instead of call for help.*

The air filled with her bitter laugh. *Because I'm safe here. Only I have no idea what happened.* Quickly, she told him what she remembered.

And do you think this attack is related to all the headaches? As if someone was trying to get inside you, your consciousness? If so what's it going to take to get you back to your body?

I didn't leave my body. I'm just resting here for a bit.

And as you know from before, that little bit is likely to become a long bit.

No, she corrected. *It did last time. That doesn't mean it will this time.*

How was he to convince her to come home? *Ronin had to become friends with Tripod to get into the house.*

Really? They've never met up to now. I've held off bringing him to the house after he made a casual comment about not liking cats.

Stefan grinned, thinking Ronin had yet to meet Tango. And what fun that would be. *Is he allergic?*

No idea, she confessed, *I didn't ask him. I was too surprised at the time.*

Yet you didn't break it off? He wasn't going to let her off that easy. If Ronin was going to be her reason to come home, then he needed her mind on him now. Enough hiding.

She shrugged. *There aren't too many interesting men that can handle my abilities.*

Then you'll have to come back, won't you? Especially before the media gets wind of this. You know how they have portrayed the reserve as being in trouble recently with all the break-ins and vandalism. If the media finds out about this state your physical body is in... The center doesn't need more bad publicity or to have the donations could dry up.

Hey, that's not fair, she said. *I'm here because I was attacked.*

And Tango and Tripod? They are guarding your place and keeping your body grounded. Your absence is hard on them.

I've already been by to visit with them. She waved her hands dismissively. *They are fine.*

So much for that tactic...

Then he had it. He smiled inside. *Except that Ronin is searching your house to find anything he can about your attacker.*

He's inside the house? Right now? She went ghostly pale. *Damn. That's so not a good idea. He could be in danger. Tango knows when someone likes him or not.*

And, Stefan said gently, *Ronin is a cop who cares deeply about you. You were attacked and if, in the course of his investigation, he's attacked...*

I'm gone.

The fog swirled around Stefan, blocking her from view. By the time he cleared his vision and swept back the cotton clouds, there was no sign of her.

***

She came to so suddenly, her body jerked from the harsh landing and she bolted upright, ready to run out of the room – and found herself in a private hospital room with a stern, darkly handsome doctor staring down at her. It took her a moment to recognize him. Dr. Marsden.

"Whoa. You're not going anywhere." Dr. Marsden reached out to stop her.

"I have to leave." She glared at him.

"Easy, Tabitha." Stefan stretched out his legs and stood up slowly. "Dr. Marsden has been looking after you."

What was Stefan doing in the corner?

"Sorry. I hate hospitals," she muttered as a poor excuse for her behavior. "And why is it you think I can't leave?"

He was wrong of course, but she didn't need to antagonize anyone further. It drained too much energy. But she really wanted to go home.

"Because you were attacked. I'd like to run some tests."

She shot him a shuttered look and shook her head. "If you know as much about this stuff as Stefan believes you do, then you understand it was a psychic attack. And that means nothing will show up on your tests."

"And you're going to do what, wait around until he tries again?" Stefan asked quietly.

Silence.

Damn. Her animals, as well as her body and her soul were vulnerable. The attack had been horrific and too damn close to being a win for the other guy to make her happy. Would he try again?

She slumped back against the headboard. "He wants my soul, not my body. At least that's what I felt during an attack.

Stronger each time. And do you have any suggestions? Some magical way to keep my soul in my body and away from this thief?"

"Did you get a sense of why he wanted it?"

The two men stood at the end of her bed, their gazes intent as if they could find the answers they wanted if they could just look hard enough. Tabitha pushed back a few strands of long hair as she tried to marshal her thoughts. "I could sense he was terrified. Angry. And was looking for someone or something."

"And found you instead." Stefan walked around the side of the bed, then picked up her hand and held it tight. "*Or* was he looking specifically for you?"

"For me." She knew that deep inside. "He wanted me."

✳✳✳

"Hello, Stefan. You used the phone this time?" Ronin grinned at the sound Stefan made on the other end. He peered through the thick wire mesh, trying to see what animal was on the other side the fenced pen. Tabitha's place was an integral part of the reserve. Anything could be on the other side of the fence.

"It saves energy. Tabitha is awake. She's afraid you'll have an argument with her cat, Tango. Apparently she left him in his cage, but she says he's wily and can get out if he has a mind to."

"Great." Horrible actually. He could already feel his heart slam against his chest. "I'm actually outside walking around the property, trying to understand the setup here." It was confusing. That there were large enclosures in the back of the house was obvious. As were the howls coming from the deep expanse.

Cats.

Why cats? He could do dogs blindfolded. This whole cat thing...not so much. At least they were all caged.

"Is she okay? Can she come home?"

"She's going to, whether anyone says so or not. The thing is she is weak, susceptible to another attack. You need to help her."

Ronin's stomach clenched. "Why me? I don't do this psychic stuff. That's your specialty. Why can't you help her? Besides, if she's that bad, she should stay in hospital for another couple of days."

"She needs both of us. And according to mainstream medicine, she's not injured. She's run down and needs to rest. That means recovering from this episode at home."

"You know she won't do it," Ronin snapped. She needed to stay safe by whatever means necessary. He understood she felt responsible for Exotic Landscape, but she had staff...good staff...and it was time for her to step back and let them carry the load.

He didn't fully understand the enormity of these attacks, but he was starting too. And that scared him. Tabitha needed protection. But how could he protect her from something he couldn't see?

He started toward the front of the house.

"No, she won't. She cares about her animals too much. And work has always been her way of escaping the rest of the world. So she's going to go home and bury herself in work – most likely paperwork at her own house."

At her house. Ronin glared at the huge monstrosity. "But she was attacked here. So how does that work?"

"Not well. I'm setting up an energetic barrier. A second security system. I'm hoping it will be enough to keep her safe. Or at least good enough to be an early warning system."

"What good will that do?"

"If she has enough warning, she'll be able to guard herself from another attack. She does have some serious skills, but last time she had no idea what was happening until it was almost too late."

"How much warning does she need?" His mind spun with the possibilities. Between Roman's security system and Stefan's psychic security system...maybe she'd be okay.

"It's only the barest of what is needed." Stefan cleared his throat, and for the first time Roman heard the fatigue running through his voice. Stefan was running on empty himself. Damn.

Abruptly, he said, "What can I do to help?"

In a hard voice, Stefan said, "Find him. Do whatever you can do to track down this asshole."

That's what he did for a living, track down perps… But how did he track down a nameless, faceless, disembodied entity?

"Search Tabitha's history. Search for any and all people connected to her who might have psychic abilities."

"Can't you see an energy signature, or whatever it's called, around her?" Isn't that what Stefan did? "Can't *you* identify him?"

"Sometimes I can. Not this time. There was nothing *normal* about this attack. She hadn't cleared away the day's energies. She was surrounded by grief and animal energies. Both completely overwhelmed her ability to notice this entity. And I can't rule out that her attacker was using animal energy to get close to her." Stefan's voice strengthened. "In fact, that's a good possibility. In which case, this person *is* working with animals."

"Fine, then that's where I'll—" There was a sharp click and his phone went dead. Stefan had hung up on him.

"Damn." Ronin stared at the house. He had work to do.

***

"Be careful with that thing. If we lose her, we've lost the biggest payday ever," Fez snarled at the forklift driver. The front lift jerked down several more feet. "Shit," Fez muttered. "We're going to kill her yet."

"Better not. I won't be happy if that happens."

The cold voice behind him sent icy shards of fear down Fez's spine. He hadn't expected his boss to show up at this moment. Then, given all the things that had gone wrong, maybe his arrival wasn't so surprising after all.

"Did Roberts come back with you?" Fez asked looking around. Roberts needed to check the delivery over. Make sure everything had survived the journey.

"No."

Fez froze at the icy dead tone.

But the boss's next words were the ones that really made his heart stop. "You know what happens to people who make me unhappy. My neck is on the line with this deal. You screw up, then I screw up. In which case you won't be looking to salvage your job because you won't care. You'll be floating down the damn river as fish food instead."

Fez nodded but kept his face turned away. Fingers of cold reached down deep inside his stomach. His boss never threatened. He promised.

Thankfully, the forklift operator unloaded the cage without any more mishaps and backed away to get the next load. They were late and time was running out. The cages had to be transferred to the new truck, which would be followed by a couple of hours of driving. Fez was taking the truck with this cargo. He sent a silent prayer to the heavens above.

Please let this job go smoothly.

Not that he expected anyone to listen to his request. They hadn't so far.

Chapter 5

Saturday, early evening

Tabitha paid the taxi before stumbling up the front steps of her house. The sun beamed beautiful farewell rays across the summer sky. Delighted to be home, she sent out a tired but happy wave of energy in greeting to both Tango and Tripod. The returning waves of deep blue and purple exuberance delighted and reassured her that all was well...or mostly well.

The front door was unlocked.

Startled, she stood in the open doorway and studied her house. She took a deep breath and mentally whistled for Tripod. Where the hell was he?

Nails skittered on the tile floors. He tore around the corner of the kitchen and raced toward her. She smiled and murmured in her head, *Gentle. I'm tired and if you knock me over I might not make it back up.*

He slowed to a skid on the tile, a deep whine coming up from inside his chest.

I'm fine, sweetie. Just seriously tired. I need to go to bed and sleep for a couple of days. "Fat chance," she muttered out loud.

"Fat chance of what?" The deep voice was an electric shock to her tired body. She stiffened as her tired gaze caught site of Ronin then she relaxed again. Strong. Capable. With his take-charge attitude. In her home.

Damn, he looked good there.

Like he belonged. Why had she been worried about having him here…?

Oh yeah, a little thing called felines...like Tango.

Her eyes filled with tears. Damn. She had to be tired to start this. She swiped at her eyes with her sleeve. He opened his arms.

And she ran forward.

His long arms wrapped around her and tucked her up close. Hidden in his embrace, she felt so protected, safe.

And dare she say it – loved?

Something she hadn't felt in a long time. She soaked up his comfort and caring until Tripod nudged her in the ribs.

She gave a small laugh and stepped back. "Hey, big guy. Let's get you some food."

With a teary smile at Ronin, she led the way back to the kitchen. She heard the front door close behind her, followed by Ronin's footsteps. In the kitchen, she stopped. There were pots simmering on the stove.

She spun around, a delighted smile on her face. "You made dinner?"

He shrugged sheepishly. "Spaghetti."

With a hand on the small of her back, he nudged her into the kitchen. A large pot in front burped. He stepped over to it and stirred the contents.

"I can't remember the last time someone cooked me a meal." Delight curled her insides. "And you've made one of my favorites."

The smile fell off his face as he studied her. Cautiously, he asked, "Really? Not your grandfather? Father? Fiancé?"

"My grandfather hated cooking. As soon as I was old enough, I took over the chore. Dennis, my father, never lived here with me."

Waving a ladle at her, he asked quietly, "And the fiancé?"

She wrinkled her nose and walked slowly toward him. "He'd never be caught in a kitchen."

"Well, I have no such issue." He shrugged those wide shoulders. "I love to cook."

Damn. She could get used to that. Her good mood restored, she said, "Perfect. 'Cause I'm starved."

"Good. 'Cause it's ready." He smiled and motioned to the table. "I wasn't sure if it was safe to leave Tripod here – nice name by the way – around the food."

"He's got great manners." She let Ronin lead her to the table and hold out her chair. "But I wouldn't trust him too far."

"That's what I thought." He quickly served up dinner under Tripod's eagle eye and carried the plates to the table. "What I don't have is a bottle of wine to go with this."

She laughed. "As much as I'd love a glass, I don't think there is a bottle in the house."

"I'll take care of that when I head out tomorrow."

Her hand dropped, her fork clattering to the plate. "Tomorrow?"

He cocked an eyebrow. "Yes. I have a few things to check on. I'll grab a bottle or two on my way home."

She flushed, and in a strangled voice, said, "Home?"

"Yep." He casually scooped up a forkful of spaghetti. "I'm not leaving you alone until this is over." And he popped the food in his mouth.

Over? She very carefully put her fork down and stared at him in shock. "Why?"

It was his turn to stare at her. "Because you were attacked?"

Cautiously, she asked, "You understand in what way I was attacked, right?"

He nodded and twisted up another fork of pasta. "Yep. Somewhat. At least what I got from what Stefan, Shay and my brother told me."

"And you think...you can help if I'm attacked again?" She didn't want to insult him, but just what was he thinking?

At the disbelief in her voice, he very carefully replaced his fork. "I know that I'm not like you and I probably can't do much to ward off a psychic attacker, but I can get help."

She stared down at her plate. "I know you believe that, but you might not even know that an attack is happening. It's not as if I'm screaming out loud."

He frowned. "Then maybe I'm going to have to sleep in the same room as you. Surely, I'd know then?"

She snorted. "Wait until you're invited."

"And how long will that take?" He grinned at her narrow-eyed look. "Hey, it was worth asking. And I've been patient."

She rolled her eyes at him. Inside, she felt the warmth uncurl in her belly. Like they'd gotten that far yet. Her grandfather's death had pushed that step back slightly. "I like sleeping alone."

Both eyebrows flew up. "And here I thought for sure you slept with Tripod." Tripod, hearing his name, gave a small yelp.

She reached out a hand. Tripod shuffled right up to her plate and sniffed. Tabitha tapped his nose to make him back up. "If you can call that sharing. Tripod is a bed hog. Besides, lots of nights I sleep with another male."

The smile slid off Ronin's face.

Good.

Then Tango roared.

***

"Jesus. What the hell is that?" Ronin half jumped out of his chair and leaned forward to look out the window.

"Ha. It's my cat. That's Tango."

He shot her a disbelieving look, catching the amused glitter in her light-green eyes. "There is no way a cat makes that kind of sound."

Tango roared again. This time though there was something off. Tabitha went to the living room and pushed some kind of button. Ronin followed more slowly and watched as the whole wall retracted.

What the hell kind of wall was that? And damn if she didn't have some kind of fine mesh cage behind that wall. Thank God.

He was half afraid she was one of those crazy people who got so super cozy with their wild pets that they ignored common sense.

Then she pulled the wire mesh completely back.

Oh shit.

And didn't the biggest damn white tiger, with a head the size of Mount Rushmore, saunter toward her.

"Watch out," he cried as the tiger jumped. Instantly his throat clogged and his chest tightened. Christ, he could hardly breathe. He swallowed. And then swallowed again. He couldn't help the instinctive clenching of his fists. Inside, insidious emotions shifted through him. Panic. Pain. Sadness. So much worse than the last time he'd been in the house.

He took a shaky breath. This was not happening.

He was halfway to her when he realized the tiger had stopped with complete control and was on his back legs, Tabitha crushed in his embrace.

Jesus.

Ronin prided himself on being a brave soul, but he was not going that close. And he didn't care how tame the damn thing was. A wild animal was a wild animal.

Unless it's not a wild animal.

Stefan. And did one ever get used to this guy in his head?

Ronin snapped out mentally, *If you're trying to convince me that this thing is safe to be around, forget it. I have too much respect for human life to believe you.*

And in many cases you could be right. In this case however, you'd be wrong.

And why is that? Has she got some kind of special powers or something? Right about now he wished she did. He'd believe that as much as anything.

No, but they do have a special connection.

See, that's where you are wrong. All pet lovers say that about their little pooches. And he couldn't help the disgust from rolling through his voice. He was a cop, damn it. And he'd seen more than his fair share of animals both domesticated and wild. Sometimes the domestic ones were the more dangerous.

Stefan laughed. *You'll have to see for yourself. And take a deep breath. You will survive this.*

"Promise?" Ronin muttered.

With a last laugh, Ronin's mind emptied. Damn, that was weird.

"Ronin, come and meet Tango."

"I don't think that's a good idea." Damn it, he wasn't a wuss. He took a couple of steps forward and stopped. And struggled to breathe. He so didn't want to pass out. Not here. Not with her. Not with that carnivore looking on. "I'll stick to dogs."

"Tripod is here, too."

He groaned silently and took another step into the living room.

Tango dropped to the floor and stared at Ronin, a howl starting deep in the back of his throat. The hairs raised on the back of his neck.

The look in those damn eyes...

Ronin took a deep breath and tried to stop the shakiness that was starting to vibrate his insides, making his stomach acids turn to cheese.

"Why is he howling?"

"I'm not sure. He doesn't normally do that." She reached down to place a hand on Tango's head. The howl changed. It wasn't the same tenor as the first time, but it was hardly welcoming.

Then all of a sudden, the howl cut off.

Thank you. Ronin much preferred the silence. Except now a dull roaring sound was in his head. Almost a buzz. He shook his head, trying to clear it.

Tabitha sighed heavily. "Come over here and meet Tango. He'll calm down once he meets you. And maybe you will too."

She tilted her head and studied him. "And make sure that gun is safely away. Tripod hates them."

"I've already made peace with the dog." He didn't move.

"And you'll make peace with Tango, too. It's much better to meet him on equal ground. If you take one step backwards, he's got you."

"Damn." Ronin stepped forward. He could feel the heat, the intensity of that deep blue feline gaze following his every movement. Like a cat watching a mouse.

Ronin had always felt sympathy for the mouse.

For a cat, the animal was damn beautiful. The markings on its head, the eyes, the shocking white fur were something he'd never expected to see up close. And never inside a house. Not sure he wanted to hear the answer, he asked, "Do you let him out of that cage much?"

"All the time. The house is his, too."

Double damn.

When he was a couple of feet away, Ronin stopped, his gaze on the cat.

"Now what?"

She grinned. "Say hi."

He shot her a fulminating look. "Just like that."

"Well, *to* him of course."

His gaze zipped back to the waiting tiger. Did she mean it the way Stefan had said to talk to Tango? 'Cause there was no way in hell he'd be dropping to his knees and closing his eyes in front of a tiger. Talk about being a sacrificial offering. Then as if to accentuate the fact that the tiger was waiting for the appropriate response, it sat down and waited.

Taking a deep breath and feeling like an idiot, Ronin said, "Hi, Tango. Nice to meet you."

No response. Then again, what had he expected? He shook his head then winced at the heavy buzz in his ear. Under his breath, he swore again.

"That ringing inside your head... It's because he's talking to you and you're not listening."

He stared at her in disbelief. "How did you know my head is ringing?"

She snorted. "Because I can sense it. Normally I only listen to my animals but now... some things have changed and I can sense more with people too. And behind your lovely front of 'I don't like cats'...I see fear."

Heat washed up his cheeks. Damn. So what if there was fear? Hell, there was a tiger in the room. Anyone with an ounce of working brain matter would understand. Besides, it's not as if he was afraid *of* cats... He knew there was fear there, he just didn't understand what exactly frightened him.

And the last thing he wanted was her laughing at him.

With a final glance at the still gaze of the tiger locked on him, Ronin decided enough was enough for this time. He'd done well but he didn't want to push it. He turned and headed back to the kitchen, putting a little distance between him and Tango. "While you're having your fun, I'll go finish eating. Unless you're planning on feeding dinner to the two of them."

Turning his back on that damn feline was the hardest thing he'd done in a long time. And he was proud that he'd managed to do it in a calm, nonchalant manner.

Then he found the two empty plates on the table and the guilty party still licking the tomato sauce off his face.

Tripod.

✳✳✳

On the road at last. Only a couple of hours late. Not too bad. His boss had driven on ahead and Fez was hauling the cargo in the big rig. Roberts hadn't shown up yet. That was a pisser. Fez had called him a couple of times but Roberts hadn't answered as yet.

The highway was almost empty. In fact, the truck was almost empty too. Good. It should make the trip easier. Faster.

Most of the cages were small. Then there was the big one. What the hell was with her?

He'd always loved his job before. Enjoyed the challenge and the payoffs. It had been easy money with plenty to keep him busy.

Only something was shifting. Maybe because Roberts hadn't shown up, Fez was afraid his buddy had 'booked it' after all. That was bad news if he hadn't planned his disappearance the right way. When the boss found out he wasn't coming back to work...

He sighed. This was a good gig. It wasn't hard. Gave them lots of free time. What was there to complain about? So what if they were moving females in cages. This type of job for many people was nothing. Besides they were paid enough to squelch any kind of misgivings.

He shifted gears and took the truck into the turn.

Please keep the females asleep. They were much easier to deal with when they were quiet. Of course they'd really start screaming when they saw where they were going. There'd be no appreciation there. But at least they'd have food and water and shelter.

See, their lot wasn't so bad after all.

And if he kept telling himself that, then maybe he'd start to believe it.

Chapter 6

Saturday evening

They served up the last of the spaghetti on clean plates and ate. Tripod had been banished from the dining room this time. Afterwards, Tabitha took her coffee into the living room, Tango at her heels. The damn softie had been trying to steal her coffee for years. Tabitha never gave in, but that didn't stop the old cat from trying, or taking advantage of every opportunity that Tabitha was distracted.

As she settled in one corner of the big settee that was from her grandfather's era, she couldn't help but see the room as Ronin had to see it. Shabby, retro, well lived in. Like her grandfather, and damn if that didn't bring the tears back up again. He'd been gone almost a week. It seemed like forever.

Ronin stood awkwardly at the entrance to the living room staring at Tango. At least he didn't look like he was going to pass out anymore. She had to give him credit. He was still there. With a smile, she said, "Take a seat. I don't have much, but what I have is comfortable."

She watched with interest as Ronin chose the chair furthest away from her – and Tango. Tripod slumped to the floor in between her and Ronin. The dog was incredibly intuitive and could sense human issues easily.

The phone rang just then. She glared at the big black square relic from her grandfather's time. It continued to ring.

"Aren't you going to answer it?"

"It's Dennis, my father," she said shortly.

Ronin tilted his head. "And..."

She snatched up the receiver. "I'm fine, Dad."

"Then why did the hospital contact me at the office to say you'd been admitted?" he snapped. "I just got the message from

Eric. Is it too much to offer me the courtesy of a follow up call to say you are fine?"

Of course the hospital had called him. He was her next of kin. He must have someone on the hospital board or an alert that rang some kind of alarm every time she went in. He always seemed to know. "I was admitted. I was checked over. I checked myself out." She sighed. "I'm fine. End of story."

"Tango?"

"Tango is fine. I'd passed out, someone checked up on me and called an ambulance. Not a biggie." She rolled her eyes at Ronin's raised eyebrow and turned her attention back to her father, wishing he'd hang up. She was lying and her father had a built-in lie detector. Like most fathers.

"Hmm."

She winced. "I have company right now. So maybe we can talk tomorrow?"

"Unless you're unconscious and back in the hospital," her father said grimly.

"Not likely. I'm fine. Just a little worn down."

"Isn't that why you hired more people? So this wouldn't happen?" he asked. "Are you sure you can handle that place? It doesn't sound like it to me."

Her back stiffened and she shot an angry look at Ronin. He raised an eyebrow and leaned forward. She shook her head. "Dad, I can handle the place just fine. I'm not fragile. I'm not losing it or whatever else that damn assistant of yours might have suggested." She tried to rein back the sweeping emotions and the fear over losing her grandfather's estate. "Eric is a drama queen," she said shortly. "There's nothing wrong with me or the Reserve."

"Germaine is concerned as well, and no one would call him that. Besides, look at the break-ins, vandalism and..." He took a deep breath. "And you having blackouts."

"I'm fine," she repeated, hating the dread reaching up to choke her. "Just finish handling Granddad's estate so I'm not in limbo anymore and I'll be even better." She drew a deep breath. "Look, I need to go."

"I'll stop by tomorrow. We'll go over the estate then."

As she hung up the phone, she had to wonder how she could have been so close to her grandfather and so distant with her father.

"You don't get along with him?"

Ronin's black gaze studied her. She shifted self-consciously. How did one explain a missed connection between generations? "We've never been close. He hates this place and I love it. I was close to my grandfather but he wasn't." She didn't expect him to understand, but he was smiling. "But he's a hell of a businessman and donates money to keep the place running."

"I do understand. I presume he isn't so hot on the animal thing?"

She laughed. "I swear he hates them. And he really didn't like the whole circus performer thing. But my grandfather, although retired by the time I came along, was a carny at heart."

"That must have been tough on your father when his father was still a performer. That's hardly the same as saying my father is a doctor or a lawyer. For some kids, he'd have had the best dad but for many others, he'd have been mocked day in and day out."

She had to wonder. Had her dad's life been the living hell he made it out to be?

"I imagine that as soon as he could, he got out of this place. But what I don't understand is how and why you ended up here without him?" Ronin studied her face for an answer.

"Now there's a story. My father had actually broken up with my mother before she found out she was pregnant. And she never told him. Apparently, she didn't want a child at that stage of her life. She tried motherhood out for a few months and decided it wasn't for her. She..." Tabitha sighed at all the childhood memories that had been so difficult growing up with. "She left me with my father."

As his eyes widened in shock, she laughed. "And as you can imagine, that was a bit more than he'd bargained for when he opened his door on a Sunday afternoon. He had a six-month-old child dropped in his arms and was told he'd make a better parent than the mother was."

Ronin shook his head. "Jesus."

She could just imagine Ronin thinking of his own life and what he'd do in that circumstance. "The thing is, my father hadn't planned on being a father either. Ever. He'd had so little relationship with his own dad that he figured procreation wasn't for him. So he dumped me on grandpa."

"Even though he'd had a poor relationship with his own father?" Ronin's brow lifted in surprise. "Wasn't that almost a punishment for you? He'd make you suffer as he had done?"

She smiled. "I think he was too desperate to think clearly at all. Maybe in a small way he figured grandpa owed him. I don't know and I don't care because it's the best thing he could have done. I adored my grandfather and I'd like to believe I enriched his life."

"Especially when you took to the animals the way his own son didn't."

"True."

"But your father still loves you."

Ronin stated that as a fact and she had to wonder about that. "As much as he can, I guess. I never saw a lot of him growing up. I think my father would have happily dropped me off and never set eyes on me again, but my grandfather was strong willed and he had strict rules about what my father's role in all this was."

"Sounds as if you might have gotten the best deal after all."

"I sure did." She laughed as she reached across the couch to scratch Tango's ear with her nails. "All the kids I went to school with wanted to be me."

"Goes to show you the difference a generation can make."

"Also, my father is conscious of appearances. But for me, as you can see…" She flung a hand at her old living room. "Appearances are the least of my worries."

"Not much point in tidying all the time if the animals have the run of the house. I'm sure keeping this place clean is an ongoing challenge."

She winced. "It's the hair more than anything. Mostly from Tripod. Tango stays in his enclosure much of the time. When he's in the house, he has the run of every room though."

"Including your bedroom."

Knowing it was likely the death sentence to their relationship but feeling that she couldn't short Tango either, she answered truthfully. "Sometimes he sleeps on my bed."

At Ronin's spluttering reaction, she shrugged. "Tango is good company. And if he isn't on my bed, you can bet Tripod is."

"No wonder you sleep alone." Ronin stood up. "And speaking of sleep, you're tired. And need rest. Do you have a spare room for me?"

"You don't need to stay over. I'm sure I'll be fine."

"Doesn't matter if you believe it or not. I'm staying."

There was no doubting the determined lock to the jaw or the glint in his eyes. She stood up. Let him see what he'd be sleeping in first. Then he could decide. She had several spare bedrooms but the beds weren't made up. One of the rooms didn't even have a bed in it. And the one room that was fully furnished and made up was her father's old room. She doubted Ronin would stay once he saw the accommodations.

Tango got up and walked toward Ronin. He backed up. "And getting this guy back into his cage would be much appreciated."

"If you're planning on sticking around, you need to get used to him being here. It's his home. I leave it up to him to decide where he wants to be." But she snapped her fingers, bringing Tango to her side.

"Shit."

Sighing, she stood up. "You can sleep in the spare room down this way. It was my father's old room."

"Does your father, Dennis ever stay here?"

"No," she said shortly.

Ronin fell into step behind her. Tango, as if seeming to know where they were going, led the way. Tripod brought up the rear.

At the entrance to the bedroom, Ronin stopped and stared. The far wall was large square mesh leading directly into the tiger's area.

"Crap."

***

Why him? He'd had enough of his ego being bashed by this damn cat thing. Ronin was not going to lose any more time on it. He hoped. "I presume the wire mesh is strong and I won't have any uninvited guests during the night." He was proud of how cool, calm and collected he managed to sound. How had Dennis liked being here with this cage?

"It's secure."

He studied the wire, walking closer to test it with his hands. It was solid. And from what he could see, there didn't appear to be any opening or hinges where the wall opened.

"I thought Dennis didn't want anything to do with the whole carny thing."

"That didn't mean he didn't want some connection to the animals. He was raised here after all. And besides, he hasn't slept in this room…" She broke off as if to consider, then shrugged. "Since… I don't remember when. Maybe thirty-five plus years."

Ronin pivoted to stare at the large room, realizing how much like the rest of the house it was. As if time had stopped. Big, old and essentially untouched in several decades.

Little had been done in the way of updating the interior or furnishings, and given where her heart lay, she'd most likely poured all the available money into the animals and their care.

And speaking of animals...

"Is this the only tiger you have right now?" He glanced around at her and saw Tango sprawled at her feet.

"Inside the house, yes. My grandfather's last tiger, Tobias, passed away a few months before he did," she paused. "In fact, I wondered if grief played a part in my grandfather's early death. Those two were so close. And up until he died, my grandfather was very healthy. He went to sleep that night and just never woke up."

"You found him?" Now that wouldn't have been fun.

She squatted and gave Tango a good belly rub. "Tango woke me up. He was howling something awful. He knew. When I heard him, I knew. There was just something different about his call. I went and checked on my grandfather and found him in bed, still curled up in his favorite sleeping position."

Ronin found it hard to believe that the damn motor coming from its throat was a purr, but it was acting like a baby house cat. "Are you and Tango that close?"

Sadness swept over her as she smiled up at him. "Yes. He came into the household when I was ten and he was just a cub. We fell in love."

"And how much longer does he have?"

"He's living on borrowed time in many ways." She sighed and straightened. "Life expectancy is anywhere from twelve to twenty years, with the white species thought to be slighter shorter than their golden counterparts."

"So he's old? How come he doesn't look it?" Then again, how would he know what an old tiger looked like? Several meters long from nose to tail with clear bright eyes and jet-black markings, he showed no recognizable signs of aging.

"He's a pampered baby." She straightened. "He's been badly affected by the passing of our tiger, Tobias, and my grandfather's deaths."

"So when did Tripod move in?" Hearing his name, Tripod nudged Ronin's hand. As mad as he'd been over the disappearance of their dinner, he couldn't help but stroke the beautiful animal's huge head. As if realizing he'd been forgiven, Tripod walked over to the bed and stretched across the bottom of it.

"He's seven now. And look... He's found your bed." She laughed. "Good thing you said you liked dogs."

Dogs were good. Much easier to deal with than this cat thing he had going on. He couldn't remember when it all started, but anyone who compared a ten-pound, fluffy domestic cat to this five hundred pound-take-your-face-off-if-you-look-at-him-sideways cat was crazy.

He might just prefer this version, but he'd rather not have anything to do with either.

Abruptly Tabitha pointed to a door off to the side and said, "There's the bathroom. I think you should have everything you need."

Then she turned to go.

"Just a question, if you do get attacked tonight, are there other animals here that I'm likely to come face to face with on my way to your room?"

She hesitated at the doorway.

He narrowed his gaze and felt his heart pound. What the hell was she hiding?

And why?

Then she laughed, a light easy laugh that made his suspicions suddenly seem foolish. "Nope, there's just the three of us here."

Dare he ask? Shit, he really needed access. And he didn't need to argue with a damn tiger when he was fighting to save her life. "And Tango? Will you lock him up in case I have to come to you?"

"He'll be in my room."

"And if he won't let me near you?" He glared at her. "Do you really want to put a cop who's going to be more concerned about saving you against a tiger that won't give him access?"

She stiffened and glared right back. "I'll be fine."

"And yet you weren't."

She walked to the doorway then paused, turned and said, "If that happens again, there won't be anything you can do about it." She was silent a long moment. "Just in case you do come across me in an odd state, try not to physically touch me."

And she walked out.

***

Fez stared into the back of the truck, hating the booming in his head from the noise. "She isn't calming down. Shit. She's been given so many drugs she should be fucking sleeping." She was going to hurt herself this way. God help him if that happened.

Where the hell was Roberts? He was the one who always dealt with this shit.

Fez knew nothing about this part of the job. He sure hoped the boss did. And Fez didn't need that added worry right now. He'd only stopped to check on her because he wanted to make sure she was okay. Now he wished he hadn't. What could he do? Nothing. Roberts had the stuff to knock her out. He did those jobs.

Not Fez.

Best thing would be for him to get back inside that truck and go straight to the warehouse. That might calm her down. And the others.

The look in her eye just then.... Jesus, that had scared the crap out of him.

"If you'd calm down and just sit quietly, it will go so much easier on you."

She still glared at him with that look in her eye... But she stayed quiet.

He was kind of glad about that. He'd listened to her complain enough already. Her throat had probably been screamed raw. If he was lucky, she'd lost her voice.

The guys he'd picked the shipment up from said she'd been tranq'd and would be asleep for hours. Not true.

Now he didn't know what to do. *Shit.* He closed the back of the truck, threw down the level to lock it in place, walked to the front of the truck and hopped up onto the driver's seat.

He could really only do one thing – carry on as he'd started.

Chapter 7

Saturday, late evening

Ronin and Tabitha were finally sleeping under one roof. Just not the way she'd hoped. Tabitha strolled back to her own huge bed and pulled the covers back as much as she could. Tango had taken up most of the space. "Move over, boy."

Instead, he rolled toward her on his back, presenting his belly to be scratched.

"That's not quite what I meant." She smiled. "Then it seems males always interpret what I'm saying in their own way."

Tango's engine kicked in. Tabitha sat down and scratched the tiger's velvety fur. "What am I going to do when you're gone?"

It would devastate her. Losing Tobias had been difficult. She'd understood her grandfather's lingering despair months later. They'd been closer than father and son. And she was closer to Tango that she was to her own father.

Tigers had been the missing link for both generations.

Her grandfather had spent the better part of his life being a servant to the large cats. She was following in his footsteps. For the most part, she was fine with that. But she didn't want to be alone forever. Her thoughts once again returned to Ronin, sleeping so close, and yet so far away. That short distance somehow made her feel even more lonely than if she had been there, alone in the house. Knowing that they were so damn close to taking their relationship to the next level also made it difficult.

She'd been falling for him for weeks. That long slow glide of attraction that was both special and disconcerting. Sure, he had this thing about cats...but when she needed him, he'd done well with Tango. Many people would have taken one look and run.

"Just you and me, huh, boy." At least for the moment.

She slipped under the covers, shoving Tango over. Not an easy task, but he rolled back the way he'd been earlier with a contented snort.

Regardless of where Ronin slept, Tabitha had to admit she did feel better having Ronin staying there. It felt right. With that thought, she turned off her lamp and slid lower under the covers.

✳✳✳

It was the middle of the night when she woke. Her heart pounded in her chest with a ferocity that had her panicked and searching the corners of her bedroom. She'd also woken alone. Tango had slipped out of her room sometime in the night. She glanced at her clock. It was 2:34 am. She'd managed less than three hours.

A shadow crossed her nervous system, accentuating the feeling of wrongness.

Then she understood. Shit.

Someone was out hunting… She was the prey.

Again.

Taking a deep breath, she sank energy lines down her legs, through the heels of her feet and deep into the ground. She had to be grounded. She desperately wanted to jump ship and hide in the ethers, but she didn't dare leave her body alone and unprotected. Not if she was the prize. Well, she wasn't going to make it easy on whoever was doing this. Not this time.

Knowing it was foolish, but unable to resist the instinctive move, she scrambled out of bed and raced to the spot behind her bedroom door. She understood it was a psychic attack, but that didn't mean her attacker wasn't here physically as well.

Except that neither Tango nor Tripod had raised the alarm. And they would have if there was a stranger in the house.

"Tabitha?" The male whisper slipped into the room, so soft it was almost silent.

Ronin? How did he know?

"Yes," she whispered.

"Are you okay?" His voice deepened as he moved closer.

She didn't know what to say. That his interruption when she'd just acknowledged that her attacker could be here physically was disconcerting. She was certain it wasn't him. There was no way. She'd have known Ronin's energy anywhere. That didn't mean someone couldn't be using him to attack her though. Stranger things had happened. And she'd let him inside the house.

A basic rule. Another of her grandfather's rules broken this last week.

But anyone who could do what this guy had almost done last time, most likely didn't need to be inside her home. He could be outside prowling the grounds. He could be miles away.

Trusting her instincts, she peered around the door. Ronin stood there in his jeans, bare chested, his gun in his hand.

Shit.

Why wasn't Tripod having a fit over the gun?

"Are you okay?" he repeated.

She took a deep breath and brushed a long strand of hair back off her face. "Yes. I think so. I just woke up a few minutes ago." She motioned to the firearm. "What are you doing here – and with that?"

He glanced around her room as if still searching for something wrong, then glanced down at the gun in his hands. "Tripod sounded the alarm."

She stared at him, then at the massive dog that strolled into her room, looking unconcerned. "Really? And what alarm was that?"

The frown as he glanced down at the dog sitting quietly, calmly at his side, was telling. "He woke me up, started whining and wouldn't quit until I followed him here."

"Interesting," she murmured. Since when had Tripod taken to a stranger like that? Normally he'd have barked until he lost his voice. Or called to her telepathically. She eyed the dog suspiciously, asking mentally, *What are you up to?*

He stared back with an innocent look on his canine face.

But she knew him. And he'd done what he'd done for a reason. The end result was he'd brought Ronin to her rescue. To her bedroom.

And she *had* woken up with that sense she was being hunted. Maybe Tripod had brought Ronin here in response to her own fears…

"I had a bad dream. That's all." She managed a natural smile. "Tripod must have picked up on it."

"What kind of a bad dream?" His voice hardened. "And don't lie to me."

She could just imagine him in an interview room. He was a good cop. And suspicion wove through his voice. He needed an explanation. She likened him to a bulldog, not willing to let go of something he wanted.

She gave in with grace. "I had the feeling I was being hunted."

His gaze narrowed. "As in an intruder, a nightmare or a psychic attack?"

She winced. "A nightmare – I hope – but…there's no way to tell at this point."

"Do you still feel that way?" He glanced around the inside of her room, those sharp eyes peering into corners looking for hiding places. Then he spun around to check in the direction of the hallway and other rooms behind him.

She shook her head. "No. The air is lighter now. The sensation is gone."

He studied her.

She stared back calmly.

"Good. Then try to get a little more sleep." And he walked around the side of the bed, placed his weapon on the night table and lay down on top of the covers. He closed his eyes.

"Uhmmmm?" She stared at him in shock. "What are you doing?"

"Going to bed. I suggest you do the same. If anyone is going to hunt you, they'll have to go through me," he muttered before a yawn took him. He rolled onto his side and looked ready to fall asleep.

She didn't know if she was outraged or honored. That he'd want to protect her went along with his cop image, but she didn't want him here in her room if it was just professional...

Wait. Of course she did. She didn't want to be attacked, but at the same time she wanted it to be more than for just a professional reason on his part. She hesitated then asked, "What if I don't want you sleeping here?"

"Too bad. Besides, I've wanted to sleep here for a while. Now's my chance."

She gasped at the smirk in his voice. She'd been wanting the same thing, but not like this.

She didn't know what to do. What to say.

He rolled over, grabbed the corner of her bedding and pulled it back so she could get in. "Come on, sweetheart, get over it. Get some sleep. You need sleep, time to heal."

She crawled into bed, her movements stiff and hesitant. "And who says I'm going to get over it?"

"I'm telling you to." He yawned again then added in a sleepy voice, "And do it fast."

She'd have gasped in outrage but he appeared to be asleep already. Damn, how could he do that? She never fell asleep so easily. She pulled the covers up to her neck, rolled over and closed her eyes. And couldn't sleep.

Frustrated, she tossed and turned.

"What *is* your problem?" he asked. "Do you want Tango here, instead of me? Well too bad."

"Ha!" She sat up again taking umbrage at his tone. "What is your problem with cats anyway? You seemed to handle Tango just fine tonight."

"Because I stayed the hell away." He chuckled softly. "Besides, I like some cats – I like you, kitten."

"Oh no, you don't." She glared at him, but inside her heart was softening. He'd always been able to do that to her. Make her go gooey inside with that deep-throated chuckle and the soft sexy tones. "This is important. I thought we had something special going on here. But cats are a huge part of my life."

The laughter fell from his face. He propped himself up on one arm so he could look at her. His bare chest gleamed in the moonlight. She swallowed, wishing she hadn't noticed. But now that she had, she couldn't think of anything else but that huge expanse of muscled body displayed in front of her. With effort, she tore her gaze away and focused on his face.

"As far as I'm concerned – I'm in," he said suddenly. And damn if those eyes of his didn't deepen and pull her into a mental embrace.

She sighed happily. "Okay then." And fell silent, not knowing where to go next.

His lips quirked in a small intimate way that sent her heart racing. She leaned back against the headboard and tugged the covers up to her waist. He reached out a hand and gently smoothed out the wrinkles of the top blanket. A heavy sigh escaped and he said in a troubled voice, "I don't really understand why, but something happens when I see cats." He stared out the window. "I don't know how to explain it. I'm not allergic, but my chest doesn't seem to understand that. It locks down and I can't breathe. At the same time, it's emotional overload. It's how I imagine a panic attack would feel. I get headaches and a lot of times there's a horrific buzzing in my head."

Now that was a different story. And one that gave her hope. "So it's not that you don't like them, but you don't like the way you react to them?"

He shrugged. "Something like that. I can handle it, but it's not exactly comfortable. And given a choice of never being in the same room with one, I wouldn't be."

"And yet you were in the same room with Tango."

"It's not as if you gave me much choice." His face twisted into a mock grin. "Besides, I didn't want to look a fool in my lady's presence. Not exactly manly."

His lady? Her insides wiggled. Maybe. Maybe this was something they could work around. And his reaction to felines, such a strong reaction pointed to several options. An undiagnosed allergy, or her favorite theory – a traumatic event in his history. Even if he didn't remember the event, his body might. And that was something that could be worked on. She'd have to mention it to Stefan.

"Do you remember when this started?"

He groaned and flopped down on his back beside her. "You know there are a lot more fun things I'd like to be doing in the middle of the night while lying on a huge bed with a beautiful woman at my side instead of talking about my problems, right?"

Tabitha grinned. *What the hell...* "And if I still want to talk about this?"

He snorted, glanced at the watch on his wrist and said, "Then get over it. You have 30 seconds, 29, 28, 27..."

She reached for her pillow and hit him over the head.

He laughed, snatched the pillow and tossed it. Then he tugged her free of the bedding before flipping her over. He quickly tossed his leg over hers, trapping her beneath him.

She was too surprised to move. Damn, he moved fast and sooo smoothly.

Then he lowered his head.

She gave in happily as his warm lips moved gently on hers. Questing, seeking, asking.

This is not where she thought the night would end up. Yet maybe she should have. Is this what she wanted? Hell yes. Was it the right time? Maybe not. But she didn't think that mattered anymore.

He lowered his head again. This kiss was no longer as gentle. It sought answers, asked permission, all while offering a taste of what was to come.

She swiftly fell under his spell. She wrapped her arms around his back and pulled him close, deepening the kiss. He resisted, keeping himself ever so slightly up and away, his lips still on hers but not devouring. He lifted his head and looked at her. "Are you sure?"

She blinked at him. Then smiled. "Yes."

His lips quirked. "In that case…"

The touch of his lips this time was sure, confident, knowing. She sighed happily and slid deeper into his embrace. She wanted him. She wanted it all.

He slid his lips across her skin, leaving a wake of heat and coolness behind. He traced the shape of her ear then dropped tiny kisses down her neck to her collarbone. Tabitha arched her back, giving him better access. He threaded his fingers through her long hair. She twisted gently beneath his gentle caress, her fingers stroking his wide shoulders and back.

He trailed his lips up her throat to reclaim her lips. His lips plundered and caressed and teased, and she was a willing victim. She shifted restlessly.

"Easy," he murmured.

"I don't want easy," she whispered hoarsely, digging her nails into his back.

He reacted swiftly, grabbing her hands and pulling them over her head where he held her gently. She didn't try to get away. Instead she twisted, dragging her lace cami across his bare chest. He bent his head and took the silk-covered nipple into his mouth and suckled. She gasped and arched even more.

"God, I love the sounds you make like this," he whispered.

She hadn't even been aware of making those tiny cries. She tugged her hands free and slipped them down inside his jeans to curve over his muscled buttocks. And dug in her claws.

He roared and bounced off the bed. In a smooth motion, he stripped the jeans off and kicked them to the side. His boxers joined them right after. She kneeled on the bed, watching him. He stood before her, tall and proud and ready. She reached out with both hands.

"Oh not. Not yet." He nodded at her clothing. "Your turn."

With a big bold smile, she crossed her arms and pulled her cami up and off. She tossed it beside his clothes. In a smooth muscled movement, she bounced to her feet, and with a snap, she dropped her panties to the bed where she kicked them in the direction of her bra.

She dropped onto the bed where he waited for her.

He reached out to stroke her smooth, silky skin from hips to ribs then down again, looking, learning, memorizing. A gentle gasp escaped as his touch sparked a trail of embers in its wake. In a surprise move, he pulled her into a loving hug and held her close.

She snuggled deeper, cuddling his erection.

He nudged her chin up to where he could see her face and took a long look. The heat in his gaze brought heat to her cheeks. He whispered, "You are seriously beautiful, you know that?"

"Thank you." She stretched up to clasp his face on both sides and kiss him, gently at first then with more enthusiasm. His heated hands slid around to her back and down to cup her cheeks before he pulled her tight against him. Rolling over, he settled between her legs. She lifted one foot and stroked the back of his calf, smiling up at him.

Dark hair, devilish blue eyes, a wicked smile...and he thought she was beautiful. What more could she ask for?

Then he dropped his head and kissed her. Oh right, he was also a dynamite kisser. He deepened the kiss and she was lost. When he lifted his head, she whimpered, raising her head to find him again. He dropped light caressing kisses on her cheeks, her eyes, her throat. She twisted restlessly beneath him. Sliding her hands over his back and shoulders, she tugged him down for another deep kiss. A gentle kiss. A loving kiss. A kiss full of promise. And found she wanted so much more.

She burned. Everywhere. Her hands had a life of their own, sparking a matching response from him. Skin slid against skin, embers flared to life as every inch of his smooth skin was stroked, squeezed and caressed.

And kissed.

Oh God, his kisses...nectar to a starving woman. She hadn't realized how much she needed this. This touching. This closeness. This connection to him.

He slid to one side, his fingers doing crazy things to her hormones as they stroked down between her legs. She gasped then moaned, her legs shifting restlessly under his clever touch. He leaned over and slipped his tongue between her lips, smoothing across her tongue. His fingers stroked her in tandem to his devilish tongue. She shivered.

She tried to touch him, pull him closer, but he shifted out of reach. "I can't let you," he whispered. "I'm too close to the edge."

Widening her legs, she hooked one leg around his and toppled him where she wanted him.

And he landed perfectly. The tip of his erection sat just inside her but no further.

It was too much and so not enough. She groaned in frustration.

He laughed, raised up on his hands and plunged all the way to her center.

Arching, she cried out with pleasure. *"Yes."*

And then he pulled back and paused.

She groaned. Tugging his mouth back to hers, she murmured against his lips, "Tease."

"Witch," he countered before his mouth closed over hers.

Then neither could talk as his hips drove him into her over and over again, setting up a tempo she matched with every beat.

Tension twisted inside, turning tighter, taking her higher. Until she couldn't take any more.

"I can't..." she cried.

"You can. Take it. Take me. More..."

He shifted slightly, hooking an arm under her thigh and plunging deep, grinding against her center – and that move sent her flying. She cried out, her head arching back into the pillow, her body still braced to take him as he thrust harder and harder.

He arched his back and shuddered, pulsing deep inside her.

A long groan escaped as he collapsed beside her.

She giggled, wrapped her arms around him then snuggled close.

He opened one eye. "You should not have enough energy to laugh after that."

"Except I feel great!" She curled into a ball, her legs layered between his and her arms around his waist. Nose to nose, she smiled deeply at his satiated glow and then she closed her eyes.

And fell asleep.

✳✳✳

She came awake a second time, her heart pounding as she gasped for breath. This time was worse. She could hardly breathe. Her chest constricted in panic.

What was going on?

She bolted from the bed and stood beside her bathroom door, only realizing at the last minute that Ronin had been sleeping soundly beside her. Ronin came awake like the big cats he said he had trouble with. Instantly. He searched the room, his gaze zipping back to her. "Tabitha?"

How could she explain? She wrung her hands as she paced.

"Something is out there." She didn't know how else to explain it. "It's hunting me."

He reached her in seconds. His strong arms wrapped around her, tucking her in close. And in that moment she knew she was no longer alone.

Thank heavens. This was damn spooky stuff.

She glanced around. The bedroom door was open. And there was no sign of Tripod. She walked to the open mesh and saw Tango stretched out on one of the many cushions, completely relaxed.

Tripod...? Surely he'd have sounded an alarm if there was danger. Yet he hadn't.

She'd met too many people with weird psychic abilities. Did someone have the ability to affect her animals? She hoped not. She desperately needed them exactly as they were – for herself.

Ronin peered over her shoulder to search the enclosure. Then he walked to her bedroom window and pulled her curtain back to search the yard out front. "How bad was it?"

"It wasn't outside. And neither is it likely to be visible to the human eye." She stood with her arms wrapped around her chest and answered his original question. "Bad, but not incapacitating."

In shock, Ronin spun around. "Has it ever been as bad as this last time?"

She gave a dry laugh. "How easily you forget. You found me in the shower unconscious the last time, remember? My instinct is to run and hide in the ethers, but I'm trying not to leave my body open to an attacker. I can protect it under most circumstances, but we don't know just what someone might be able to do in this field. And Stefan is afraid that my body might be exactly what this person is after."

"Your body?" He reached up and pinched the bridge of his nose as he searched her face. "Really?"

With the sensation fading, she could afford to smile. A little one. "Yes. Some people are dead. Their souls don't want to cross over. Their souls are, in fact, trapped here and are looking for a way to live again. They only need a physical body. And some are trying to stay here forever."

Ronin's breath rushed out. He shook his head as if trying to deny her words. "And they can just slide back into a life, into another body again?"

"If they can take control of the body, then they can take over and live again." She nodded. "Yes. It's odd and shocking and crazy but it's...true. Ask Stefan. He's seen cases like this. Hard to forget."

Ronin shook his head. "Wow. Every time I get close to these freaky 'woo woo' cases, I have to wonder how any of this could happen while the rest of the world is completely oblivious."

"They are *mostly* oblivious," she corrected, "but at the same time, there are more and more people waking up to the psychic potential within themselves."

"And therefore to the potential for these horrific attacks," Ronin said.

"Of course, but also the potential for skills and healing beyond anything most people can imagine."

"Dr. Maddy, for instance." He smiled. "Now she is something."

Tabitha laughed. "Isn't she though? And she's not alone in what she can do." She walked toward him. "There are people who can see through solids, hear a pitch lower and higher than most animals. Some people can appear as one thing while being something different altogether." She shook her head and studied the emotions sliding across his face...shock, disbelief, curiosity. He'd been exposed to some of this mess through the other friends in their circle, but this was a bit much for anyone. "It's a whole different world once you see below the surface."

She walked closer and almost reached his side when she felt it again.

The hunter. Searching for his prey.

"Shit," she whispered. "He's back."

"Who?" Ronin immediately stepped to her side. "And where?" He turned around in circle, his eyes searching for the predator.

She shuddered as her spine froze. Inside, she felt as if a spotlight shone down on her. "He's found me."

"Hide," Ronin ordered, his gun once again in his hand as he stepped protectively in front of her. He searched the area. "Where is he?"

"Everywhere," she whispered. "He's everywhere."

Ronin spared her a single look. "And so how do I find him?"

"I don't know." She spun around. "He's not showing an energy signature." Knowing Ronin wouldn't understand but not having time to explain, she studied the air in the room. But there were no strange energies.

Then another wave reached for her, over her. This time it was so strong. Even as she stood in place, the emotions hit her.

Fear.

Panic.

Hatred.

She cried out as she dropped to her knees.

Ronin dropped beside her, wrapping an arm around her shoulder. "What is it? What can I do to help?"

"It's him." She screamed and slapped her hands to the sides of her head as the same claw-like sensation dropped inside her skull.

She struggled to set a bolt of energy, her ground, deep through her house, deep into the earth beneath her – as strong and as deep as she could manage. And just like last time, it was almost impossible to hold on. She struggled against the fear, knowing that fear was the most debilitating. Her fear. Ronin's fear. Her attacker's fear.

The combined energies were enough to kill them both. Maybe all three of them. Oh God, had she put Ronin in danger too?

"Tabitha?"

"I'm trying..."

She bent over, trying to shut out the roaring buzz that was increasing by the second, she whispered over and over again, "Stay centered. Stay grounded. Stay balanced."

She had to survive this.

Don't fight.

She didn't know where that thought came from, but she realized she was going about this the wrong way. She was trying to fight off the attack. When she should be giving in to it, then detaching from it.

Observing it.

She straightened slowly, hearing Ronin cry out in the background. "Tabitha? What are you doing?"

"I'm going to try something," she whispered, her voice barely audible. "Don't touch me while I'm doing it."

And she sank within herself, emotionally, physically and psychically. She slipped into her own energy, feeling her way through the heat of her body to the heat of her soul and grounding herself inside.

Another wave of emotion whipped at her, closing in on her soul. It grabbed on and gave her energy a good shake.

She lost her center of balance, scrambled to get it back, then lost it again. Panic swept through her, crying out to her, calling, pleading, begging, for something...someone...to help.

She gasped.

They wanted help.

A scream of anger blasted through her mind. And the pain in her side near her belly region made her want to cry out at the top of her lungs. Something else pricked her side. She barely felt it with everything else that hurt. After a moment, the pain eased.

Only to be replaced by a rage that wouldn't quit.

She felt it at the DNA level.

Then it got worse. That same hand reached deeper into her psyche, deeper into her soul, latched on...and yanked.

Just like last time, she was pulled up through the top of her head.

She screamed as her body collapsed to the floor while from her waist up, she was lifted up and free of her body.

No! She was desperate to stay.

Ground. Ground. Struggling against her own panic, she poured energy deep inside her body and through it to the ground below. She could do this.

As if enraged at being thwarted, she was given a second hard yank... and she was pulled higher up.

There was so much rage behind the energy assault, she could hardly deal with it. Emotions swamped her as she was bombarded by colors and emotions. The pain was so extreme that she was buffeted on all sides even as she shuddered deep inside. She couldn't get a coherent thought to stay long enough to understand it.

And then it was buried under the pain of the next wave.

There was so much fear, it crippled her. She had no time to adapt. To accept. To detach. She couldn't adjust. She wasn't used to this level of panic or this pain. And she definitely wasn't used to the overwhelming sensation of captivity. Imprisonment. Death.

Another heavy yank and she was pulled higher until her knees were now at her waist. She screamed her own scream, a sound of horror and inevitableness. He was too strong.

Too desperate.

And he grabbed hold harder and ripped one more time.

And pulled her loose.

The last thing she saw was her body folded in half on the floor, with Ronin hovering helplessly at her side, his arms wrapped protectively around her. He was trying to save her – but he was trying to save the wrong part of her.

Then she knew no more.

***

Helpless, Ronin could only watch as Tabitha slumped to the floor. She'd been in the same position for a few minutes already, but this last change was shocking. As if she'd been suspended by some kind of string that had been cut, and her lifeless body collapsed to the floor.

He checked for a pulse.

And couldn't find one.

His heart ripped open. Dear God. What was going on?

How could this be?

It was not possible.

Instantly Tango started roaring, the sound loud enough and haunting enough to raise the hairs on the nape of Ronin's neck. Tripod appeared at Tabitha's side and sat on his haunches. He tilted his head back and howled, the sound slicing through the atmosphere with shocking clarity.

Tabitha was in trouble.

Big trouble.

This was so bad. Tabitha wasn't just out cold... She appeared to have moved out permanently. That couldn't be.

She'd be dead if that was the case. And maybe she wasn't dead yet, but she was most definitely dying.

"Stefan? Where the hell are you?" he yelled to the empty room. He pulled out his cell phone to dial when a tired cranky voice answered him – in his head.

Does no one sleep anymore?

"It's Tabitha," Ronin said starkly. "She's gone. This time it looks really bad."

Stefan never said a word. The air around Ronin warmed, moved. Like, what the hell? Ronin hovered protectively over Tabitha as he caught movement out of the corner of his eye.

"Jesus. What is that?"

What? Stefan asked.

"Movement. I swear I can see something moving off to one side but it's not there when I turn my head. As if it's not really there."

It's me. Close your eyes, realize I'm here in spirit form, then open your eyes again.

Ronin followed the instructions even as his mind said he was crazy. When he reopened his eyes he saw a deep blue cloud at Tabitha's side. "Jesus." His mind balked and as it did – the cloud disappeared. "Hey, where did it go?" He spun around. "Where did you go?"

I didn't go anywhere. Your belief system kicked in and changed your perception. Work on it later. We have to help Tabitha now.

"And how do I do that?"

She needs to go back to the hospital. Get Dr. Marsden. Have him meet us there.

"That I can do." Ronin called for an ambulance. "Can anyone else help her?"

Yes. I'm calling them. You calm the animals while I help Tabitha. Stefan, in a somber voice, added, *this time, I don't know if I can save her.*

***

"How bad is she?"

Fez pulled on his gaping neckline and tried to school his face to project a confident smile. His boss narrowed his gaze on him.

Rushing into speech, Fez said, "She's had a rough trip, no doubt about it. But I'm sure she'll pull out of it." *Like hell.* He prayed she didn't do anything major like try to escape or die on his watch. Counting on Roberts to handle this stuff before had been way easier. He didn't like being responsible. Especially when it wasn't his job.

"Is she eating and drinking?" His voice, so cold and clipped, cut off Fez's hopes instantly.

"Not when I left. If Roberts would show up, he could fix her." The boss's gaze turned flat, dead looking. Ah shit.

"Roberts won't be back. You'll have to handle it."

No. No. Where was his partner? What the hell had happened here? And Fez didn't know how to do Roberts's job. Shit. Shit. This was not good. Could Roberts have booked it like he'd suggested he might? Or had the boss 'taken care' of him.

Shit. He shouldn't have mentioned his missing partner. But now he was starting to worry about his own skin. Especially if he was expected to look after the cargo without Roberts. He didn't show his concerns – instead smiled brightly. "I'm sure she is drinking and eating now."

"I'm not. Go back and watch over her." That gaze became lethal. "Or else..."

Oh crap. "I came to get my pay—" Fez, perspiring heavily, wiped his brow with his sleeve.

"You'll get paid when I get paid and that will be when she's delivered safe and sound," the boss said flatly. "If anything stops me from getting my money, you can be damn sure you won't be getting yours either."

And that nervous feeling since Roberts went missing deepened to much more. Somehow this gig had gone south and this job was bad news. And he wanted no part of it. Well, no further part in it.

He hadn't gotten this far in life by being stupid. He knew when to listen to that gut instinct. Too bad his instincts hadn't kicked in earlier. He could have left with Roberts.

His partner must have some money stashed to have pulled off his disappearing act. Fez wished he'd asked more questions because Fez was broke. He needed this payday.

And pushing for money right now just might be the stupidest thing he'd ever done.

Better he did as he was told and keep this female alive. At least long enough for the sale to go through.

Then the boss could eat his dust.

Chapter 8

Sunday, wee hours of the morning

Hunger. Fear. Panic.

Emotions rolled through Tabitha as she was buffeted from side to side by her experience. She beat back at the pain and struggled to retain consciousness.

It was all too impossible.

But at least she was still alive.

Or was she?

Could she have died?

And was this....death?

No. At least not any form she'd understood death could take.

Another sound of rage rippled through her. She shuddered but the agony was at a visceral level. She couldn't escape. This agony had become hers. Not her attacker's.

Something was happening to her.

To her body. To her soul. To something that was an inherent part of her.

She couldn't move away from either the attacker's or her emotions, but she didn't feel a physical pain. It was there, but in the distance as if it was a cloud away. A cloud? Listen to her. She was talking as if she were dead. And that so couldn't be.

Why couldn't it be? her conscious mocked. *What's so special about you that death wouldn't find you? He found your grandfather and so many of your friends.*

I'm not ready, she whispered. Too damn bad. And something tugged at her. That same grabbing sensation. As if someone needed her. Or wanted something from her.

She tried to identify it, but blacked out before she could identify it.

***

The smell hit Tabitha first when she stirred back to consciousness. Rank, old and stale. Cigar smoke. Animal odors. Feces. Of many kinds. Fear. The dominant smell was...blood.

Instinctively, Tabitha wrinkled up her nose.

Memories flooded her. She'd been attacked again. Hadn't she?

She'd only surfaced a few minutes ago. But surfaced to what? Where was she? And if she could move her nose, was she here physically? She desperately wanted to stretch. Her body felt cramped, imprisoned in some way. It was a horrific feeling, but she didn't know if the sensations were physical sensations or psychic ones.

How was she to tell?

The stench was horrific – and that was physical. But her house didn't stink and that meant she wasn't at home. Her hopes fell. And if she wasn't at home, then where the hell was she?

She tried to assess her surroundings but she couldn't open her eyes. She felt heavy. As if her body was too big to move. As if whatever had happened to her was so bad she shouldn't look.

Beneath the sensations ran a thin river of anger. A molten lava river ready to burst into flame at the right moment. Her tense muscles sang in readiness.

Tension? Muscles? What the hell was going on? The last thing she remembered was being ripped from her body while Ronin was at her side. *Ronin?* Where was he? Had that been a bad dream? Or was *this* the bad dream? She knew it was impossible to sort through realities if she didn't ground herself in one of them. She'd tried to ground herself in her house.

But she either hadn't been – or had her ground had moved.

And that terrified her. She hadn't realized that was a possibility.

In the distance, she heard sounds of a door opening. Her muscles came to life. Waiting...

Maybe she was at home? No. She couldn't be. She had to remember that. And if she wasn't at home, she wasn't in her own body, and therefore the muscles she could move as if her own – weren't hers.

Talk about a mind bender.

She had to consider that this was a possession – one where she had somehow possessed someone else. How could she have been forced to do that against her will?

She'd never heard of it happening to anyone else without their effort. Of course not. That would be too easy.

And that idea of possession was obviously not the whole answer because in order for her to possess someone else, they'd have to be here too.

They'd have to be sharing the same body.

And that just creeped her out. How could anyone drag a soul out of its body and into their own? And even if they could – why would they? That just didn't make any sense.

Especially when she didn't want this.

She'd never considered possession in the sense of wanting to possess another soul. She'd heard Stefan talk about other cases where possession had happened. Where someone else stepped in and took over a person's body…regardless of the original owner.

Is what she was going through the same sensation of what a person trying to possess another felt like? Did they want to feel strong young muscles tightening beneath them instead of their current existence?

Or was this something else again? Damn, but she wished she could see. Something. Anything. But her eyelids wouldn't open. Why? Then it hit her. Because they weren't her eyelids?

Yet.

A door slammed shut. She heard a muffled sound that was oddly close. Her body shifted, tightened. Apprehension rippled through her. Nausea climbed her throat. But was it hers or her host's?

Separating host from visitor would be impossible if she couldn't detach. Tabitha tried to shut out the many conflicting sensations and just listen. And footsteps were striding across a hard floor toward her. Steel-toed boots on concrete maybe? At least a work boot. Heavy. So it was likely a male approaching, one with a slightly uneven gait. So she definitely wasn't at home. She could think of many other places that she'd been in this last year that might sound like this.

She could sense her body – or the body she was in – tightening, as anger and panic built. The footsteps strode closer still. Her body quivered. Then a sharp clatter sounded. She jumped back. It was close. So damn close. And it wouldn't quit. As if this person walked with a pipe dragging along the side of a cage and made sure to bang on every pipe in the metal cage. *Clack. Clack. Clack.*

Cage? Hell. Was this person, now her, a prisoner?

And the footsteps would then belong to her captor. *Asshole.*

She shuddered and felt an answering ripple from all around her. So weird. Yet in a strange way, almost comforting. She and her host were connected. Their emotions and reactions connected. It was hard to be disturbed by this as she could sense the other person's reaction to her every emotion.

It meant she was not alone in this body. Only there was also some sort of disconnect between them.

The sounds grew and grew and changed tone as if someone raked a pipe along several different cages. Her stomach cramped with every step taken. If he was trying to psyche her out, he was succeeding.

She wanted to hide. To back into the furthest corner where he couldn't find her. But somehow she thought she might already be as far back as she could go. It was hard to tell.

She could sense the panic rising inside. Not her panic. Yet it was her panic. She was terrified. Only she didn't know of what. And that made it worse.

"There you are. How are you doing now, my beauty?"

Tabitha frowned. Was he talking about her? Damn. She wished she could see. Was she blind? That would certainly add to the horror.

"Still won't eat or drink, huh? Well, we can't have that. You're worth far too much money for me to have you be stubborn to the point of hurting yourself."

She wanted to hide away from the silky insidious evilness in his voice. She wanted to. But nothing she did made the muscles react. Not to her commands. Or to her fears. She really was living inside someone else's body.

His words finally penetrated her beleaguered mind. Just what did money have to with this?

Then the possibilities pummelled her brain. White slave trader. Sex trader. Kidnapping. Extortion. Blackmail.

Her mind spun with the horrible possibilities. This poor person. The emotions ripped through her in waves of pain and loss and revulsion.

"So are you going to have a better day today?" The voice that spoke was really close. A horrible voice. And that was when she realized there was a solid dark blanket or some kind of covering over her prison.

"Yah need to. We have some more traveling to do. Just a short trip from here. And you need to be in good shape when we arrive." There was a metal click. "Then you're his problem."

The voice got closer, encroaching on her space, pushing against her boundaries. She backed up to the corner of her cage. The cover over her prison was pulled to one side and she heard a small pop. She fell back and there was a stinging sensation in her shoulder.

She bounded to her feet, opened her mouth to scream...but...instead...out of her mouth came a horrific...roar.

✳✳✳

Stefan couldn't explain the compulsion to come to Tabitha's house. Tabitha herself was in the hospital in critical care. Dr.

Marsden, who'd seen so much, had been shocked at her condition, telling Stefan over the phone, "I have no idea what is keeping her alive."

And that's why he was here.

To find answers.

Stefan, Tabitha's friend and mentor, exited his car and climbed the stairs to Tabitha's front door. She'd invested no money in outward appearances and had put everything into the animals and their protection. She'd had a decent security system, but Roman was boosting it for her. Then yesterday Stefan had beefed it up yet again. Apparently that hadn't been enough either. The contents of her house were precious in more ways than one. The energies of its inhabitants were special.

He closed his eyes and waited for the energy of the house to calm. It automatically picked up the pace of its movements with the arrival of any stranger – person, animal, or thing. As Stefan stood there, the energy would eventually recognize him and his attachment to the house's energy.

He let his energy soften, soothe and expand. Using an adaptation of a technique he'd learned from Shay, he thinned one layer of his aura to spread like a blanket of comfort over the interior energy of the house. Within seconds, the house energy calmed and the two energies did a dance of recognition before assimilating into one.

He smiled as the door in front of him opened on its own.

He stepped through to the front hall.

Tripod waited a good ten feet in, his long tail sweeping a wide arc on the floor, a full throated whine wailing from his throat. Hearing Tango in the background, his voice just starting to pick up full strength, Stefan sent out a wave of comforting soothing energy to the tiger. And a greeting. He'd met the big cat many times on an energy level. It was inevitable when he spoke with Tabitha telepathically. Tango's energy was all over her. This would be the first time he met the huge cat on a physical plane.

Stefan walked forward and bent over to give the big guard dog a scratch behind his ears. Waves of grief and anger poured from the big animal. "Sorry, Tripod. I'm here to help. We're doing everything we can. You keep her in your thoughts and I will too. Together we'll keep her grounded so she can find her way home." At least he hoped.

The dog whimpered. Stefan understood. He could sense the dog's distress. And the dog's confusion. "You probably haven't been fed either, have you?"

He checked out the dog's energy. There was a thread of hunger but it was suppressed under the distress. Even if he set food out for the animal, chances were good the dog wouldn't eat.

He walked into the kitchen and found dry kibble. He poured several cups into the dog dish. Tripod could eat when he wanted to. If he wanted to.

Sue, from the center, could also deal with that problem. She had pitched in last time Tabitha had been incapable.

Sending out a second wave of soothing energy to Tango, Stefan strode calmly to the back enclosure. It spread from floor to ceiling at the back of the house and was connected to a larger outside enclosure to give the tiger more roaming space. Stefan stood and waited.

Tango's roar reached him before he saw the elderly white tiger. Did Tabitha even know how old this guy was?

Tabitha was in her late twenties and this guy had been in her life since she was little. Tango's father, Tobias, had been with her grandfather for decades before her. And Tobias's mother before that – probably given another name starting with T as well. Stefan remembered Tabitha mentioning something about it being a convention her grandfather had used after his wife, Tansy had passed away.

She'd been the impetus for this house and enclosure having been as crazy about tigers as her husband. Stefan also understood Tango had been here all his life. He was also born with a minor defect in his leg – if Stefan remembered correctly.

The massive animal sauntered toward Stefan. The cage wall was the only thing between them. He knew Tabitha spent most of the time with Tango. In fact, her bedroom had some kind of doorway as well. The large cat had never known freedom in the sense of being wild.

And times had changed. There were large reserves around the world that were dedicated to taking care of animals like Tango. Exotic Landscape covered acres of land – and yet it was never enough. The property value of a piece this size within commuting distance to Portland was astronomical. And Tabitha couldn't care less about its monetary value. The property value to her was all about the amount of space she could give to each animal.

Tango? How are you?

The roar of pain rippled through Stefan's mind. Tango was afraid. For Tabitha.

There was so much information rolling off the big animal yet it appeared to be emotional in nature. Stefan couldn't see if Tango actually understood what had happened. He'd know Tabitha wasn't here though. And that was enough to throw both animals out of their comfort zone. All animals were intuitive, but beloved pets even more so.

Stefan had no idea what would happen to Tango if Tabitha didn't survive. Her father was alive but had as little to do with the place as possible. And from what Stefan understood from Tabitha, Dennis wouldn't keep it running if anything happened to her.

Tango was too old to move to another reserve. He was past his twilight years. And his energy said he was close to going. Tabitha had broken down in tears more than once over the thought of losing her feline companion.

The old tiger didn't appear to be in any actual physical pain. But then, Tabitha was a strong healer, with animals her focus. It made sense for her old friend to live so long and be so healthy if she'd dedicated a certain portion of her healing energy to that purpose.

He could see an odd thread of energy heading from Tango to Tabitha's bedroom. Then maybe that was to be expected. Maybe the big guy was searching for her, too.

Animals had such interesting abilities that no one, especially humans, understood. Stefan hoped they would eventually understand all. But like humans, some animals appeared to be so much more capable on an energy level than other animals. Reassured that Tabitha's animal family was fine, he made his way to the bedroom easily by following the trail of turbulent energy through the house. He stopped just inside to see if there was any foreign energy. He didn't think she'd been physically attacked, but he was here to make sure.

The room was essentially clean of energies. Ronin, Shay, Tabitha, Tripod. Tango.

Keeping his energy close and tight, he checked out the bathroom where she'd been attacked the first time. The same energies hovered, but there was an extra one.

Dark and faint and at ceiling level only.

What was happening here? Another truth filtered forward.

That ceiling-level energy belonged to an animal.

***

Ronin stood at Tabitha's bedside at the hospital and cursed under his breath. Talk about a panicked trip – again – to arrive back at the same damn room she'd just left. He couldn't help but think she needed to stay here awhile this time.

He already hated this woo woo stuff. That was fine and dandy when it was other people and he could do his cop stuff to help out, but this time it was more personal. Way more personal. And they belonged together, damn it.

He felt so helpless. And so lost.

He loved her and yet he hadn't been able to protect her.

Surely, there had to be something he could do. He'd been working on breaking the vandalism side of the case but when no one saw anything, no one heard anything and no one was admitting to knowing anything...he could only hope his brother's new security system would turn the tide. Ronin felt the break-ins and damage had to be an inside job, but after running through all the new hires, he'd come up with zilch.

Tired, he ran a hand down his face. He'd been here all night. And now he had to go to work.

"Tabitha, where the hell are you?" He stood up and whispered, "Please come home soon."

Ignoring the curious look from the nurse who was walking past the open doorway, he strode out to start his day.

And stopped at the hospital room door. *What was that*

He thought he heard a sound of some kind.

He spun around and stared narrow-eyed at Tabitha. There was no change showing on her face. He walked closer to make sure. No. She looked the same.

Then what had he heard?

Feeling like an idiot, he leaned in until his ear was almost touching her pale lips.

Then he heard it again.

He straightened. No way. It couldn't be.

But...unable to help himself, he leaned over again. And there it was.

He shook his head in disbelief as he collapsed at her bedside. Numb, he leaned over for a third time. And heard nothing. He sat back up and stared at her slack features.

Damn. He could have sworn he'd heard what sounded like a terrified roar.

***

Fez listened to the telephone conversation going on in front of him. He desperately needed sleep. And that wasn't going to happen any time soon. In fact, not until the sale went through.

His boss sat at his desk, his hand clenching and unclenching. He'd already snapped the pencil in his hand. From the shouting going on the other end of the phone, the buyer was even more pissed.

He'd sent a representative to come and see the product.

The buyer's voice screamed through the phone. "Who the hell do you think you're talking to? I ain't giving you shit if I don't like the product. Do I look stupid? I ordered a healthy, whole female for breeding, not an old sick one."

The yelling had Fez sinking deeper into his seat. Oh shit. He wished he'd just called in an update instead of showing up in person. And he really wanted to find out about Roberts. He'd seen something in the river behind the warehouse this morning. Looked like a floater – someone he couldn't identify but his gut said he didn't need to…because he already knew.

He wanted to ask the boss, but hadn't found the courage.

He was pretty damn sure it was a man caught up in the log. When he'd made his way closer it had come unstuck and floated further down.

But he was damn sure it was his old partner.

Had that been the boss's handiwork? Fez hadn't been part of it and he didn't know if the boss would do his own dirty work. There was a new guy at the warehouse. An older scrawny guy named Keeper. Why the boss had hired him, Fez didn't know. Hell he wasn't big enough to do any work.

The boss shifted in his old wooden office chair, glaring at the phone. He shook his head, ready to blast back when the angry voice snapped again, "And I want her now. Don't you dare try to pull a fast one on me. I'll fucking take you out if you try to stiff me. I paid a hefty deposit. Give me the healthy female I ordered or give me my fucking money back, with interest."

"Do you know what we had to go through to get her in the first place?" the boss said in a hard voice.

Fez really didn't want to be here.

"I don't give a damn. My order was very clear," the disembodied voice snorted. "From what my man saw, this damn thing is almost dead, for crying out loud. Deliver what I paid for or else—"

"She's just stressed. She needs to settle into her new home and adapt to her surroundings. She'll pick up in no time. We've seen it before."

"Then you can hang onto her until she's healthy again. If she doesn't pick up, then sell her somewhere else. Or sell her in pieces for all I care. The Chinese are always happy to buy them in that form."

"We can't keep her. You know that." The boss clenched his fist around the stapler, his knuckles growing white. "We bring them in specifically for the client. You don't want it, that's your problem. No refunds. Read the fine print in the contract."

"Like hell. I want my money back if she's not delivered in good health and on time." There was a sharp click as the buyer hung up.

The boss glared at Fez. "You heard him. I'm in the supply and demand business. If I don't come up with the goods, then I'm screwed. And if I'm screwed then you're screwed. So make sure she looks good and is delivered on time."

He smiled in a dark cold twist of his lips and added, "Do you understand?"

Then he made a dark slashing movement across his throat to cement his message. Chills rippled down Fez's throat and he swallowed. He turned and walked out of the boss's office silently and for the first time he understood the phrase 'quaking in your boots.'

And now he knew. There was no question in his mind. Roberts was dead.

Fez was going to be next. Maybe not today. Maybe not tomorrow. But if the boss had taken Roberts out because he'd found out Roberts was planning on skipping town...then Fez had better watch his every step.

He had a measly hundred bucks in his pocket and knew he'd never see another dime from the boss until this job was done. The hundred might get him a bus ticket, but only to the next damn state. Not far enough to avoid the long reach of the boss if he came after Fez.

He considered his options as he walked to the truck. His boss's truck. If he stole that, the boss would never stop looking for him. After a few moments, he realized there were no good answers. But the easiest way to get away alive was to get his full pay by completing this job.

And that meant making sure this deal went down. His stomach acids gurgled, making him slap his pockets for the open packet of stomach aids. Damn. Where had he put them? He slapped his back pocket. There.

He yanked the roll out and opened it, popping two into his mouth.

At least one part of him would feel better soon.

To make the rest of him feel better, he needed money. And for that to happen, they had to get the female to eat and drink. And maybe find a nutritional booster of some kind. Anything to have her looking strong and healthy long enough to complete the deal.

He needed that damn payday.

So he could escape while he still had the chance.

Chapter 9

Sunday morning

Tabitha choked, twisting frantically as she tried to control the noise, but the roaring continued...out of her mouth...or rather her soul and whatever mouth she was physically attached to. So loud it would have hurt her ears – if they'd been her own.

Then the sound cut off. And her shoulder started to throb. She swayed in place, struggling to stay upright, then stumbled and collapsed on her side. What was that? Had she been shot? There wasn't much pain. But she didn't feel well.

Or right.

Something was off. A half laugh choked free. She was captive in another's body. What was normal about that? No, her host felt off. Drugged. And given the sluggish sensation that felt like it was rippling through her veins – the host was unconscious.

It would help so much if she could see. Why the hell couldn't she?

Then as if just by asking the question, clarification came. She had to accept the body of whatever person she was in and see through *their* eyes.

So far she'd been fighting her host. Fighting against understanding it.

She should have been doing the reverse of that. In the beginning, her panic was understandable, but her awareness was here now. And she was late in figuring out what was happening.

The simple rule of energy. Become one with the energy. Be that energy. Be one.

Instead of fighting, she had to become one with it. Then she could use the host to show her what was going on. She'd done similar things before. Essentially reading the energy of any animal was a similar process. She had to change her energy to blend with theirs, become one with theirs, and then they were

94

essentially one with her it would make sense she could then see their energy.

She would *be* their energy. She wasn't a separate observer, although she knew people whose abilities ran in that direction. In her case, she had to join with them in order to get the clearest vision of what was going on.

Closing her inner eye, she sank deeper into the unique and frightening experience. That overriding fear made this horrific experience difficult to accept. She took a deep breath and searched for a ground. She was alive spiritually, so therefore she was attached to something.

Tango? Tripod? Her body? Although the latter was in doubt. But she had to believe it was there for her. That her friends were protecting her.

Mentally she reached for Tango. And hit a blockage. Someone else kept crossing her path, interfering, calling to her.

She called to Tripod.

And found the same thing.

Therefore, she had to ascertain what interfered first. Connect with it, then move it to one side.

Stilling, she quieted her mind and waited.

There.

Another energy whistled through her mind, requesting a response. A connection. She'd never had such a thing happen before. Never knew it could invite her like that. Who was this entity? And why was it connecting to her?

A whisper of a sound. A cat's cry, muted, but crying out in pain...and fear.

Tango?

No. Not Tango. A different energy. A feline energy though. Another cat.

A big cat. But not Tango.

Then she understood. Although she had no idea how this came about, she thought she understood where she was.

Inside a large cat. Potentially a tiger. Potentially one that might be connected to Tango and through him – to her. If such a thing was possible.

And its spirit was calling to her.

She'd always understood her animals were equal to humans in many ways. She'd seen their interactions, their caring, their intelligence. She hadn't given them credit for being capable of energy work though. Or that they could have energy abilities like this.

And perhaps she was giving this one too much credit.

Maybe this animal hadn't consciously cried out to her. It was just crying out emotionally. In need. To whoever would listen.

That meant to her. Relief washed through her as she understood.

Thank God.

Then she sensed something else. A lighter energy, softer. Younger. Somewhere close by? Were there other felines in this room? She could hear slight movements, rustling around, but nothing like the screaming and pain she'd heard from her host.

Tabitha hated the pain that rippled through her system. It was cloudy, confusing. There was no cub here. But she could see in her memories – the tiger's memories – cubs. In days gone by.

The tiger was old. Sick. And maybe dying. But there was something else... She couldn't quite grasp it.

Something had triggered her need to communicate. Something had sent her crying out.

Tabitha thought of all the problems inherent in moving a large cat like this one, especially if she'd been caught in the wild. She'd have been tranq'd right from the beginning. Somewhere along the line she'd have woken up and found herself captive in a foreign world. With foreign smells, sounds.

When she'd woken up, the tiger would have screamed with rage...and panic.

And had somehow snagged on Tabitha's energy and dragged her here. Into the cage with her. Why? How? She didn't know. But the female cat had. And now Tabitha was caught inside. With it.

And what could she do about it now?

Soothing the animal was paramount. Maybe then she could get the cat to relinquish its hold on her.

Tabitha also needed to check out her host's body. See if there was anything she could do for her. To heal her as much as she could and to find a way to escape. But having a tiger run loose in whatever part of the world they were in was a whole different story than being free in the wild. She knew that's where the tiger desperately wanted to return, but Tabitha had no idea if they were in India or the U.S.A. For all she knew the tiger had been captured in China.

She could physically be anywhere in the world. Energy traveled across the world in a heartbeat. That she'd connected as strongly as she had *should* mean the location was close by her home. But nothing about this scenario was normal so she couldn't bank on that.

Just as important, she needed to check in with her own body and keep it alive – if possible.

The same questing energy that she'd sensed earlier pulsed again.

Tabitha opened up her mind to the soft wave of it and sent out a probe to the energy. There was a hesitation, fear, but also a request for reassurance.

There was another feline. A young feline.

Very young.

Her heart ached as she understood this animal's panic. She sent out waves of calming energy, healing energy. Energy to ease the animal's fear. She'd dealt a lot with similar issues over the years as animals were brought into the reserve. Some had to be tranq'd for the trip; others were completely accepting.

She gentled her own energy more, aligning hers to the young male's, adding soothing thoughts and above all else, caring, compassion and empathy. She loved all animals and when one was in pain, she lived it with them.

She sensed this link of energy was another reason she'd locked on Tabitha. And if it was a feline, as she suspected... maybe it understood Tabitha had a soft spot for those, too.

She searched out the cat's energy pathways and stroked along the meridians, trying to figure out if it was physically hurt. The shoulder pain she'd noticed first appeared to be where she'd been shot by a tranq dart – probably on initial capture. The site was sore, puffy, but not serious.

Pain drew her to the back right leg – the older tiger's back leg. There was something wrong there. An old injury perhaps? If she could open her eyes she could take a closer look, but that meant the cooperation of the feline.

She sent warm healing energy to the spot. Tabitha *could* heal at this level. Instantly there was a lessening of the tension in the space they shared. As if the cat knew, understood and responded to her energy. Maybe it didn't know Tabitha was there, but the energies were blending naturally now. That would also help the animal to calm down. Having a foreign energy inside the cat's body would not be comfortable or easy on either of them. Especially if the energies couldn't find a way to exist together peacefully.

Animals normally responded quickly to treatments. At least the cat appeared to be willing to accept her initial attempts.

Still emanating even, calming waves, Tabitha tried to get a better idea of what was wrong in the cat's world.

And getting her vision back would be major.

She sent out her energy in the direction of the cat's head. And into the skull and eyes. There was some resistance, but she thinned her energy to the density of the cat's energy and became one with it, helping it become comfortable with her energy as she became comfortable with its energy. She settled in. With a sigh of acccptance, of knowing, she sank deeper into the experience.

Then the cat opened her eyes.

To bars.

Rusted bars of a small cage. Only big enough for the cat to stand, take a few steps and turn around. A plywood floor. An attached water dish was perched halfway down the inside of the cage. It was full. The cat was thirsty. But she was too scared to drink.

Tabitha didn't blame her.

There was darkness all around. A cover of some kind surrounded the bulk of the cage, but one end was open.

She stared at the large paws crossed in front of her. A dirty gray paw with slight stripes. She was sharing space with a tiger with some variant coloring. There were many white Bengal tigers...but her coloring wasn't quite right.

There was gray and a lot of it, but that could be dirt. Or it could be something else. A thread of excitement wove through her consciousness. There was an extinct species of blue tiger, the Maltese tiger. Some scientists believed it never existed in the first place. Rumor said their slate gray fur shone blue in some light. There were also black tigers, but then this tiger's fur was too light for that. If she could see more of its body, she might know for sure. She'd never expected to see a blue tiger in her lifetime.

The tiger was slowly adjusting to its latest drug dose. Whoever these captors were, they were more concerned about the animal staying quiet and not hurting itself than having it actually eat and drink to stay strong and healthy.

It was obvious this tiger had been hunted and taken from the wild. There was no sense of comfort or familiarity with cages or humans. There was no understanding of the confinement or the lighting. The water dish was new. Images of creeks and ponds flashed through her mind. The cat was desperate for water.

But it was more desperate for its freedom.

She moved back and forth as the big cat struggled to its feet and staggered throughout the small space. It roared in anger, a weak defiant sound echoing through the large space.

And that brought up another issue. If the tiger couldn't be controlled, it would most likely be killed. Or kept so confined, it wouldn't survive anyway.

Unless it was destined for a zoo. No. That wouldn't be. Not this way. If the animal was being imported through the proper channels there'd be vets, trainers, people to look after the tiger, to see to its comfort. All efforts would be made to reduce the animal's distress – and not through the overuse of tranquilizers

Of course, it may be for a zoo in a third world country where the restrictions were lax and the paperwork wouldn't be looked at very closely if at all – for a price.

This was likely a black market deal.

As the thoughts took her to other animals in her world, Tabitha lost her focus. And couldn't see anymore.

She closed her own eyes and breathed into the big cat that surrounded her and reconnected with it.

Then opened her eyes once again.

The room appeared in shades of beige and shadows. Cat eyes. Cat vision. It was likely to be dark in this room. Shadowy. Her human vision would have seen one thing and interpreted it with her human eyes, but her cat's vision was different altogether.

And maybe that explained the color of her fur. Maybe dirty white fur looked like slate gray when viewed from a cat's eyes.

Then she was distracted again as the big head swung from side to side as if looking for an opening, a way out. She studied the change in view as the head swung. The large warehouse was full of empty cages. There were double doors up ahead, but she didn't think the cat understood them to be an exit...as in maybe it didn't understand the concept of doors. But then her mind, or rather its mind, was groggy and dominated by confusion.

Tabitha struggled to stay connected and yet separate. To keep in tune with the tiger but also to allow Tabitha to think on her own. Not an easy thing to do. But she had to keep clarity of her own thoughts and actions. Somehow she had to stay separated from her host so she could do something for both of them.

What she really needed was to find out their location. In what city was the animal being kept? The man had spoken English. Guttural and slang, but English nonetheless. That might help narrow the country down. The man had said something about more traveling to come.

Meaning they could be anywhere in the world – including the U.S. And as helpful as it would be, she didn't want to believe the tiger was in – or destined – for the U.S. Money drove the markets and poachers were in the supply-and-demand market. That meant global markets in today's world. So the tiger could be destined to be shipped anywhere.

She figured if she could free the tiger, the big cat would release her. She could be dreaming, but that was her goal. A hope – and she needed something to hang onto right now.

On top of that, she wasn't sure how her own physical existence was doing. How could she check? Would her attempt to return to her body trigger the tiger's strong emotions so she would be yanked back?

How could she let the tiger know what she needed to do? And that she wouldn't desert her. She wanted to help the tiger.

A roar ripped through her head. Of rejection. Of loneliness. And fear.

She tried to calm the tiger down again, but this time the tiger wouldn't let her. She was too agitated.

Pulling back, Tabitha eased her own feelings down inside the tiger's ballooning emotions – so the big cat would feel Tabitha's emotions.

She wanted out. The tiger wanted out too. They both wanted their freedom.

How did she argue or try to show logic to a panicked animal? How could she prove she was trustworthy? That her word could be counted on when she was pretty sure tigers understood instinct and action, response in the present. Not promises of future acts.

Especially when she couldn't guarantee that she could come back. Thinking through energy laws, she realized she could always find a trail back here. She'd use anchors to make the travel easier and faster.

But she had to go deeper to place them. Deeper into the tiger's psyche to make sure they stayed in place.

Only deeper was more dangerous. For both of them.

But that recourse was likely the only answer.

As she tried to descend to where she needed to go, emotions pummeled at her and images filled her. Images of the tiger's old life, the trees, tall grass. The wind. Racing across a field. Basking under the sun. Freezing in the snow.

Still caught in the tiger's memories, there was a sudden pain in her shoulder and hip. Loud noises followed. Confused and hurting, the large cat had stumbled in a daze of pain. She struggled to escape. To hide. Only she could hardly move. The tiger's body burned. She wanted it to stop. She could hardly breathe. Or run.

The tiger hadn't gone down easy. And they'd shot her again. Only the cat had reacted badly to the drugs and she was sick. Tabitha saw the sweating as a separate issue now. Not caused by a sense of panic, but more by drugs. The cat's body had reacted. Swelling. She found it hard to breathe. And she was so thirsty. She was already old. And now with the drugs...she was in a bad way.

The poachers didn't seem to know about her distress – or maybe they didn't care. But a dead tiger wasn't worth much. In the Chinese medicine industry it was, but if capturing her was for that, they could have shot her dead up in the mountains. That would have been much easier. And much faster.

The drug reaction explained the debilitating weakness, the fever and confusion. In fact, Tabitha would swear the big female was dying. And that made her own heart ache.

But there was still something else in there. Tabitha went deeper.

And found the other feline energy she had sensed earlier.

What she understood at a primitive level made her want to rage against these men. And made her want them to pay.

And made her want to help the tiger in a big way.

Because, and against all odds – the old female tiger was pregnant and carried one cub.

Had the poachers known? No. That would have changed the deal entirely.

Tabitha had to help.

But how?

As she considered the almost full-term cub, she realized the energy of the cub was distinct, separate – and yet at the same time it was one with the mother.

That made sense, as all energy was connected.

Parts of other people's energy gravitated naturally to a person they connected with in some way. In her case, it was the energy of people she'd been closest to through her life and those that stayed close to her...some of their energy stuck to her. So therefore Tabitha should be able to find some of those energy fragments and follow them home. She'd already found Stefan's signature, but it was so faint that it wasn't usable, as if it couldn't quite reach her.

Instead of an energy line, it was more a sensation of him being there, searching for her. Or maybe that was wishful thinking.

But there was no denying Tango's energy. Whether it was the feline connection or something else, Tango's signature was strong and loving in Tabitha's heart.

She sent warm loving energy to Tango. He'd be lost if she died. In fact, his energy vibrated at a tense level that said he was already nervous and heading into seriously scared territory. And the color had deepened to a dark blue instead of the lake-blue it normally vibrated with.

She smiled. Maybe she did know what to do.

Sending out a wide green band of healing energy, followed by a gently loving band in lavender, Tabitha surrounded the caged female tiger with energy that would make her feel good. Make her calm. Not afraid. Not alone. Letting Tabitha slip away. At least long enough to check on family and...her body.

Next, Tabitha carefully wrapped her own loving essence around Tango's energy. Added layers and layers of loving, healthy energy like wisps of colored cotton candy until the entire thing was thick and solid looking. Then she blew a breath into the center, making a hollow, and sank into it. Became one with it. She shifted deeper and deeper, feeding the energy trail as she slipped along the pathway, following it back and back and back hoping to find the reality she recognized. Faster she flew as energy warmed, reconnecting to the animal that had shared so much of Tabitha's life.

He'd been there for her after a trying day at school; he'd cleaned her face on the day she'd graduated; he'd been ecstatic over the arrival of Tripod. A kindred soul, in so many ways. A playmate for Tango when she was gone from the house.

Tango had been there listening to her spout off joyfully when she'd gotten engaged, and he'd been there listening to her tears after she'd been jilted. He'd been there for her every step of the way.

She knew him as well as she knew herself. As she thought all this, she fell into Tango's space.

His energy kicked into overdrive. If he could have twisted his lithe body around her, he would have. Instead she was the one wrapped around him. Inside him. Outside him. She was him.

He jumped and spun and howled. And his roar was deafening.

His joy...her joy. Both brought tears to her eyes, if she'd had eyes...or tears.

She cried out his name repeatedly. She couldn't seem to stop. The sense of safety and being home overwhelmed her. Such a relief. Such a feeling of joy. It was finally over...

Only not quite. Reality intruded. She was in Tango's body now. Not her own. Still, she'd managed to leave the other tiger – mostly.

Tango, I need help.

The purr increased to deafening proportions. He'd always understood her moods. And she his.

I need to get to my body.

She stopped and thought about what she'd said, what she was doing. This was stupid. Tango couldn't go to her body. He was trapped inside his own massive physicality. She needed a way to get from here to her body.

Then she heard footsteps. And a voice.

Tango? Are you all right?

Stefan!

***

Stefan wandered through Tabitha's living room looking, seeking something that had to be there, but not sure what. The house was old and empty, but there was a disturbance in the atmosphere that went beyond the lack of furniture. Part of the house had felt empty on his first pass – as if Tabitha had disappeared completely.

Tango had lain despondent in a corner of the large enclosure. Not eating or drinking. Tripod was acting the same. Just like any well-loved pet would, given the absence of their beloved owner.

Stefan wandered back through the house again. He'd learned a long time ago to not ignore his instincts. That prodding voice that said to keep looking. He was here because he was supposed to be here. If he was lucky, he'd understand the reason why. Soon.

He wandered over to Tango's cage once again. He searched for a change. Something to understand this nudge inside him to keep searching.

Just then Tango came racing through the pen into the main area where the caged wall was all that separated him from Stefan.

But he looked different. Happy. Energized.

Stefan narrowed his gaze and studied the tiger. It was almost delirious. Rolling on the ground, rubbing his back on the floor, all four legs in the air as he tossed his head with abandon. It was a joy to see.

The cat looked...ecstatic. *And how could that be?*

"What do you know that I don't, Tango?" Stefan murmured, studying the big cat's aura. Sure enough, the color had shifted, brightened. Was now surrounded by a lavender sheen.

Tabitha?

Surely that was her energy mixed into the big cat's energy. *Could it be?*

He stepped close enough to press his face against the heavy gauge divider.

"Tango?" he called out. "Come here, boy."

Tango jumped to his feet and bounded to Stefan, rubbing his side along the cage. It was if he understood Stefan. Or someone connected to Tango understood and brought the big cat close. *What were the chances?*

Tabitha? Is that you? Stefan asked telepathically. *Are you with Tango?*

Yes!

✳✳✳

Fez walked calmly into the warehouse. At least on the outside he hoped he appeared confident and in control. At least someone needed to be. Keeper was there waiting for him. "How is she doing?"

"Not eating, but maybe had water."

Fez brightened up. "Water is good."

"And the bleeding stopped."

Fez closed his eyes briefly then said in an ominous voice, "What bleeding?"

"From the original poachers. They shot her with tranq darts, but one site seemed to close over, only she gnawed on it and ripped it open. But it's stopped again."

"That's a good sign." At least he hoped it was. "We need her to eat." He lifted the blanket slightly and the rank odor of meat gone off filled his nostrils. "No wonder she's not eating. What is this crap?"

"I'm hardly going to put good stuff in there to go bad. When she's hungry enough, she'll start eating. Then I will get her fresh stuff." Keeper spat on the old wood floor and walked away as if the conversation was over.

But it wasn't. Not by a long shot. Fez didn't know where the boss had found this guy but he wasn't worth the pennies he was paying him.

Fez grabbed him by the shoulder and spun him around. "She gets the best. And she gets it now. You aren't paying for her food. We are. Now go and clean that shit out of there and bring her fresh meat."

"You ain't the fucking bos—"

Fez punched him in the nose. "I'm the boss when the boss isn't here. I'm following his orders and you will follow my orders. Now get to it. And give her fresh water too."

When Keeper shot him a resentful look, Fez smiled cruelly and said, in a soft voice, words that echoed the boss, "And do it now – or else."

Chapter 10

Sunday noon

At the sight of Stefan, a wave of sadness washed through Tabitha. Hers or Tango's? She didn't know or care. There could also be vestiges of the other tiger's energy floating through her energy space. And that tiger also had homesickness as a major issue.

The poor thing.

What thing? asked Stefan accurately, reading her mind.

She quickly explained who the other tiger was and what had happened to her, then tried to explain what had happened that Tabitha had ended up inside of the tiger.

There was a long shocked pause from Stefan. *Tabitha...are you sure...that's what happened?*

Doesn't make any sense, does it?

Not only doesn't it make sense, it requires a level of unprecedented power to do something like that.

But it also explains how and why I was hooked and grabbed. Think about it. The most logical way the tiger found me was through Tango. I already have a strong open connection to Tango. She nodded to herself as she realized something else. *I used to connect to Tango while I floated in the ethers. If this other tiger could connect to the ethers, theoretically it's possible she'd connected to Tango. It was just an easy step to me.*

And that would explain how there were no strange human energies here, Stefan added thoughtfully. *I saw the animal energy but couldn't see whether it was from other animals you'd worked with. I never thought your attacker would be a tiger.*

She laughed. *And yet look where I am right now.*

But you also have Tripod and any other number of animals in your life.

But not as close and as loving as Tango. Or in as much distress. Tripod would be a very close second, but Tango has been in my life so much longer.

So you're thinking that the tigers are connected? By love? By circumstance?

Unless we want to contemplate that psychic tigers exist.

She heard Stefan's whoosh as he exhaled. *Yeah, a bit of a mind bender, isn't it?*

Definitely.

We have some incidents involving animals to draw on, but nothing like this. Stefan paused then added, *I can't say it's a comforting thought to consider that any animal at any given moment can reach out and yank their beloved owner into their own psyche when they hit a bad spot in life.*

Probably not any animal. Special ones, yes. Consider this possibility too. An animal in the wild looking for anyone to help them – and they grab a hold of those of us open enough to be accessible. She felt his shudder. This mind-link thing with Stefan was so intimate at times she could sense his very movements.

As I can with yours, but since you are inside your tiger...yeah, that's more than what I was expecting to find when I arrived at your door today. He gave a half laugh. *And it feels weird on my end so I can't imagine how you are feeling.*

Just why did you come here now? she asked. *That you'd be here when I arrived...*

Remember there are no such things as coincidences. When you are in tune with the universe, you will always be in the right place at the right time. You just might not always like the lesson to be learned by the experience you get to go through.

She snorted. *Like getting yanked out of my body? What the hell, Stefan? I figured out how to come back to Tango by building on our bond, but how the hell do I get back to my own body?*

There was only a long silence in her head as Stefan contemplated her through the cage. *You should have gone back naturally on your own.*

Yeah, but I tried that – it didn't work.

I have no idea then. You've already defied psychic laws as we know them because it shouldn't be theoretically possible to live without the cord attached. How to reattach a severed cord has always been considered impossible. Not that yours is detached. I don't know what it is.

If it were, in theory I'd be dead. And I'd have disappeared to the ever-after long before now.

What's the chance you are still attached but stretched so thin no one can see it? He gave a small laugh. *Or could it be masked, hidden in some way? Not that many could see it normally anyway.*

I don't think so. Could she have hidden it instinctively, something so natural and fast that Tabitha hadn't been aware as the process happened?

Could...Tango? Stefan asked cautiously.

Tango? Tabitha wanted to laugh. It was ridiculous to think of an animal doing something like that. But was it? Look at what the female tiger had done. She wanted to shake off the concept of her animals having any kind of ability. To harm her or help her. *Such a foreign concept.*

But is it a wrong one?

I don't know, she whispered. *It's been so hard to deal with this as it is. To try to understand that an animal had that level of competence...*

I think we're giving the animals too much credit. Whatever they're doing would be out of pure instinct. He walked across the room, his head bent in thought. *You could have helped this tiger without severing the cord, so why do it this way? And if the cord is still attached, why hide it?*

I have no idea.

That's what we need to understand. There has to be a reason. Find that reason and we'll understand more about what's going on.

She understood that, but it wasn't helping her get back into her body.

What about the other tiger, does she know that you've left? Stefan asked.

Yeah, that's the thing, I'm not sure I'm totally gone. She took a deep breath. *I feel splintered into many little bits and pieces.*

Have you split your energy? Stefan asked curiously. *I've been trying to do something similar but it takes a lot of energy to maintain.*

I don't know, Stefan, she cried. *I just tried to build a stronger bonding energy with Tango so I could travel here, but I can still feel the older female.*

The other tiger is an older female? Older than Tango?

Maybe a little. I don't know. Why?

Could she be related?

No, I don't think so, she answered slowly then remembered the odd coloring, *I'm not so sure they are the same variant. She's got an odd tint to her fur.*

More likely she panicked and sent out a cry for help on the ethers. Stefan paused again. *Tango would likely be open and responsive and like you said, through him, she found you.*

Stefan studied Tango as if trying to see her face, at least that's what she thought he was staring at. In truth, through Tango's eyes, Stefan looked odd. Gray, yet distinct.

Stefan asked, *Has Tango ever done this before?*

Not like this. I've connected with other tigers – Tobias being one example – but I haven't noticed other tigers connecting to me. At least I don't think they have. She shrugged mentally. *But maybe it was natural for them and felt natural to me so I never noticed.* It was starting to sound like she'd been unaware of a lot happening lately. Had her life disintegrated so much that she'd been this far off balance?

So what's different now? Stefan asked.

There was a long pause as they both thought about it. Tango lay down on the floor and rolled on his back, happy and content. Tabitha laughed. *He's so not bothered.*

Have you done this with him before?

Sure, she said.

He paused. *Sure what?*

Yes, I've been communicating with him since forever, and there is no closer communication than telepathy. But because he doesn't use the same language, I found it easier to hop into his energy and spend time with him that way.

The shock coming through the airwaves made her pause and ask, *Why?*

It's very unusual. You know that, right?

What is?

The jumping in and out of other people's psyche.

Well, I'm not jumping into anyone. Only animals. And Tango was open to the idea at the beginning and now we both love our time together. It's a wonderful feeling. She shrugged. *We played our version of hide'n go seek too. I'd disappear and he'd come find me.*

Sure, he said humorously. *But that just makes the situation all that more unique. Have you done this jumping in and out with other animals?*

Yes, if they were doing poorly and I couldn't figure out why. I can enter their energy systems and check out their bodies. Dr. Maddy does a similar thing.

Similar, yes. But she doesn't jump into other people's minds and take possession.

Shocked, she jumped back, affronted. *I'm not taking possession. Holy crap. That would be just wrong.*

He stood in front of her, his head tilted to the side. *So what is it then?*

I'm not making Tango do anything. I'm a visitor. Spending time with him. He can't come to me so I go to him. I don't make him sit up, roll over, or roar. She hated that feeling of justifying her actions. She'd never do anything to hurt Tango. *I'm here like you and I speak telepathically with Tango in a similar way.*

I'm not accusing you of going too far or of doing anything wrong. What I'm trying to understand is the ease with which you do it. He shook his head. *I can slip into people's minds and speak with them, show them images, give them information – but I've never tried to persuade them to do anything. Because to me, it is morally and ethically wrong.*

Me too. She let her breath out on a long sigh. *Sorry. I didn't mean to snap at you. I hadn't considered that what I was doing was wrong. Tango and I are so close that it never occurred to me that I wasn't welcome.*

Given the complete look of happiness on that overgrown tabby cat, I'd say you were very welcome.

Mollified, she said, *I hope so. I'd never do anything to hurt him.*

And that bond between you is obvious. It's also probably why this other tiger, once she caught scent of your connection, had no trouble yanking you into her space. You were already used to it.

No. That's where you're wrong. Tango never yanks me.

Stefan laughed. *But if you look at the times you're in his space, I'm sure you'll see a recognition of what you're doing on his level. Whether he ever initiated the contact or just put out the suggestion and you responded by jumping in, this other tiger did no less. When you didn't respond initially, she reacted with a stronger message.*

True. And... She thought about the number of times she felt compelled to be with Tango after her grandfather had died. Had that been at her instigation or his? *I never thought of our bond in that way,* she admitted. *But now that I take a closer look, I guess that's reasonable.*

The real trick is to figure out how to break the connection. As far as we know, if you are in the person when that person dies, then you are likely to die too.

Especially considering that we're not sure how I'm still alive at the moment.

Stefan took a huge gusting breath and added gently, *If you are still alive.*

***

Stefan waited a long moment. From the shocked silence and then a weird blankness in his mind, Stefan understood Tabitha had withdrawn. How far back, he didn't know. He pinched the bridge of his nose and sent her a warm hug. He had no idea what to say to help her deal with her situation. He could only hope time would help. He just didn't know how much time she had.

Nothing was ever what it seemed, and most people lived out their lives never understanding this other layer of existence going on around them. An underground society was probably a better way to look at it. Maybe it was just as well. Those that were aware were often too overwhelmed by the circumstances their intimate knowledge brought them.

As if the ones with awareness were forced to step up and deal with things others had no inkling of.

He turned around to survey the room. It was colder than when he'd first arrived. He glanced back at Tango and found him asleep.

Hosting a second being in your aura had to be draining – a hell of a sleep aid.

Still, as long as Tango wasn't being hurt by the visits, who was he to judge? And as he studied the old cat, he realized Tango was likely enjoying an extended life because of the way Tabitha'd handled him physically and psychically. Tabitha would have taken care of even the tiniest ailments her beloved pet might have experienced. Even pushing off the discomfort that old age often brought.

So Tango might have the best deal after all.

Was she doing the same for the ailing old female she'd joined, too? If so, they might have a little more time to find a way to help Tabitha there as well. Once that female died... Stefan shook his head. He didn't want to imagine the consequences of that connection to Tabitha being severed.

They had to find the host tiger and help her. Maybe then Tabitha could be released.

And he knew just who to ask for help in finding that tiger.

Ronin?

Ronin bolted to his feet, accidentally kicking the hospital chair backwards. The question came out of the blue and was so sharp and clear it couldn't be anyone other than Stefan. Damn that guy anyway.

Sorry. I just thought you'd like to know that I spoke with Tabitha.

Ronin walked to Tabitha's side. He'd stopped at the hospital on his way to the office, wishing to hell he knew how to help her.

"How can you speak with her?" he said, casting a glance around to make sure he was alone. "I'm staring down at her unconscious body and there is no way in hell she's awake or even conscious."

She's inside Tango.

"She's *what?*" he asked incredulously. He studied the pale, waxen features of the woman in front of him. So not possible.

And yet, apparently it is. Because I'm at her house and talking to her.

There was only so much woo woo stuff any normal guy could stand, but being a cop who'd recently had that whole believe-it-when-I-see-it thing going on, he was still adapting.

Staring at Tabitha and wishing to hell she was berating him again for his attitude on cats was a whole different thing than understanding she was inside that damn tiger.

Except...that's where she was. At least part of her.

Ronin pounced. "A part of her? What part?"

He stared down at the main part, her body, that hadn't moved since he'd arrived.

Part of her consciousness. So I know this is going to be tough, but we need your help as soon as possible. Here's why.

Stefan gave as clear and as concise an explanation as possible – and left Ronin completely confused. He struggled to sort through the bizarre concepts. "So let me get this straight. There is most likely an old tiger captive in a cage, most likely hunted down by poachers, most likely getting ready to be sold to yet another person, in some country somewhere in the world, that I'm supposed to track down."

I guess that sounds a little bizarre when you put it that way, Stefan said.

"You think?" Ronin snapped. "And how do you expect me to help here at all?"

Um yeah, Tabitha says they are in a warehouse with lots of cages.

"Oh, that's great. Does she have any idea what country she is in? Do you know how many countries could have an English-speaking captor?" He paced the small room. "A little more information would help, you know."

That would be too easy, Stefan said, his voice all business. *What I can tell you is that if that sick tiger dies while connected to Tabitha, well...I wouldn't give a penny for her chances of surviving this trip.*

And he was gone.

Shit.

✱✱✱

The tiger didn't look so good. Fez winced. She'd slumped into the far corner. And didn't move – even when prodded. They needed a vet in here and fast.

But who'd pay for it? His boss should. They'd hoped to make this deal happen faster than this. He didn't understand what was taking so long. None of them had time for this. Especially not this female tiger.

He glanced at the haunch of fresh meat lying untouched beside the water. So not good. At least the asshole, Keeper, had done what he was told.

He studied the tiger's still form. There was still blood on her flank. Maybe there was something else going on. He wouldn't trust those damn poachers to not have shot her with real bullets. Hell, she could be riddled with buckshot and no one would know. It's not as if she'd received the care she needed from the beginning.

It was all too possible they'd left it too late now.

There wasn't much in the world that made him feel so low and like such a loser as what he was doing with this female cat. Going into it, he'd looked at all these jobs as easy money. He'd only been working for the boss for five months and it was four months too long. At least now that he'd seen that thing in the river. And understood he himself was living on borrowed time. This job could be the catalyst for his own deep swim.

The tiger was caged. But he was starting to see bars in his own world. How could he get out of this mess? There was nothing nice about seeing a floater.

All Fez could think about now was getting the hell out of here – with no holes in his damn skin.

Go back East. Find a job where he could hold up his head. Instead of this. The animal was tearing his heart out.

Who'd have thought he still had one?

Chapter 11

Sunday early afternoon

Tabitha burrowed deeper into a ball. She didn't give a damn whether she was hiding from her problems. The ethers had always been her comfort zone. Her escape from the painful reality of her physical existence. Okay, so it wasn't the same type of escape as for other people. But she'd dare anyone not to do the same, given the shock she'd just been given.

Was Stefan right?

Was she dead?

God, she hoped not.

If she'd had a body, she'd be shivering uncontrollably. As it was, she felt shivers sliding up and down her nonexistent spine. How did that work? Surely that meant she was still connected to her body. Surely…

She desperately wanted to see her body. Could she? When she'd been alive and doing out-of-body experiences, she could. But then she'd been attached by her cord. What was she now?

Even if her cord was hidden or spread thin, it should still function the same.

She closed her eyes and thought herself to her body.

When she opened her eyes, it was to see her slim frame lying under the hospital sheets, machines moving noisily at her side. She looked like she was comatose but according to Stefan, the machines were there to keep her alive, to keep her breathing in case that all stopped. She shuddered. She so didn't want to die.

If they unplugged that machine, she would. She knew it.

And that so couldn't happen.

A weird clacking sound caught her attention.

Ronin. Typing furiously away on the laptop on his knees, his phone open in his hand. Sitting vigilant at her bedside.

God, she missed him.

Tears came to her eyes. Or it felt like they did. Suspiciously, she reached up to her astral cheeks but there was no wetness there. Duh. She leaned over her body and damn if there wasn't a sheen of moisture in the corner of her eyes.

She *was* still connected! Hadn't she just proven that?

Somehow.

If that was true, she had to trust the process and that she'd find a way back into herself soon. As soon as she could help the tiger.

There was such a sense of connection to Ronin. Watching him there by her side, she fell in love a little more. Knowing he was sitting and watching over her gave her an insight into his feelings she hadn't seen before. How could she resist that?

She slipped behind him, and unbeknownst to him, she kissed his cheek.

Ronin straightened, almost dropping both the laptop and phone in the process.

Whoa.

Had he felt her?

Ronin searched the room, his gaze dark and narrow. Then he put a hand to his cheek.

She gasped.

He spun around.

She stared into his dark eyes.

And Ronin stared back.

She swallowed. Then whispered, *Ronin, can you see me?*

He cocked his head to one side, as if listening intently, and his eyes lost their focus.

Such a reaction could only mean he was hearing something, maybe even seeing something but didn't know what or how. And being analytical, he might be struggling to understand instead of going with his heart.

Ronin?

His gaze narrowed, then suddenly he spun around and stared at her body prone in the bed. He carefully placed his laptop on the floor and pocketed his cell phone then walked to her bedside. He stared down in confusion, then his gaze caught on her face. He reached down to touch a tear.

"Tabitha, is that you?"

Yes!

But he couldn't hear her.

"Stefan? Is that you?" Ronin asked.

No, Stefan said, *it's Tabitha trying to talk to you.*

Tabitha could hear Stefan speaking in a three-way communication system that she imagined could only work with psychics. But she could hear Ronin, could see him lift his head and speak out loud to the empty room accusingly, "Damn it. I thought I heard something. Why can't I hear her clearly?"

He pointed to Tabitha's body. "And why is she crying?"

Tabitha was mortified. It was one thing to react honestly with true emotion while believing herself alone; it was quite another to have someone else explaining it to a third party. Then her sense of humor popped up. At least there was a translator. She should be grateful for small mercies.

I am a lot of things, but not a small anything, Stefan said with a light smile.

"Huh?" Ronin asked, turning around. "You people are making me crazy."

Then tune in, damn it, and save all of us this trouble, Tabitha muttered. *And fast.*

He can only learn and believe and grow at his pace. Not yours or mine.

His twin is psychic. That Ronin can even sense me means he has the basis for so much more — so why isn't he learning?

120

He can. Stefan answered imperturbably, *but consider that Roman had no idea what he was doing until it was brought to his attention and didn't believe it until he was forced to use his skills to help you.*

So why is Ronin so blockheaded? she grumbled. *Hit him over the head or something.*

Is that a serious suggestion? His grin slipped through in his voice. *Even if I wanted to do it, I'm not exactly close enough physically to carry out that request.*

"Carry what out? What the hell is going on?" Ronin snapped. "I feel as if I'm only get half a conversation."

You are. Tabitha is the other half. She was talking to you and she wants you to wake up your psychic senses so she can contact you directly. I believe she mentioned how a solid blow to the head might help.

Ronin spun around. "What?"

Tabitha laughed, but it was a hollow sound in her heart. Of all the things she missed, not being able to talk, touch, and love Ronin topped the list. She could talk to Tango and Tripod, and Stefan was always there for her whether she was dead or alive.

Thanks.

It is comforting, she insisted. *No matter what happens, I know that you are there.*

Yes, but if you die, the best thing for you is to go onward, not stay here because you can communicate with me. He sighed and added, *and I suggest you try to contact Ronin as soon as possible.*

I did. You saw the results.

No. I heard the aftermath. He heard you. He just doesn't know what he heard.

Damn it. He's so frustrating.

Stefan laughed out loud. *That's only true because you care.*

Oh, I care. Then there's the fact that he doesn't like cats. That does slow the development of a relationship with me, for sure.

Stefan stilled then he started to laugh. And laugh some more.

It's not that funny, she muttered.

Yes, it i-is. Stefan came to a stuttering stop. *How can you let something like that stop you?*

It's hardly a small issue, she gasped. *Look at where I am at the moment.*

He smiled, and humor still threaded his voice. *True. But does he have a reason for not liking cats?*

We spoke about it briefly. He actually gets a physical reaction. Shortness of breath, his face flushes. She tried to remember what else he'd said.

Could be several explanations. Allergies. A trauma he was in associated with a cat. Even a reaction to an event so long ago he doesn't remember.

That's what I thought. But there's been no time to get deeper into the issue.

Well, maybe you should make time. And with that, Stefan slipped away.

Time. She had nothing on her hands but time. It would be a good time to focus on Ronin's story. But she had no way to communicate with Ronin. She'd only ever been able to communicate with Stefan and her animals on an energy level.

***

Ronin had already started researching the people close to Tabitha after the first attack, and that research hadn't borne any fruit yet. Nothing that connected to what was happening at Exotic or to Tabitha herself personally. He'd left a couple of messages with his buddy Jacob, but hadn't heard back from him yet. Jacob had a long history in undercover work and was often involved in setting up sting operations. Some of them had gotten him into trouble with Internal Affairs. He was involved in something heavy right now. The office rumor mill had supplied that information. Something very hush hush.

Still, that wasn't helping solve the incidents at the reserve. The break-ins. The vandalism. The thefts in the medical side of the building. An inside job perhaps. That said someone close to the reserve. Close to her.

Her grandfather's only relative besides Tabitha and her father was a brother who'd died when Tabitha was a child. Ronin had started searches on her close friends, and most of them were psychics, lending weight to their involvement if he were to connect the two problems involving Tabitha – only there was no proof they were connected.

He'd also reviewed the information from Stefan. That the attack came from a tiger was beyond anything he'd ever heard. It blew him away. How could he reconcile what he knew to what he was learning?

In a way, he couldn't. He had to take it on faith...something he'd done a lot of since he'd met Stefan and his group of friends.

But considering that a tiger would attack anything vulnerable if it had the opportunity, maybe it wasn't all that impossible. He hadn't understood that such an attack could cross such great distances. Surely it would be more reasonable to look closer to home first.

This stuff and his inability to understand all of it – so he could resolve the case – was making him crazy.

Once again, he couldn't bring any of his cohorts in on the problem with a full explanation. But he could ask a few questions and get some idea of whether smuggling endangered species into the country was also a local problem.

If he made the assumption that the tiger could connect with Tabitha because it was close, he needed to narrow his search down to smuggling rings in the U.S. Apparently psychics connected better to events that were closer, geographically, so Tabitha connecting to the tiger made sense that way as well. There were no guarantees, but he had to find a way to narrow this problem somehow.

And if he was narrowing it down even more within those same parameters, he'd start with the West Coast. It was the closest destination for many shady import and export companies looking to tap the U.S. market, particularly those from India and China.

He suddenly remembered those pictures Geoff had handed him. The two detectives he worked closely with, Geoff and Carmichael, both with some experience in animal smuggling, had offered to go through animal smuggling cases. He picked up the phone and called Geoff.

"Geoff, have you got any leads on the animal smuggling?" If only he knew what kind of tiger Tabitha had connected with, he could narrow the field slightly.

"Not much, except it is big business. The animals are flown in, shipped over in containers, driven to their destinations. You name it and people are trying it. Of course much depends on the species. Just last month there was a case of a guy's suitcase completely stuffed with snakes from South America. Like who does that?"

"Crazy," Ronin said. "What about bigger animals? Tigers, lions, that kind of thing?"

"There's always a black market for those. You can buy them locally to some extent, but people always want something not easily obtainable. Transporting them is another problem. Just think of the logistics involved in bringing over big cats. Can you imagine the howling going on in there? You'd have to keep them drugged up the whole time. And cats are fussy. They don't do well in transport. Just ask my wife. Every time she takes Fluffy into the vet, it takes days to regain her trust." Geoff laughed. "Like you'd know. You hate those damn things, don't you? Why are you asking?"

Ronin smiled. "I guess a lot of you guys know about my cat thing, huh?"

"Hell, yeah. So what gives?" Geoff wheezed on the other end of the phone.

"Just a line I'm tugging on a different case. Searching for a smuggled tiger. Wondering what the black market in trading live big cats looks like."

"Like always – it looks like money. Good money. Just don't get caught." He laughed. "Like you know, anything illegal will pay off big if you have someone willing to pay – if the stakes are high enough."

Ronin thanked him and hung up. Now, if only he could connect with Jacob. That detective knew everyone and anyone. He'd worked the docks for years. Several years ago, he'd been part of a huge sting that stopped a large human-trafficking ring. Since then, Jacob had kept a pretty close eye on everything going on. He could be a big help. And those pictures Geoff had dropped off were just as likely to be from that big sting. Why someone would try and get Jacob in trouble could also be due to any number of undercover jobs. If anyone recognized Jacob in these pictures, they could easily assume he was a dirty cop.

With this reasonable explanation, the tension in his shoulders relaxed. Someone was seeing exactly what they were supposed to see if Jacob was undercover. He was supposed to look like he was involved in shady deals. When Ronin got a moment, he'd explain go over that with Geoff.

First, he called Jacob again, and this time he actually got through. He explained his problem.

A long whistle sounded through the phone. "Animal trafficking is big. But a tiger is usually by special order. They are available domestically so the order would be for something unique. Think about it; it's not exactly something you could keep in the basement until the market improves. There are some companies that do special orders of that thing, but they've been skirting the law for so long we've had a hell of a time trying to pin anything on them."

"Names, please."

"I might be able to come up with a couple." He listed off several that Ronin didn't recognize. "Keep in mind, this is a supply-demand chain thing. They don't bring in a product on spec and even if you could catch the supplier, you'd have a hard time connecting it to the buyer."

"What's the chance of seizing the animal?"

"If you're lucky, it's possible. It would be easier with a tiger than, say, a monkey or something even smaller – like snakes. Huge market trafficking snakes."

"Why?" Ronin shook his head. "I just can't see that many people wanting dangerous snakes."

"People will always want what they can't have. And will go to great lengths to get it." He coughed and cleared his throat. "I presume you have a reason for asking about this tiger thing?"

"Yeah, a big one. And time is an issue. Keep an eye out, will you? Let me know if you hear any whispers anywhere along the road."

A second long whistle slipped through the phone. "Will do. Just think a fully grown tiger can jump...what...thirteen to sixteen feet with prey in its mouth."

"I'm expecting it to have been drugged and kept in a cage the whole time." Taking a chance, he added, "And I'm looking for a more or less old warehouse in a deserted part of town."

"It would have to be. Transport and delivery would have to happen fast to avoid detection, so an empty warehouse makes sense. I'll think about those, and write up a few possible leads I can think up to off hand." Ronin could hear him scratching down some notes. "I can check on a few around here." Silence again. "Another angle to pull on is the documentation required to pass it off to the authorities, too."

Ronin responded drily, "In this day and age, anyone can get the required documents for anything." He rubbed the bridge of his nose. "Send me an email with names of people who do that kind of forged paperwork too if you have them. I'll add them to my list and follow up."

"I'll let you know if I find anything." Jacob hung up.

Ronin's brain circled and ran with possibilities. Leaning back, he stared at the now-unresponsive woman who had become so important in his world. "Damn it, Tabitha, I wish you could at least figure out where you are physically located at least."

Stefan had run out of ideas on how to find the tiger with such a dominant energy that it could suck Tabitha into its own space.

He'd dumped it on Ronin and hoped the detective could do his thing.

Animals were not up his alley.

They were Tabitha's thing.

Or at least, until now, they hadn't been his thing. He wasn't sure he had the luxury of excluding them any longer. He'd never had pets. He did know that because of his different energy, most animals reacted to him, one way or another.

Sometimes positively and sometimes negatively.

He was sure that Tango and Tripod accepted him because Tabitha was so well blended with his energy. The animals would sense that. But that didn't mean this strange tiger would be as accepting.

Should he try to connect? He sensed a blockage down that path, but that didn't mean connecting was impossible...

Or would he end up in the same condition as Tabitha? If so, how would that help anyone? Could he walk the ethers, a theoretical halfway point, and call Tabitha? Would she hear him? Would she be able to use him as a guide to bring her home?

Still, if she had anything to add that would help them locate the tiger, then maybe...

He stared around at his open living room where the sun shone so innocently in through the myriad of stained glass panes and had to wonder.

Nothing lost, nothing gained.

Except your soul, snapped a testy voice – a testy astral voice.

Stefan glanced over. *Lissa.* Of course it would be her. Stefan had many ghosts in his life, but none as persistent or as caring as this one. She was the deceased sister of another good friend and since a terribly nasty case he'd helped resolve, she'd been a regular in his life. She claimed it was because he needed someone to watch over him.

And you do.

He laughed. Young and full of life, Lissa was the antithesis of most ghosts. *What could you possibly do if something does go wrong?* he asked her.

Marshal the troops, Lissa said with a laugh. She'd started calling his group of friends a team or a troop, as if they were psychic crime fighters.

That was a joke.

No joke. You can't defy fate. If it's going to happen...

So not.

She laughed. *Look at what you're trying to do now.*

Tabitha needs help.

There is always someone in your world that needs help. There always will be.

He frowned. Even though he knew that, he liked to maintain the fantasy that he had a choice in this regard.

You made that choice a long time ago.

He glared at his wispy visitor. *And I can change it too.*

You can try! She laughed and started to fade away.

Wait, Stefan called out. *Do you have any idea how to find this tiger?*

Tiger? She brightened. *There's a tiger involved? Awesome.*

Her response reminded him that she was still a teenager. *There could be all kinds of animals involved.*

Then why not use another animal to track it?

As quickly as she appeared, she disappeared.

Stefan stared after her in shock. 'Out of the mouth of babes…'

So simple.

When hunting humans, they used humans.

When hunting animals, maybe they should use animals?

He wasn't much of an animal lover, he knew many who were, such as Kali, another psychic friend, and her search and rescue dog. Or Shay and her ghost cat Morris. Stefan still didn't understand how that worked.

Maybe Tango could go after the tiger. Stefan had been considering that, but it wasn't something he could do easily.

And if he couldn't – who could?

***

Keeper walked over, a worried frown on his face. Fez shook his head and said in exasperation, "Now what?"

"The tiger is acting funny."

Fez hunched his shoulders. No, not again. He said ominously, "What do you mean by funny?"

"I mean she's acting funny…" He shrugged. "Weird like."

Fez rolled his eyes. "Is she eating? Drinking? Is she hurting herself in any way?"

"No. She's lying down relaxed and calm. Almost asleep. If I didn't know better, I'd have said she'd been tranq'd with a different kind of drug. She seems almost content. Happy. But we didn't give her anything."

"That's supposed to be a good thing – right?" At the other man's shrug, Fez added, "Keep an eye on her. Just in case."

The other man sauntered back to the cages. Fez didn't know what to think about the tiger's condition. Maybe the tiger had finally calmed down enough, after she'd had several good meals and water. Maybe she'd finally decided that everything was going to be okay.

Then he remembered the look in the big cat's eye. He tugged at his collar again and swallowed hard.

Yeah, that wasn't likely.

The last time he'd looked into her eyes, he'd seen into the heart of her. She might look relaxed and calm, but there was no way he'd trust that look. She'd had a look in her eyes that he'd never forget.

She had murder on her mind.
And he was the prime candidate.

Chapter 12

Sunday mid afternoon

Tabitha studied Ronin as he worked. How long had he been sitting there? Shoulders back and sitting straight in his chair, his fingers clicking away on the keyboard. Every once in awhile he'd frown, then shift and carry on. A man on a mission.

How, when she could only communicate via cats, could she communicate with Ronin?

She could use Stefan, and that worked – somewhat. It didn't stop this gnawing need to be held in his arms and be told it would all be okay. There was only so much she'd share through Stefan.

She glanced over at her body and shuddered. So close and yet so far. Then she frowned. But was it?

If she could communicate through Tango, why couldn't she get back into her body the same way? With all the times she'd traveled into his space and home, she'd damn near created an energy highway.

Why the hell hadn't she thought of that? She'd been so focused on reaching Tango, she'd forgotten to use him to extend her travels. Excited, she closed her eyes and thought her way back into Tango.

He slept heavily, as if he hadn't had a good sleep in forever. And he probably hadn't – at least for several nights.

With a slight release of her nonexistent breath, she sank back into his mind. And smiled. He was racing across open fields in joy. Not chasing anything, just stretching out and using his muscles like they used to work when he was younger. He'd gotten old on her.

Very old.

She'd done all she could but had yet to find a way to stop death from taking those she loved. And she'd tried.

With a wiggle, she realigned her energies with his, gave him a mental hug as she always did, and then traveled back the way she'd always gone before – when her life had been normal. Only always before her actions had been instinctive. There'd been no doubts. No questioning of how. She'd taken one road in and the same road out. Without thinking about it.

Only now she couldn't do that.

Energy wasn't a highway, in that it had no definite directions of travel. Energy floated all around and crossed dimensions and time. To find the same pathway back would be almost impossible. She should be able to close her eyes and think herself back home, but having tried that, she knew it wasn't working. Something was stopping her.

Most likely the connections to the tigers.

Maybe they were keeping her contained? Could she use them to get home instead? She was at the origin. Tango. So what if she could get Tango to find her? She could travel with him back into her body.

God, how bizarre.

Was it even possible? It was because she'd experienced Tango in her space already, but how could she get Tango to actually do the traveling? Prodding a sleeping tiger was never a good idea.

She almost laughed.

Then sighed. He was sleeping so soundly.

She grinned. How about directing his dreams? She whispered gently into his mind, *Tango, come to me. Tango, please come. I need you.*

Tango's paws jerked, but outside of a slight shimmer, his energy remained still and quiet. She didn't want to scare him or have him thinking she was desperately in trouble. That could backfire in a big way.

She smoothed his energy as she planted images of how she'd seen her body the last time in the hospital. Then she placed overlaid images of the two of them playing, of walking through his acres of space. Together.

You'd like that again, wouldn't you, boy?

His feet jerked and his legs shifted as if he were already running. *Just go and get me. Tell me it's time to get out and play our game.* She kept murmuring the same suggestions over and over again. Tango slept on, completely oblivious. *Damn it, Tango. Why won't you come to me?*

She sat back, and if she'd had arms and knees she'd have crossed them over each other. Instead she sat in a whirly ball of energy. Unsure of how and where to go.

As she pondered her quandary, she almost missed seeing the solution. Some of Tango's beautiful dark blue energy lifted and drifted lazily away. Other strands had been doing the same thing with every thought and every action he took in his dreams. But this strand of energy seemed to have purpose and was thick enough to be out there and do something useful.

It shimmered as all healthy energy did, but... She studied it. What was different about it?

Then she got it. There was another energy intermingled with Tango's. A warm chocolate mixed and twisted in a caring way. It was Tripod's energy. Surprised and charmed, she watched as Tango's energy went out in search of Tripod sleeping soundly on the other side of his caged enclosure.

It dipped over Tripod, stroked along his back, and appeared to nuzzle up against the side of his head.

She'd never seen this before. If she'd ever wondered about the relationship between the two of them, this blew her earlier understanding away. They were *that* close.

As she watched the gently caring energy smooth over Tango's canine brother, she realized that she knew so very little about animal energy work. She'd never been in a situation where she'd have even looked for something like this. And usually not looking, in energy work, meant not seeing. The mind would be completely overwhelmed if ninety percent of the energy activity wasn't filtered out.

Tripod never moved except for a huge, gusting breath coming from his chest. He seemed to sink deeper into sleep. Happy and content.

"Tango, how lovely to see you checking up on him."

Then the energy picked up and skirted the huge dog's body and headed out into the hallway. Curious, not letting him know she was riding there because then he might change his actions, she followed just behind him. As they'd been so close for so long, her energy would also appear as his energy. That was the nature of loving energy.

The energy slipped out into the hallway and down the long corridor to her bedroom.

She smiled with delight when she realized Tango was coming to check up on her.

Tango's energy swirl lifted to cover the top of the bed. It settled down on top.

She waited. And waited.

Damn it. She'd hoped he would realize that she wasn't really there.

After a few moments, the energy became restless and slunk over the surface of the bed and around to the other side. It paused, lifted, then hesitated in the air for a moment before circling around up above, almost creating a tornado. She could see the energy spread until the ceiling was completely covered. She had no idea what Tango was doing, unless he was still looking for her.

Then it hit her. Tango had found her as she was right now – hiding behind him.

Clever boy, she whispered. There's no fooling you, is there. Tango's energy seemed to nuzzle up against hers. She kept her field of energy tight and thin. Unwelcoming. She didn't want him to receive the same comfort he'd expect if he actually found her. She wanted him to run to her body looking for the same thing.

Just like that, the energy zipped off.

Pulling her with it.

Tango had no hesitation in his direction. Guided by instinct, he was searching the ethers for her, following the instinctive need to find her. His energy raced forward.

Then he came to a stop. At her bedside.

Tango's energy nuzzled her body in a warm loving way. Blending with her energy, sinking into it just as he'd so many times before.

Smiling, she closed her spiritual eyes, cried out a happy welcome, and sank into Tango as he sank into her space.

She was home.

***

Ronin looked up from his laptop. He'd only been here for a half hour. He'd been running around all morning. Had ended up in some of the seediest areas in town looking for smuggled animals, checking out names and locations Jacob had sent him, feeling like a fool because he didn't even know if the tiger was here in the U.S.

But he had to do something. And of course there was always his job. He had cases stacked up. Not the least were the break-ins at Exotic Landscape. But he hadn't been able to resist checking on her again.

He walked over to the bed. She looked...better? He bent over. Yes, her cheeks were rosy and she was breathing easier.

How and when and why hadn't someone contacted him? He spun around, wanting to race out and yell at the overworked staff...but at the same time he didn't want to leave her side.

As he turned back, she opened her eyes and stared straight at him. Her lips twitched in a tiny smile. "Hey."

"Hey." He grinned, his heart pounding inside his chest. "There you are. It is damn good to see you."

"Same," she whispered. Her eyes drifted closed. "I still feel a little rough."

"Nothing like going for a trip on the wild side."

She winced. "Now that was bad."

"Then again, when you crashed, as you did, after our lovemaking session… That was bad too. At least for me." He tried to make it humorous, but as her gaze widened in shock he realized he'd failed.

"It had nothing to do with you," she gasped. "You did not do this."

"I know that much." He picked her hand up and brought it to his lips. "But maybe if we hadn't been so passionate, you'd have gotten more rest. Been less susceptible. Stronger."

He hadn't allowed himself to focus on the possibility, but it had eaten away at him. Just below the surface.

"No." She shifted her head from one side of the pillow to the other. "Besides, I'm fine. And while I've been in the ethers I might have figured this out. But I'm not sure."

"I hope so." He gripped her hand. "This has been incredibly difficult."

"Ya think?"

He laughed, mostly out of relief. "What did you figure out? See anyone?"

"Yes," she said in surprise. "I heard them. They speak English. I saw a couple of faces, but no, I didn't recognize anyone. And honestly, I didn't get a clear view." She explained what little she'd heard about the buyer and about the tiger's pregnancy and her overall health, ending with the fact that they were afraid the deal would go south. Tabitha wrinkled up her face. "I guess that doesn't help much, does it?"

"Everything helps, but descriptions would be better..." He raised a brow in question then he leaned over and kissed her. Hard.

"Definitely, but I might know a faster way." She smiled. "Stef—" And then she cried out, her back arching high up on the bed.

He reached out. "Tabitha, honey...what's wrong?"

"It's happening aga—"

Her body went rigid, her face froze.

"Jesus. Don't fight it. Do what you did last time and come back."

"Help me," she gasped painfully. "Better yet – help her."

She twisted from one side to the other, tugging at the sheets and covers. Her face scrunched up in a horrible rictus and she collapsed backwards on the bed.

Then her face went slack. Her mouth fell open.

Someone came running in behind him.

"What's going on—oh Jesus. *Move. Move!*"

Ronin stepped back out of the way as the team checked her over.

He knew what had happened, but how could he tell the medical staff?

He had to find that damn tiger. Maybe then Stefan could find a way to separate Tabitha from her – and fast.

Chapter 13

Sunday late afternoon

Pain ripped through Tabitha's mind as if she'd been stabbed. She understood what was happening, but not why. Psychic pain was amplified by one's lack of understanding. But once that awareness was there, the pain should have been almost eliminated, instead it was almost worse. Of course...

She immediately shut off her mind. It was her consciousness that was struggling. As she stopped trying to control it, the pain eased and the journey sped up until she was there.

Back inside the tiger.

Screaming in rage.

Tabitha adjusted more quickly this time and her eyes were open. The tiger had been so calm before. So what the hell happened to change that?

As if in slow motion, she watched two men struggle to subdue the tiger.

"You should have gotten here earlier, Timothy." One of the men puffed with effort. "She's been sleeping comfortably all morning."

"Until we approached," the stranger said. "The tranq should have taken effect already. At least I'm looking for a better reaction than this. She should be calmer. I just need to make sure she doesn't have an infection and that the wound is clean."

Tabitha could feel the tiger's pain. A collar had somehow been placed on her neck while Tabitha had been gone, and she'd been tethered down. A type of muzzle stopped her jaws from opening. She heaved up on her back legs.

"Jesus, Timothy, did you get a blood sample yet?" the first man panted. "I'd like to get out of here in one piece."

Then she realized she could see the men's faces – barely. Tabitha desperately tried to study the men's features. If she could only ID them... She was pretty sure she'd seen one man before. The Timothy guy might be a vet, which meant he had a license and there'd be paperwork to help them track him.

Unfortunately, the tiger was in full-blown panic now and was going to get herself knocked out again.

Timothy groaned. "Shit. You said this would be easy."

"Well, if you'd arrived when you said you were going to, it would have been."

The tiger's emotions swamped Tabitha so she sent out wave upon wave of soothing, calming energy. She needed the tiger awake and calm so Tabitha could see the damn men, but because of the shape the female tiger was in, if she sent out too much calming energy she was liable to put the tiger to sleep.

The tiger finally stilled. Tabitha could feel her chest still heaving, but the soothing energy she'd sent to the tiger had stopped her struggles and that was what was important.

"Jesus. Finally," Timothy said.

"At least she won't hurt herself this way. Hurry the hell up, will you."

"Okay, got it." Timothy shifted. Tabitha could feel a hand on her haunch, assessing her injury. The tiger's old injury. The new guy had to be a vet, and that would be a good thing.

One of the men stepped back.

"Weird coloring. Must be something wrong with her." The first man turned his back on them and walked away. Tabitha tried to find something memorable about him to tell Ronin, but what did one say about a tall, skinny, homeless-looking bum who wore clothes pulled from a garbage can? He looked as if he hadn't seen a toothbrush or hairbrush in years – the same as every other homeless guy she'd ever seen.

His buddy, whom she'd heard and seen before, was better dressed but still he didn't look dressed up in his rough jeans and denim jacket. He was bald and more round than tall and made a great comedy counterpart to the first man – only nothing they were doing was funny to her. He walked with a gimpy leg. Not bad, just off in the stride. She filed that information away.

The vet was young. Had to be a student or a young graduate. Italian looking. She struggled to see the details.

Only she couldn't control where the big cat looked. The tiger made that determination and now that she lay quiet, Tabitha could only see in one direction.

And she couldn't get a decent look at any of their faces.

The tiger's anger stayed inside, riding just below the surface, letting Tabitha know that if any one of them let down their guard and she had an opening, they'd be dinner.

And speaking of dinner... She had to persuade her host to eat and drink again. The tiger, in the family way, needed more than she was taking in. Tabitha could feel the thirst in her mind. The tiger didn't know what a watering bowl was and the idiots had made sure it was small and hard to reach. Best if they'd left her a large open tub of it. Still, it was water and she needed it. And there was food – if not for herself, for the babe growing inside her belly.

She'd protect her cub and herself by any means possible. And that cub...

Tabitha couldn't believe how intimate the sense of love – the bonding – that raced through her as part of the tiger's experience.

It was so special. So loving. Tabitha hadn't experienced anything like it. Her connection with Tango was the closest thing she had to compare this to. But Tango was her friend. He wasn't her baby, no matter that she treated him that way.

If that's what all mothers felt during their pregnancies, especially at full term, maybe she should consider having a family. That level of connection would be hard to experience any other way.

She wanted to know what it was like to care for someone so much that she'd do anything for them. Even die.

She felt privileged to be here, living the experience inside the majestic cat; privileged to be part of their bond, even for only a few hours.

And it would be only a few hours if she didn't get this tiger to drink again. She closed her eyes and filled the tiger's mind with images of water and creeks and lakes and ponds. Then showed them pouring that water into the water dish at the side of the cage. Then she repeated that visualizing process, over and over again.

Several long minutes passed before the suggestion showed any effect. The tiger finally lurched to her feet once again and inspected the foreign dish. She dipped her nose into the water then started to lap it up.

Relieved, Tabitha waited until the tiger's thirst was quenched. She realized the bald man had stayed to watch her.

"There's a good girl. Fez isn't going to hurt you. I'm doing my best to keep you safe." He took a step closer and pointed out the chunk of raw meat at the side and said, "Now how about a nice bite of roast?"

Only Tabitha had lost track of what he was saying. Her mind had caught on the one word in there of interest. Fez? So Timothy and Fez, possibly someone called Keeper, but she wasn't sure about that last one. Besides, any names these guys used probably changed depending on the situation.

But at least she had something tangible. She needed to tell Ronin.

Somehow.

✱✱✱

Ronin slammed the door on his truck and walked across the Exotic Landscapes parking lot. He worked a case until he got to the bottom of it – until he had someone to pin to the wall. In this case, he felt like he was running around in circles. He'd probed into the black market buying and selling of endangered animals and hadn't gotten anywhere. He'd also been working the break-ins at Exotic Landscape – and so far, nothing. They might not have anything to do with the current problem, but still they were part of the file.

He'd just finished saying he needed more information, more avenues to pursue, when he received a call from Sue at Exotic Landscape.

How did another incident – cut fences to the lynx pens this time – have anything to do with this? And damn it, why did this case have to involve more cats?

A dumpling-shaped, middle-aged woman walked out the front door to meet him. Tabitha had told him about Wendy, but he'd yet to meet her. He'd met Sue and several of the security guards but not this new manager. Considering the problems in Tabitha's life, he wondered what kind of a background check Tabitha had done on the new hires.

As much as she needed more staff, she didn't need to add the wrong people to her roster.

He held out his hand to her and smiled briefly. "I'm Detective Chandler."

And had to wonder at her speculative look.

She rushed to say, "I'm so glad you're here. We just found this a couple of hours ago." As she explained, she walked in the direction of the double front gates of the enclosure. "The side of the pen has been damaged. It appears that the person was trying to release or to steal the two female lynx."

Either case likely pointed to neighbourhood kids playing a prank or something more serious. He asked, "The females are unharmed?"

"Yes. They are in this pen only a short time while adapting to their new surroundings. They'd been checked by medical, but we've waiting for Tabitha to get back before the surgeries were done."

"Surgeries?"

"Most of the animals are neutered after they arrive – if they haven't been already." She motioned in a wide arm sweep. "It makes the animals easier to deal with and generally stops people wanting them for breeding purposes. We list that on the website hoping it will stop the inquiries."

"What kind of inquiries?"

She shrugged. "I haven't been here for long. We ask for donations or virtual adoptions for the care of the animals. Many ask for visitation rights, home visits, and even more want to purchase the animals. Sometimes for breeding purposes."

He frowned. "And that's not allowed?"

"No. No they stay here their entire lives. Not at all. This is their home forever. They get all they need here and have room to roam in a decent space created for them. No cages unless they have medical needs that are being addressed. Each animal is safe and secure from the public."

Ronin had to smile. She was a walking billboard in support of Exotic Landscape. Maybe Tabitha had made a great hire. Except many of these incidents could have been carried out as an inside job. He studied Wendy but she didn't look strong enough to cut the fence. That didn't mean she wasn't in partnership with someone else who wanted the animals though. She could have found a buyer for them…

The B&Es could have been an inside job, too. He'd taken a close look at all the staff already.

"Of course. These break-ins will slow down donations. Nothing like bad press to make those dry up."

He shot her a sidelong look. As they came around the corner, he switched his gaze to the pen. There was a big patch showing where the gaping hole had been.

Damn. Whoever had done this meant for the animals to go free. But why these ones in particular? Why not any number of her pens? Or was that just for convenience? These pens were closest to the road. Had they run out of time? Or… He spun around searching for cameras. They were still there and that meant there could be a record of what had happened. He could hope.

The question was – why had they done this and did they plan to do more?

He glanced around. Wendy had disappeared. But then the offices weren't normally open today. Still, he wanted to see the security feed.

Could he find someone here who knew how to access them? Tabitha had new hires, but the security system was even newer.

He dialed his brother – and got no answer. Damn it. He vaguely remembered there being some shindig of Shay's he'd planned to attend.

Checking his watch, he realized he could check the feed on Monday when the usual security people were here.

His phone rang. Stepping outside, he answered Jacob's call.

"Ronin, I've got someone willing to talk," Jacob said. "Six o'clock tomorrow morning, at Land's End."

"Hey, Fez."

"What?" Fez turned from the back of the truck where he was unloading the day's shipment. Most of the food was raw meat for the big cat. The last of the other animals he'd transported had been picked up yesterday.

"I think you should come and see her," Keeper said from behind him. "She doesn't look right."

Not again. Jesus, Keeper was simple. He was repeating the same phrase over and over again. "I'll be there in a minute."

He finished storing the meat, wiped the sweat off his face and turned back into the warehouse. The black cloth was covering the tiger cage. He lifted a corner and tried to peer inside.

And came face to face with the tiger's eyes. Her massive jaws opened up. *Rawrrrr!*

"Jesus Christ." He bounced backwards, almost tripping over his own feet as he raced to put distance between himself and the tiger.

The other man was laughing like crazy, bent over and slapping his thighs.

"Oh, my God. You look so funny." Keeper howled again and pointed a finger at him. "You damn near shit your pants."

Damn near felt like it too. But he wasn't going to say that to this asshole. "Did you do that on purpose?"

"Do what? Hell, I just told you to come here because she doesn't look right. I didn't say go lift the corner of the cloth where she's lying and scaring the shit out of her."

Fez barely stilled the impulse to beat Keeper's head in. Asshole. "Well, she looks damn normal to me."

"Well, she isn't." The other man sobered up instantly. "Not at all. She's abnormally calm. I just don't know how that can be."

"Well, maybe you should just be thankful that she is," he snapped. "Besides, that's what you said last time."

"No. She's *too,* content. I think someone is slipping her drugs. It's the only explanation. I know I didn't do it. I don't think it's you, so who the hell is drugging her?" He looked around the warehouse as if seeing it for the first time. "And does that mean the boss is doing something that doesn't include us? Or is someone else involved, maybe one of the delivery guys?" He lowered his voice. "The security here is pretty lax. I know we were counting on no one knowing what we really had...but what if someone finds out?"

"And what good would drugging the tiger do? Sure, it keeps her calm but that would benefit us and no one else." Fez had to think about that. In this lowlife location, their movements could have been tracked. It wouldn't have taken much for a curious someone to figure out what they held captive.

"Unless it also makes her more docile around the guy who drugged her, too," Keeper said. "In which case, it would be easier to steal her."

"And there is someone else who knows she's here. The young kid you brought in. Timothy. Maybe he slipped her something we don't know about?"

Keeper gasped. "No way. He's just a kid. Besides, why would he? No one knows about the tiger. He wouldn't tell, so there's no point in giving her an extra shot."

Looking around as if afraid someone would overhear, he added, "Besides he said the blood tests came back positive. The old girl is pregnant."

"What?" Fez couldn't believe it. But it was damn good news. That meant the boss would be happy. The buyer would be happy. And the damn deal could go through. Then Fez could get his damn money. "Now that is very good news."

"Maybe and maybe not. Someone could be trying to scoop their sale." Keeper nodded wisely.

As if he knew anything. But Fez did know there'd been trouble with the boss and the buyer. But that's 'cause the tiger had been ailing.

But a pregnant ailing tiger was a hellavu bonus.

And Fez took that one step further. What if the buyer really wanted the tiger but decided to not bother paying? With the pissing contest going on between the boss and the buyer, the buyer could do that out of spite.

In this business, lots of people just took what they wanted. Especially if they didn't like doing deals with certain people. Especially if they felt they were being screwed in the first place. If the buyer found out about the pregnancy, there was no guessing what he might do.

To Keeper, he said, "We need to boost security around this place. We can't take the risk something will go wrong."

"You mean something else going wrong, right?" Keeper groaned. "There is no way to increase security. Short of camping here overnight."

Fez just stared at him, waiting.

"No way." Keeper shook his head. "You can stay overnight if you want. I'm going home for a decent meal and a beer."

"Sure," Fez said mildly, "then get your ass back here for the first watch. I'll relieve you at 2:00am."

The other man groaned. "You aren't serious?"

"Return in *four* hours or don't bother returning at all." Keeper needed the money just as much as he did. The man stared at him, stomped his feet a few times, his mouth working, then stormed out to the other room.

Fez watched Keeper leave. He'd be back. He turned to stare at the cloth-covered cage. "Looks like it's just you and me, girl."

A deep howl started from the far end. There was no way she'd be able to get out. Just the fact that she'd reacted this way though...

"Shit." He gave into the fear and backed up several paces then turned and ran to the far side of the warehouse. As the door closed on his heels, he swore he could almost hear the damn feline laughing.

***

Stefan opened his eyes, though sleep still clouded his mind. The bedroom swam and twisted in front of him. The air swirled in black clouds, taking him somewhere...else.

He had no idea where he was or where he was going.

The clouds cleared. Blue sky and sunshine shone above him. He floated in the clouds above a generic countryside. He zoomed in faster and faster, seeing the land come rushing up toward him. He zipped down to follow a blue ribbon slashing across the land.

Closer and closer he went. Faster and faster he flew, swooping lower and lower until he was skimming across the water. He hadn't recognized any landmarks while flying down, and now at water level there were no buildings that he could see. Faster and faster, the wind whipped past so hard it brought tears to his eyes.

And then he stopped and hovered in place to study the surroundings. He didn't have a time frame either. Was this the past, present or the future?

He was still traveling forward, but almost in a slow gliding motion. He was coming up to a town. Not a town. A city. *Portland.*

With the tears flooding his eyes, he could barely see. And then he came to a sudden stop. A dirty river. Derelict buildings. And empty streets.

But it was the body floating in the water that caught his attention.

A man.

Dead.

But the dead man was important.

Even so, Stefan could feel his energy zapping his system. He had to travel home soon. If he could just get a closer look at the man's face…

Pulling on the last of his reserves, he dove lower until he was lying parallel above the body and gazing straight into the dead staring eyes.

Stefan hit the end of his rope. He was sucked back in time and space through the wind and the clouds and the sky – back through a long black tunnel – and slammed back into his body that still lay on his bed.

Chapter 14

Sunday early evening

Tabitha curled into a tight ball of energy. She had no idea what to do or how to do it. She could go back to Tango and potentially back to her body – unless she'd died the last time.

Only the connection to the tiger went both ways, and now she was attached to her existence here and fearful for her life – and the tiger's life. How could Tabitha leave her alone?

She'd heard the men's discussion about drugs. Were they talking about the effects of her calming energy on the tiger or had someone else entered the warehouse and attempted to drug the tiger? She didn't feel anything new, but Tabitha had felt a wash of wrongness in the tiger's body since she arrived. The body felt different from Tango's, but then he was tame, happy, and healthy. Trinity – Tabitha had named the tiger following her grandfather's naming scheme of all pets starting with T's (and, damn, she hadn't wanted to ask about her own name) – was wild, hurting, and on death's doorstep.

Trinity was tired. Hurting. Scared. Almost to the point of giving up.

Tabitha rocked back and forth in her virtual space, wishing to see a way forward. The tiger was a victim here. But then so was Tabitha. She hated that feeling. And her awareness was so much stronger because the tiger's feelings were bleeding into Tabitha's emotions, amplifying them, making Trinity's feelings Tabitha's. This amplification connected her to the tiger in a big way – they were both victims.

Her mind stalled.

Victim. That's what she felt like. That's what she'd become. That's what she was.

Because she'd slipped into the victim mentality.

She was letting the circumstances dictate what she could do. She was reacting...not acting. She was letting the situation get the best of her. Instead of doing something constructive about it.

That had to stop.

Trinity slowly eased her legs down to stretch out in front of her while Tabitha's mind wrapped, shifted, and reformed the new reality of the situation. There was no way in hell she was going down as a victim.

Not in this lifetime. Unless her life was already over. But she couldn't go there. She didn't dare. She had to figure out how to take back control. And that started at the emotional level. Then the mental, and finally she knew she could manifest intent in her physical life.

She took a deep breath and released it. Then took another. As she started to feel better, she realized that her energy was uncurling, stretching away from her, relaxing too. Her energy was changing as her mental shift grabbed hold. She smiled as the tension slipped down her spine and into the ground, opening her consciousness.

Fear had sunk so deep inside Tabitha, she hadn't recognized it when it crept up and took hold. But it was there, almost rank with its stench.

She shone a little light on her fears, letting them breathe, letting them swell before releasing it to the ether.

As she released all that in front of her, she could see them. See what she'd held deep inside, hidden even from herself. Things that were clogging her soul. Things that were holding her back from the next step. The hurts were all there too.

Tobias's death.

Her grandfather's death.

Tango's impending death.

Tripod's eventual death.

Her uncertainties over Exotic Landscape.

So many regrets. So many fears. And along with those, so many fears of what was to come. So many hurts she'd hidden from herself. So many losses and wishes and dreams. She was like a water slide, with all these memories and dreams and thoughts gushing from her out of this big pipe – as if the process was releasing everything that had held her back. It was what she needed to do to lighten her soul and let it breathe again.

Let her soul live. And stretch. And thrive.

And act.

She waited, feeling the power surging through her. She didn't need to be confined in here. She could go anywhere. Any time. Including to her body.

It was fear not reality that had held her back.

Now she knew what to do.

She needed to go to the source. And that meant the tiger's source.

Tabitha pushed gently into Trinity's memories, easing into it, one gentle pulse at a time. She had the names Fez and Timothy, now she needed the faces. Tiger vision was different and she'd seen the general outline of the men, but not their features with any clarity.

She wished she could transmit the images to Stefan. He'd be the one to translate them to paper. But there was no guarantee she could.

Damn it, where was Ronin? She needed him. In so many ways. More than she'd understood before. She sent out another gentle pulse into the old tiger's memories and watched as the curtains of the big cat's mind opened slightly. Tabitha was taking a dangerous chance doing this. She didn't want to open the memories too wide or deep. If Trinity had many traumatic instances in her life, reliving them could bring back the same shock and stressors as she'd experienced in the wild. In fact, given the state Trinity was already in, any number of these could kill her.

And most likely Tabitha along with her.

Taking a mental step back, she approached the next layer of energy with love, sending out warm caring thoughts to tamp down the fear. She wanted the memories to be like an old black and white movie. Something distant and hard to relate to.

Not something that would cause Tabitha's heart to race or her adrenaline to kick in.

Trinity lay at one end of the cage. She'd responded well to Tabitha's suppression energy and that had calmed her aggression, eased her fears, and worked to save her from feeling pain. It was easier on them all this way. But dangerous too, especially if the men assumed it was safe to approach the tiger – if that were to happen, Trinity's instincts would override Tabitha's work and, given the opportunity, she'd attack her captors.

Tabitha knew Trinity would never be happy in captivity. She could live on a reserve to the end of her days, but the caregivers would never be able to let down their guard. Tabitha also knew she might be able to do some energy work to help Trinity adapt; she certainly helped the animals on her reserve that way. Anything that helped the animals live a healthier and happier life worked for her.

Humans could learn a lot from them. So could she.

As that thought crossed her mind, the layers of Trinity's memories pulled back and she watched a stream of disjointed images ripple past at super speed. She tried to slow them down but nothing she did worked. The film raced by in a never-ending stream of hunting, feeding, mating, birthing. Then the film started to crackle as if it was breaking. It got deeper, darker, and more sinister. A loud pop sounded so close that Tabitha could feel the sting as something bit into her hip. She gasped and could feel the burn and shock and terror Trinity experienced during her capture as if it were today. Trinity had survived a lot in her life, she was old for a wild tiger, but she hadn't been expecting to run from a gun. She hadn't even seen that coming.

When she'd woken up, Trinity had been caged.

Tabitha watched the rest of the bad-quality film, searching for something usable. From inside the darkness, she could hear sounds in a distance and understood the animal had been kept sedated. She had no idea for how long. To Trinity, with the fear and rage rippling through her, it seemed endless. She'd been kept drugged for far too long. Tabitha understood the need from the poacher's point of view, but for the tiger...it was an endless myriad of pain and fear.

Tabitha had to wonder where Trinity came from. Not that it mattered, but someone had obviously gone to a lot of trouble. The fur on the tiger's paw was a dirty gray and black. Tabitha hadn't had a clear view of the rest of her body. She could be a white Bengal. White tigers were rare in the wild. They were legal to own and breed in many parts of the U.S. but the color came with its own set of problems. White tigers, with their distinctive recessive gene, were so inbred that the breed had multiple problems.

But what if this wasn't a white tiger? What if she was a rarer variation? What if that slate gray on her front leg and paw were the same all over? What if she really was a famed Maltese tiger?

There'd been reports since forever of blue tigers, but confirmed sightings were few and far between and none in the last several decades. Then there was a rare black tiger species – although her coloring didn't go that far.

But if she was any one of these rare breeds, she should have been treated much better. The world would want to know that one of the species had been found in its natural habitat and it would be protected – as were all extinct and endangered animals. And the penalties for smuggling it would be stiff.

From the memories she'd accessed, she knew this tiger had been captured in the wild.

If it was the breed she suspected, it was one of the last of its kind.

That made Trinity even more special. It made her...a rare find.

"A floater?"

Stefan's tired voice sounded flat, disembodied. Ronin had observed the famed psychic on just enough calls to realize he'd probably just climbed out of another vision.

It was late on a Sunday. He should be back at the hospital, not still at the office, but he'd needed to check in. There'd been a surprising number of people here. He tried to focus on Stefan's conversation.

"Do you have a location?" Ronin asked.

"Portland, but nothing more detailed."

But a city was good. If the floater was related to Tabitha's problems. "Does this guy have something to do with the tiger?"

"I'm hoping so." This time there was a thread of humor in Stefan's voice. "It could be another case though."

Ronin paused to digest that. So, a body somewhere in Portland... he thought, but could they count on that, considering he didn't get a good look. And maybe or maybe not related to Tabitha's predicament. Couldn't these psychics make it easy for once? "Have you any idea how little help this is?" he asked in frustration

"No. And I don't want to know. Thanks." Now his voice was sounding positively cheerful. "I just pass over the information. It's your problem now."

Ronin pinched the bridge of his nose and took a mental step back. Since meeting these people, he'd learned that nothing ever fit together in a straight line...at least not until they solved a case. Then the puzzle pieces fell nicely into place. But the path getting there was beyond twisted. The stuff they found out in the pursuit of their answers made him realize a long time ago that most people lived their nice happy lives blind to everything around them. When it came to the area of psychics, there was a whole other world just under the surface.

"Please tell me you have something more."

"Check your email."

And he hung up.

Ronin groaned. He'd turned off the notifications on his phone a long time ago, hating to be always attached to the damn thing. He walked back to his desk and opened his laptop.

The email program took a moment to load before he saw Stefan's email. With an attachment. He opened the attachment and was reminded, Stefan was an *artist*!

The scanned black and white pencil sketch might as well have been a photograph. The lines around the man's face were so well blended, the shading so realistic that if he hadn't understood Stefan's talent, he'd have assumed he'd taken a picture of the dead floater.

Behind the first sketch was a second one, of the surrounding buildings.

Bringing them both up on the big monitor beside him, Ronin studied the images. He sent them to the printer and waited.

He'd pick them up in a minute. The old rundown buildings along the edge of the river were interesting. The buildings had no identifying names or numbers. He had no clue where the buildings were located, but he thought some of his buddies might.

Ronin knew a couple of techs that might be able to help. He whipped up a few emails and sent them off with a note saying he was on his way over to talk to them. But first, the printer.

The big printer was in the outer office. Beside the coffee. Several of his buddies were standing around and talking when he entered the room.

He searched for the printouts. The one of the river was there, but not the floater. Crap. He'd have to go back and reprint it.

"Hey Ronin, is this yours?" Brent held up the floater's image. "Where the hell did you get that?"

"A contact." He deliberately kept Stefan's name out of the discussion. "Quite the sketch, isn't it?"

"This is a sketch?" one of the men asked.

"Looks like a photograph."

"Of a dead guy."

"Yeah. He had to have been there to have seen it in this kind of detail." The paper was passed from hand to hand as they studied the artistry.

"Anyone recognize the dead guy?" Ronin asked. He glanced up at their faces, and damn if there wasn't a shadow crossing Geoff's face. "Geoff? Do you?"

He shrugged his shoulders. "Damn if I know. The guy's face is all distorted."

"Yeah, he's a floater."

"We've had a few of those come in the last month. None around this guy's age that I know of though."

Brent said, "How can you tell what age?" Brent peered more closely. "Guy could be anywhere from twenty to sixty."

"The water is never nice to flesh, but this guy doesn't look like he was in all that long. I've seen worse."

With that announcement, several of the guys grabbed their coffees and headed back to their desks. Brent handed the picture back to Ronin. "Good luck."

Ronin watched him walk away. He would check on the recent floaters from the morgue and check with the lab techs to see if they could help improve the image.

Ten minutes later, he knew that wasn't going to work.

"Sorry, but the guy's features are too distorted," said the lab tech. "We can set up a facial recognition scan and run it through the database looking for someone, but it's a long shot."

"Run it anyway. Besides, I have a second problem for you. Is there any way to figure out this location?" He handed over the second picture.

They fell into a discussion about the minor landmarks in the picture. Finally the lab tech shook his head. "Sorry, Ronin, but there's not much to go on here. No skyline. No physical landmarks. It's just a few old buildings."

"Yeah, that's what I was afraid of." Ronin picked up the picture and walked out.

What was the chance that Stefan could return to the same place and find some landmarks this time? Possibly keep his eyes open, for heaven's sake.

***

4:30 am

The warehouse was steeped in darkness. And silence.

The darkness was a bit too dense to see much. Fez wanted to open a window, maybe turn on a light. Something.

Tonight this place was giving him the creeps. He'd come in and relieved the idiot, Keeper, about a half hour ago. Keeper had been asleep when Fez arrived. Now, alone at 4:30 in the morning, Fez wished he'd left Keeper asleep and just stayed here to keep watch over the tiger.

He'd never been afraid of the dark before. Neither had he been afraid of being alone.

Tonight, he had to admit to both.

He was tired and chilled with a powerful need to constantly look around. He just needed a good night's sleep. Keeper had slept through his shift – lucky bugger. Sleeping wasn't exactly the best way to stand guard, but it sure as hell helped pass the time.

Happy with his decision, he curled up in a far corner of the warehouse where he had a good view of the front entrance and the tiger's cage and closed his eyes.

Every sound was amplified in the dark. Somewhere in the far side of the warehouse he heard the scurrying of little feet. Probably rats. The damn place was infested with them. The dampness from the river brought them in. At least it was dry in here. And a few rats didn't bother him.

It's not as if there were any animal control or health inspectors that came around this corner of the world, and if they did stop in, there was always money to grease the wheels to make them go away.

He struggled to get comfortable, shifting his fat bottom on the cement floor, wishing there was at least a chair to sit on. He leaned back against the wall and closed his eyes.

Then opened them. *What was that?* He caught his breath as he heard something over by the tiger's cage. *Voices.*

Quietly Fez regained his feet and tiptoed toward the cage, his head cocked in the direction of the sound. He stopped and waited breathlessly. Then he took another step and thought he heard it again. He took several more steps toward the tiger's cage and waited. The warehouse seemed alive with weird sounds. Air whistled from the blowing wind. Timber creaked with age. And he swore there were sounds of people moving.

What the hell was going on? He hopped to his feet and walked over to the tiger, peering into the cage. The tiger lay sleeping on her side. Calm. Quiet. Peaceful.

He turned around to face the empty warehouse. Shadows seemed to shift even as he watched. Now he knew his imagination was working overtime, and that pissed him off as much as it scared him.

Seeing nothing to justify the sounds, he slowly retraced his steps back to his spot. Then he heard something that sent shivers down his spine. Breathing. As in human breathing. As in a person. So loud he imagined the hairs on the back of his neck lifting.

He willed himself to turn and see who it was. Wishing he had a gun, he spun around.

The blow came out of nowhere. It smashed into the side of his head.

And he dropped like the heavy weight he was – to the ground.

Chapter 15

Monday early morning

Now that she had some inkling that Trinity had come from the wild with this coloring, she suspected Trinity to be a Maltese tiger. Tabitha dredged through her memory for all the information she could find about them. And there was damn little. Maltese tigers hadn't been seen in decades in the wild. She knew of none in captivity, but that didn't mean there weren't any. It was an endangered species and the whole world would celebrate if they knew Trinity existed.

If they knew.

Which, considering Trinity was being smuggled, they weren't likely to ever learn. And she was old. By any medical standards, being pregnant at her age was rare. Not that Mother Nature cared what humans deduced. She was forever throwing up new and wondrous things. But did the smugglers truly understand what they had?

Understanding the problem and the precious cargo helped, but not enough. So what if there were buyers and sellers and good guys and bad guys out there? If she couldn't see any to identify them or find a way for others to find her, none of that mattered. Somehow she had to get Ronin the information she'd found. But what was that? Just a name. And a vague face.

She needed more.

She wondered if she could create enough energy disturbances to upset the asshole standing guard. She'd learned his name was Fez and she'd managed to stretch her energy out enough to raise the hairs on the back of the guy's neck. But he'd gone back to sitting down. She'd been trying to get a good look at his face, but there were so many shadows she couldn't see it clearly enough. She'd tried, but unfortunately didn't have a photographic memory.

But Stefan did. She'd been trying to tell Ronin the details earlier but she'd been yanked away before she could say anything. Now maybe she had a better idea.

She closed her eyes and sent out a strong message. *Stefan. Stefan? Stefan!*

Taking a chance, she told her subconscious to transmit the images to Stefan. They could be the answer to saving Trinity. And for good measure, she told herself to send anything else that might be useful.

What the hell? Where are you and why? Stefan's voice growled in her head. Faint and odd sounding but still identifiable. The diction was off, but it was clear enough to hear.

I need you to see some images. Pictures I can see but can't remember.

Silence.

Not sure that will work.

You can often connect in such a way that you just see into my mind and save me from trying to explain. Why can't you do that now?

Because you aren't here in front of me. You're in someone else's mind.

Damn it. I've seen one of the men that's holding the tiger. His name is Fez. I can see his and Timothy's face, but I'm no artist.

You know every step away from the original blurs the details. You'll have to try and grab the details.

He was right, but she didn't like it. *Suggestions?*

Clear your mind and use the energy. Try to remember and come home. I'll tell Ronin.

Crap.

Stefan disappeared and the fog moved in again.

She needed another look. She stared through the tiger's eyes out at the warehouse. It drained a lot of her energy to do this but the rewards could be worth it.

She closed her eyes and stretched a bit of her energy away from the tiger's cage toward where she'd sensed the asshole the last time.

The idiot appeared to be sleeping. She stretched out a little more, trying to get a look at his face, but there was something wrong. There was blood around his head. Lots of it.

He'd been attacked.

And she hadn't heard it.

That terrified her. Had she been so focused on contacting Stefan that she'd missed it? Or had the attackers been so quiet, she'd not have heard them?

The shock zapped her back to the tiger where she curled up into a ball. A new fear took over, blending with that of the tiger's. Who the hell had hurt Fez? Were they still here?

In the background, she heard a door rattle.

✳✳✳

Ronin had walked a lot of seedy streets in his time, but these slums were pretty bad. He'd already seen several drug deals go down. Life here was a whole new world. The hookers strolled the sidewalks, looking ready to call it a night. Businesses thrived down here, but at this hour of the morning it appeared only the underbelly was alive. During the day, it teemed with people from all walks of life. Many were visiting. When this was your life, escape was damn near an impossibility – so many never did.

He walked around the corner to find Land's End Cafe. From the outside it had that tired, worn down look – the same as so many of the other local businesses. Open twenty-four hours, there were likely more cockroaches eating at the restaurant than clients. Still, he ordered two coffees and watched the grizzled waiter pour them. As he accepted the steaming cups from him, he was surprised to see the rich color. He wasn't sure what he'd expected. He'd taken his chances on the coffee here – it could've been anything from sludge to a tea-looking brew.

The diner was empty, but the traffic outside was steady. From a table in the corner, he watched the world walk by. His eye caught on an old couple holding hands. His smile warmed. He'd planned on having a wife and a family to grow old together. The growing old together was what he was looking at. The comfortable reassurance that they knew each other inside and out. That their love had been the light they'd walked with for every day of their lives.

He had to admit, he wanted some of that for himself – with Tabitha.

But that girl seemed to thrive on trouble. He didn't feel in sync with her world. As much as he wanted to be, that didn't guarantee he'd find his place in it. And he hadn't been able to help her. Yet.

"Ronin?"

Ronin glanced up. A scraggly looking man in oversized pants and jacket, with a full and unkempt beard and an old flattened hat stood in front of him. Just a middle-aged man down on his luck. Nice disguise, except the man's eyes were clear and direct. And faintly familiar.

Ronin nodded and motioned to the seat across from him and the waiting cup of coffee. "Take a seat."

"Thanks." The man sat in the chair.

Trying not to stare, Ronin studied the coffee swirling in his mug. "What do you know?"

The man took a sip of his hot drink first. "There's some talk about a rare cat. Doing poorly."

Now they were talking. Ronin leaned forward. "Where?" he asked in low undertones. He didn't know if it was a rare cat Tabitha had hooked up with, but that made sense. He should have asked her. The various states had different laws regarding owning and breeding large cats, but he'd also learned that anything was available for the right price.

The other man shrugged. "Can't be sure."

"What *can* you be sure of?"

"It's rare. It's hurting, and there is some in-fighting going on between buyer and seller." The older man inhaled the caffeine fumes, then lifted his cup and took another sip, then sighed happily.

"Names?" Was he an informant or an undercover cop? That Ronin couldn't tell said much for his disguise.

The other man took his time then shook his head. "That I can't do." He put down the empty cup and stood up. "Thanks for helping an old man out. Appreciate it."

He shuffled passed Ronin and went out the door.

With a snort, Ronin stood, pissed at not having more. As he turned to leave, he saw a crumpled piece of paper on the table. He could've sworn it hadn't been there before. He snatched it up and raced out the front door so he could see which direction the old man had gone.

There was no sign of him. He'd disappeared.

Ronin glanced down at the paper in his hand. He smoothed it out. And found what appeared to be a phone number scribbled across the sheet.

***

Stefan woke from a deep sleep, silently, stealthily. Alert. As if he was under attack – or preparing to attack. Only there was no sign of anything. Or anyone. He shifted his vision to search the energy in the room. It all appeared normal. His guards were still in place. The house remained safe. His security system untouched.

So where was the danger?

Faint images of a collapsed man filled his mind. He sorted through the images, trying to figure out who the man was. And why was Stefan receiving the images?

He grabbed his pencil and sketchbook and went to work. The picture came together relatively quickly.

After a few moments, he closed his eyes to bring the image up again. And caught that same scent of wrongness he'd felt on waking.

He sent out a probe, searching the ether for what had disturbed him. Nothing. He lay quiet for a few moments, listening. Nothing obvious, but still...something was wrong. He couldn't identify it. But that didn't mean it wasn't there.

Tabitha? He wished he knew for certain. Too often he dealt with multiple cases at once. There could be any number of things wrong. Restless, he set the sketchbook aside and stepped out onto his deck as the early morning light was cresting the horizon.

He took a deep breath of the crisp air. There was still a bite in the cool morning, but not enough to ease the rising temperature of worry. If only he could figure out what was wrong. He stared across the property. He was far enough out of town that he was often visited by wildlife. No animals moved.

He cocked his head to the side, turned to glance back into his bedroom, then walked through to his front door. He threw it open. Then stared. There was the merest whisper through the large bushes in front of him. He shifted his vision to search for energy. Blues and greens swirled in the early morning dawn. He used colors to help his plants grow. Those not native to the country utilized the energy to adapt. The colors helped stabilize, helped them to adjust. In part, that was why they'd done so well here.

Tabitha's face rose from the colors, letting him know he was between realities. She opened her mouth, but the words flew from his lips. "My grandfather's box."

***

Fez sat quietly in the corner of the warehouse. His head was killing him – and his boss looked like he wanted to finish the job. When he'd first arrived, he'd had a genial smile on his face that made Fez's blood run cold.

Now he was talking to the buyer. Only Fez didn't understand the conversation. And yeah, that might be from the knock on his noggin. He reached up a tentative hand to touch the wound. Blood was still dripping down the side of his neck.

He needed medical attention but had no money. He was also damn sure the boss would toss him in the river rather than help him. The longer he listened, the more he realized the boss was dousing his chances of ever getting away.

"No," the boss said into the phone, "I'm sorry to say, she's definitely not improving. I don't think she's even going to make a week even. I should be able to refund this transaction by the weekend."

This time Fez couldn't hear the buyer's half of the conversation, but the glint in the boss's eye said he wasn't backing down. None of this made any sense. He groaned and leaned back to rest his head.

For whatever reason, the boss wanted to back out of this tiger deal. And that was seriously bad news.

His boss continued. "No. There's no option at this point. I'll make the arrangements."

When he hung up the phone and stared at Fez, Fez said querulously, "We did everything we could to make this deal happen. Now you cancelled it?"

The boss snorted. "Damn right I did. She's pregnant. That changes everything. There is no way in hell I'm going to sell short the best deal of my life." He smiled, a cold, hard smile. "She's worth so much more now."

Fez didn't know what to say and couldn't think straight either. Money...he needed money. "But...my paycheck?"

"Oh you'll get paid. No worries there." His boss pulled out a small notepad and dropped it on the floor in front of Fez. "We're going to run a private auction – contact a few more people. Some high-end collectors."

"I need money now," Fez protested. "And this buyer... What about when he finds out?"

The boss opened his wallet and pulled out some bills. He threw them at Fez. "This will tide you over for a week. It won't be longer than that and you'll get your full pay."

Fez leaned forward, shuddered at the pain, and picked up the money. "And the buyer?"

"This buyer can go to hell," the boss said calmly. "Once I give him the money back, he's got nothing to do with this anymore. If he wants her after that, he can bid in the auction. If he asks, I'll tell him she's made a miraculous recovery and is pregnant to boot." He smiled. A twitch of his lips that made Fez's heart quake with dread.

"And if he doesn't like it, too damn bad." The cold smile turned to ice. "I have solutions for assholes like him too."

Chapter 16

Monday morning

Tabitha had to get home again. It was early, she'd heard something out in the warehouse a while ago, but it had calmed down.

In fact, outside of trying to grab something useful for Ronin to help her and the tiger, she'd had no real reason for staying as long as she had. Except to provide comfort. Trinity was calm and peaceful when Tabitha was there beside her.

But once she left her, Trinity's energy would thin and she'd feel the fear and panic that much stronger – even with Tabitha's suppression energy.

Tabitha understood Trinity was sick. In a way that was beyond healing. Heartsick. And maybe soul-sick. There was only so much she could do to make Trinity's remaining time as easy as possible. Given the situation, that wasn't much. If they could get her to the reserve, she'd do better but any measure would be only temporary. As for the cub inside...

If it could survive this nastiness, then there could be a decent life for it. Tabitha already felt the same warm maternal feelings the tiger did, as if the cub were her own. It would be brutal if something happened to it, but she also knew the dangers of getting this attached. The cub most likely wouldn't be able to stay with her, although it could live at Exotic Landscape quite nicely. She'd have to fight for it. Better these assholes had left her in the wild.

Tabitha sent a warm, loving energy jolt to the tiger's energy chakra and then to the baby. She poured protective energy around them both as she backed up and away before finally turning and sweeping into the ether to find Tango.

As her energy had never left Tango's, he only gave her a surprised greeting as if to say, 'What is your problem, I was sleeping here?'

She laughed with joy at the familiar surroundings and gave the big cat a warm hug. His energy rolled through her, around her, warming her and bringing tears to her eyes. She felt so sorry for all the lonely people in the world who never had a chance to connect on this level. She'd been truly blessed. Her father was one of those who'd never connected, and as such had missed out on one of life's truly great experiences.

She shifted back to check on Tripod, who barked a warm greeting, before she dashed back to her physical body. This time she slid back inside effortlessly.

She opened her eyes. And saw she was back in the hospital.

This trip had been much easier on her body and on her soul. Her room was empty. She had no idea where Ronin was, but he couldn't be expected to stay here forever. Knowing that, she wanted to return to her house. Even connected as she was and knowing that the tiger could pull her back at any time, Tabitha would be better off at home. She could only hope that the protective healing energy she'd left behind had the power to keep Trinity calm for a day or two at least. That would hopefully free Tabitha long enough to sort out her life here. She did not want to get tugged backwards like she'd been twice, but that appeared to be the only thing the tiger knew to do to make herself feel better.

And Tabitha would have done the same thing under the same circumstances.

She threw back her covers and gently sat up, letting her legs swing over the side. The room swam in front of her. She clasped a hand to her face and shuddered. Then groaned. "I feel like I'm going to puke."

"Oh dear." Footsteps raced to her side. "Let's get you back into bed."

Strong arms reached around from behind Tabitha and helped her shuffle backwards to lie down again. "Now, let me raise you up a little bit and see how that feels."

The nurse pressed a button and the top half of the bed rose slightly. Then a little more. As it moved up again, Tabitha protested, "That's good." Not quite what she meant to say, but the nurse appeared to understand and lowered the bed slightly.

Tabitha took a deep breath, grateful when her stomach and the room behaved. With a small smile, she whispered, "Thanks. I guess I wasn't really feeling as good as I thought I was."

"You just need a day or two to recover."

Tabitha gave a broken laugh. "That much time I don't have. I have an hour or two at the most."

"I don't think there is going to be a doctor here for several hours." The nurse patted her hand. "Just rest." She walked out.

Tabitha let her head roll to the side. She wouldn't let something like the lack of a doctor stop her. She'd leave the minute that she could stand and walk that far.

You should wait until you're strong enough, Stefan announced in exasperation.

She smiled tiredly. *That would be sensible, but just think...you wouldn't recognize me then.*

No, but I'd be totally okay with you trying the sensible route once in a while. Especially if it would keep you safe.

"Well, I'm not strong enough to walk across the room yet."

Good thing. You also need to speak with Ronin.

She bolted upright – only to cry out as her head started pounding. When the pain eased, she threw back her covers for a second time. Dizzy or not, she did need to speak with Ronin. *I'll call him. I have a name and a twist in this psycho situation.*

Good. And I have another piece of art. I sent it to him a few moments ago.

"Do I get to see it?"

You need to. Confirm if it's your Fez character.

She gasped. *You did it.*

Maybe. Not sure it's a decent likeness. Had no idea cats saw in that perspective. Grays and blacks.

I know. But her night vision has been a blessing in the dark. Tabitha...

She froze at the warning tone in Stefan's voice. *What? What do you know?*

I saw you early this morning. You were trying to say something about your grandfather's box.

She straightened, her mind racing. *My father has it. There were documents in it. I thought he'd need it to handle the estate. Then this nightmare with the tiger started and it slipped my mind.*

It's important. Find out what's in it. Having said what he needed to, Stefan slipped away.

She searched the room for her cell phone and found it on the little portable table.

She dialed Ronin and got his voice mail. Rather than leave a message, she redialed. Again, there was no answer.

Calling the Center, she caught up on work with Wendy and learned about the sabotaged fence.

That was majorly bad for a lot of reasons, but the biggest was that normally that type of disturbance on the reserve was something her psychic radar should have picked up on, on an energetic level. The mess with Trinity was screwing her energy radar around. If she'd overlooked that incident, what else might she have missed?

At least the lynx hadn't run from the pens, which meant the protective energy she used to calm the animals had worked – partially at least. Please let the new security system have caught this person on camera. She pressed Roman's number on her phone to see what he knew.

"Tabitha," he said. "Sorry to hear you're in the hospital."

"Me too. I'm on my way out of this damn place. Never to return, if I can help it." She went on to explain about the vandalism and the location and asked about the cameras in that area. The damaged pens were on the side of the center but reached back into the trees.

"Do you have someone else who can check the feeds while you are in the hospital?" He paused. "I'll check mine here, and I can send it to Ronin. If there isn't a feed, I'll run by this afternoon and make sure all the cameras are working."

She frowned. "I'm on my way there so will check it out first thing. This has to stop. I seem to be plagued with problems on all sides."

"Maybe it's all the same problem."

"Maybe." Distracted, Tabitha hadn't realized she'd made it to the cupboard and pulled out a large paper bag with her belongings in it. She dressed quickly.

With a last glance around the empty room, she slipped out the door and down the hallway to the exit. Like hell she was sticking around. She had to pay the bill, but she could call them from home.

Outside, weak but gaining strength with every breath of fresh air, Tabitha searched the parking lot for a cab.

Only to have a truck pull up in front of her.

Ronin.

With a stern look, he asked, "Going somewhere?"

***

Ronin studied Tabitha. She looked terrible.

He didn't know if he should show her the pictures he'd printed off right now or later.

Stefan had sent him a new one. He'd passed it around the office but no one recognized the guy's face. A black and gray sketch of a man's head and shoulders showed. The man could have been sleeping except for what appeared to be a pool of blood at the top of his skull. If he wasn't dead, he wasn't in good shape either. His pudgy cheeks sagged and his eyes were closed, adding to the corpselike look.

According to the email, this was one of Trinity's guards. He thought about the next part of the email. Then he'd been thinking about that part a lot. Stefan had said, 'Tabitha saw the image through the tiger's eyes and I could see this variation through my connection to her.'

How was that possible?

Tabitha slumped in the corner, her eyes closed. He wanted to bring her up to date on all he'd been doing to try to find the tiger, but would telling her he still had no solid leads depress her more?

He'd tracked the phone number the homeless man had left behind down to someone who dealt in the black market, and he was hunting him now. There'd been no answer at the end of the phone, and given that this guy dealt in what he dealt in, maybe that was normal. He wouldn't have recognized Ronin's number.

Ronin had been on his way to the office when he decided to swing by the hospital. He'd just had the feeling that he should go...

Damn good thing he did.

Because she looked like walking death. He cast another glance at her slumped in the corner of the truck and wondered if he should just turn around and take her back to the hospital.

***

Stefan stood in his studio staring at his blank canvas.

He'd tried a lot of odd and original stuff lately. That was the one thing about psychic abilities – there really was no level of comfort, of knowing the capability of your skills because they were forever changing. Forever growing. He'd done things in this last month that he'd never considered possible – stuff he'd never considered doing before. His abilities never put a judgement on such things. He could only try something when the idea struck him and often, new things didn't work the first time. If he gave it a rest and tried again a few days or weeks later, sometimes it did work. It was as if his first attempt was more a notice to his abilities, telling them that this was something he wanted to be able to do. Informing his skills and abilities that the next time he tried this he wanted it to work. So the ability had to evolve the new maneuvre. And yes, Stefan had no illusions of how people would react if he tried to talk to them about this.

Thankfully his group of like-minded friends was growing. As were the crazy situations.

Look at this Tabitha nightmare. A tiger had actually psychically grabbed her with enough desperation that Tabitha had been helpless to resist. In fact, that had been the first time Stefan had any understanding of the power of an animal's will. His friend Sam, who lived just out of town, could help see the injuries sustained by an animal by connecting to the animal and seeing the damage. Tabitha connected to an animal on their energy level and worked her magic from there. That was the same method that Alex, another friend, used with plants. He himself did something similar with his garden but with a few other tricks thrown in.

Still, this was the first time he had seen an animal as the instigator in a psychic trauma. The connection was less Tabitha's energy work and more about her very intimate connection to Tango. He'd sensed yet another energy in her house, too. Although it appeared to belong and also appeared to be animal in nature, he couldn't help but wonder if that new energy wasn't connected to all this as well.

Or was it simply the new tiger's energy brought back to the house with Tabitha? Why and how? He had no idea.

He stared at his canvas and wondered what that idiom 'we're all connected' really meant. He'd been trying to paint from the images Tabitha sent, but could he connect to Tabitha and the tiger so he could see the man through the tiger's eyes and capture his face? If he could, this would be much more accurate.

How differently did a tiger see from a human? He knew there were differences but was not sure how that would all translate to his brain. To his own psychically artistic brain.

He picked up a paintbrush, surprised to realize he really wanted to know the answer to that question.

***

"Did you see it?"

Timothy had barely entered the fancy office when the man sitting behind an ornate desk jumped on him verbally. Add that hard stare and cold tone, and Timothy wished his damn tuition wasn't so hard to come by. It was obvious, this guy would slice his throat if he didn't like his answers. It was barely morning by the world's standards and Timothy hadn't gone to bed yet. This guy looked as he'd been up for hours already.

Then again, he ran his business like a captain ran his ship. Tight. Timothy had been approached by a middleman. Someone who'd found out that he'd checked the tiger over. Now he was reporting to the buyer. At least he hoped that's who was glaring at him. And if he'd realized who that boss was prior to this, he'd have walked away. As it was, he wanted to get the hell out now.

But as always – he needed the money.

"Yeah. I did." Timothy nodded. "The tiger didn't look bad at all. I don't know where the rumors came from, but the female was lying in a corner of the cage sleeping soundly when we arrived."

Silence. Timothy stood straight, knowing that to shift or show any uncertainty would possibly cause him more problems than this was worth.

"So there was nothing wrong with her?" The man leaned over the desk and gave him another hard look. As if lying to him would mean the end of Timothy.

Timothy had no wish to lie, but he didn't have much to add either.

"I didn't say that." Timothy shrugged. "I aint no vet, just a pre-medical student, but she looked to be okay. There's an injury on her hip that could use a bit of attention, and a shot of antibiotics would probably help there. She had the remains of a good-sized bone in there covered in chew marks. So she's eating and I presume drinking after all this time." He held his hands out, palms up. "Honestly, she looked fine to me considering..."

He hesitated.

The man raised that snake gaze and held him captive. In a soft dangerous voice, he asked, "What is it?"

Timothy shrugged. "The blood tests said the tiger was pregnant."

The other man's gaze widened in surprise then settled with a satisfied look. "Is she now? That's very good to know." The man gazed out the window at the tiny rays of morning light creeping in. He absently said without turning around, "Could you identify the species?"

"Only that it was unlike anything I'd seen before. She was gray." The younger man didn't care and didn't want anything more to do with this. The tiger was alive and well and as far as he could tell, she didn't even appear to be under any stress. He figured he should tell this guy everything. He might get a bonus. "They are probably giving her something to keep her calm."

"Do you think so?" The boss's gaze sharpened and he nodded slowly. "Smart. She won't hurt herself by fighting this way."

"So we're good?" Timothy asked, backing toward the door. He just wanted to get the hell out of here.

The boss nodded. "For the moment. When we do the snatch, we'll need you to check her over." He pulled an envelope out of his pocket and handed it over. "I'll give you a call tonight or tomorrow. This needs to happen fast."

Timothy accepted the envelope. "No problem. I'm in class all week." Careful to keep the casual look on his face, he turned and walked out, choosing the stairs over the elevator.

He'd thought the warehouse where the tiger was kept was rundown and cold. Spoke of back room deals and shady clients. Bookie style. This guy and his rich-ass office probably owned this whole building. Well, what did he care? He carefully tucked the envelope beside the first one in his jacket pocket. Playing both sides might get him killed, but everyone had to make a living. Some of them did a better job at it than others.

Like him.

Chapter 17

Monday noon

By the time Ronin drove up to Tabitha's house, she was almost wishing she'd stayed in the hospital. Her energy had long since flagged. She watched the driveway appear and hoped Ronin knew to slow down. She wasn't antisocial, but she didn't appreciate uninvited visitors in her personal space and so hadn't made any improvements to the private driveway. It badly needed gravel. She ran a tight ship at the reserve and the animals never suffered, but to compensate, she barely kept back enough to live on. She took home the same salary as the other employees.

"Looks like you have company."

She straightened. "Oh hell," she murmured. "It's my father." That's the last thing she needed.

She ignored Ronin's sharp look as he parked beside her father's BMW. "Is that a problem?"

"Not always."

He hopped out and walked around to open her door. "He has keys?"

"Yes." She didn't add anything more. She didn't have the energy to spare. Ronin opened the front door. *Where was Tripod?*

She called out, "Dad?"

"In the back."

She walked through to the living room, wanting nothing more than to head to bed. Even the hospital bed sounded good right now.

Her father was sitting with Tango at his feet.

She felt Ronin come to a halt beside her. Right, the damn cat thing. "Dad, Ronin. Ronin, this is Dennis, my dad."

The two men nodded at each other. She watched her father's cool eyes assess Ronin. "Ronin is a detective." Perversely, she watched her father's eyebrows shoot up.

"You need a detective?"

She sighed. "Why are you here, Dad?"

"You collapsed again," he snapped, as if that were reason enough. And maybe that would be okay if they had a normal father-daughter relationship. But theirs was anything but normal.

"Wow, your intel is as sharp as ever."

"No need to be snippy." He frowned. "You know I only want what's best for you, right?"

"Sure." She walked over and bent down at Tango's side. He opened one eye and his big engine kicked in. She glanced around. "Where's Tripod?"

"I let him out back."

On cue, Tripod started barking like mad from Tango's room.

"Tripod!"

He arrived just as she finished speaking. He howled and jumped for joy.

Knowing she shouldn't encourage his bad behavior but unable to resist, she patted her shoulders and opened her arms wide.

He planted his front paws on her shoulders and proceeded to clean her face. She laughed until tears rolled.

"I do wish you wouldn't encourage him," her father said in exasperation.

Maybe that's why she'd done it. So it would piss him off. The older she got, the less grownup she appeared to be. With a last hug, she pushed Tripod down. As soon as she did, Tango jumped up and took Tripod's place.

Only Tango draped his forearms around the back of her neck and rubbed his head against her.

Tears welled up again. These last few days had been difficult. So close to the tiger and unable to hug her physically. Tango understood. She could feel the waves of empathy – sorrow even – roll off him. She hugged him hard and burrowed into his thick fur. Emotion hit her hard in waves of unending sadness. The old ailing female, her unborn cub, her grandfather and...Tobias, her grandfather's tiger that died six months ago.

She'd loved that old tiger. At the memory of her old friend, the tears started to pour. She tried to stifle the sound but knew her shoulders were shaking. No amount of control could still the shakiness. She just didn't have anything more inside.

A strong hand wrapped around her waist. Ronin – and he'd come this close to a cat. But she could see her father in front of her...and she didn't miss the look of disgust on his face.

She'd battled that look all her life. With her grandfather alive to run interference, she'd managed to ignore it as much as possible. These days, everything seemed to bug her.

Then she realized there was an unnatural stillness in the arms wrapped around her. Bone and pliant muscles had turned stiff, unyielding... A silent quest for dominance had suddenly reared its head.

"Easy, Tango."

Tango's eyes glittered. *Shit.*

"Ronin, back up slightly."

She sensed the unwillingness in him. What a time for Ronin to decide to face his fear.

"Tango?"

And felt his neck ripple and cord as he opened his mouth, a roar ripping from deep below.

After a long nerve-wracking moment, Ronin stepped back. But only a bit.

Still in the way of male animal, it might be enough. She sent warm loving energy to Tango. If she had to, she could drop him in an instant. Energy worked both ways, to heal and to hurt. Or in Tango's case, to discipline. When he was young, she'd been forced to overwhelm him to the point he couldn't move a time or two until he understood. She hadn't had to do it since.

Then everyone was off kilter and over protective right now. Between her father's energy and Ronin's energy, her own scattered space...everyone was acting out. "Tango..." She sent a strong mental warning to him. He howled. She scolded him. "Leave him alone; he's a friend."

He whined. Then he cocked his head and looked down at her like a petulant child denied a toy.

He dropped down and padded back to his pen to sulk. "Thanks, Tango."

Her father stood and watched as Tango headed through the flip panel to the outdoors. "That animal is dangerous," her father snapped. "He's going to kill someone one day."

"And yet you let him into the house to sit with you." She so didn't need this right now. Her emotions were too raw.

"He knows me." Her father turned to glare at Ronin. "He obviously doesn't know or like you. Since when do you try to challenge a tiger? If it wasn't for her, you'd have had your hands full."

Tabitha closed her eyes as her father started showing his testosterone.

Abruptly she turned and headed to the kitchen, Tripod at her heels.

She put on a pot of coffee, wondering if she was going to have to feed the men too. If so, too damn bad. She stared into her empty fridge, wondering if fuzzy blue cheese, eggs and wilted peppers would work as an omelette. Even the concept sounded bad. She slammed the door, stole a cup of coffee from the pot and turned to lean back against the counter. Closing her eyes, she let the steam bathe her tired eyes.

"Bedtime?" Ronin asked gently.

She laughed, a broken sound that came off harsh and cold. It wasn't his fault. And it wasn't fair to take it out on him. She pulled on her flagging energy and said, "It's too early, as much as

I'd like to. I have to go to the office and touch base. Your brother might be coming by to check the cameras. And I need to assess the cut fence and go over the security feed."

"Isn't that why you have hired help?"

"Oh, that's funny." She took a sip of her coffee, loving the heat as it slipped down her throat. "New complex security system and new staff don't work well without training. And I haven't had time to complete that aspect. Soon." Very soon, she added to herself.

Ronin poured a cup of coffee for himself. "Do we offer your father a cup?"

"He doesn't drink coffee." And she didn't say anything more.

He studied her face. "Food? You haven't eaten."

She took another sip of coffee. "There isn't much of anything here to eat." And damn if that didn't bring tears to her eyes.

He put his cup down and then removed hers from her hands and placed it on the counter beside her. He tugged her into his arms and just held her.

She nestled in close, just wanting to hide away until she felt better. Until she was strong enough to handle the shit flying through her world. After a moment, she cleared her throat and looked up at him.

"Thanks."

He nodded and stepped back. He reached inside his coat pocket and pulled out several large pieces of paper folded many times over. "This probably isn't a good time to ask, but I'm not sure waiting is any better. I need to know... Do you recognize any of these?"

She took the first one from him and frowned at the image of a bloated dead man. "No."

He handed her another one. This time it was a series of derelict buildings backing up to a creek.

Again she shook her head and handed it back. "No. Not at all."

"And this is the third picture."

"That's Fez!" she said, "after he'd been attacked."

"Good. How about this last one?"

Another man lying down on the ground as if asleep.

She frowned and turned the paper slightly. "No, I don't think so."

"Damn." Ronin took the paper back and held it up to see it better.

"That's Bruce Tappet." Her father's voice spoke from behind her. "What the hell does that lowlife black market dealer have to do with my daughter?"

Bruce Tappet. Interesting. That was the name registered to the phone number he'd been given.

***

Ronin checked his watch as he walked into the station. He'd told Tabitha she had two hours before he'd return to make sure she knocked it off for the day. He'd used up twenty minutes just getting to work. Plus he needed to shop if he hoped to get dinner tonight.

"About time you got here. Figured you'd gone on vacation or something." The laughing comment came from the left side of the hallway as soon as Ronin walked into the office.

He smiled good-naturedly at Carmichael. "Not likely." At his desk, he logged on to his computer and checked his emails. Nothing useful. He set up a search on the name of Fez and Bruce Tappet. There were no hits on Fez, but Tappet had a long record. Small stuff though. There was an address on record so Ronin wrote it down then he sent an email to the coroner, attaching the picture. A moment later he picked up the phone to call her personally. "Dr. Candace?"

"Well, well. So how's my favorite detective?"

"Looking to see if you can recognize a couple of faces. I just sent the sketches by email." He paused as he heard her click on the keyboard. "I'm thinking one might be your floater."

"Sketches? I presume your artist knew them personally then?"

Ronin laughed, but it was without humor. "I f you knew Stefan, you wouldn't ask that."

"Stefan Kronos?" She clicked on several keys. "In that case, I'll take a look. That man is something else."

Not knowing if she was talking about Stefan's psychic skills, art skills or his good looks, he stayed quiet.

"Wow. Damn, he's good."

"Do you recognize any of them?"

"The last one is lying on my table right now."

"That man has been tentatively ID'd as Bruce Tappet." Ronin's heart sank. He'd been hoping the guy wasn't dead. Hard to get answers from a corpse.

"Nothing tentative about it. His fingerprints are a match. According to Detective Carmichael Woodrow he's got a long rap sheet."

"When did you get him and do you have a cause of death?"

"Not yet." She gave a rasping cough. "I'll send you both copies of my report when I'm done."

As he put down the phone, Ronin had to wonder what his old friend's interest in Tappet was. He decided to find out. Carmichael's desk was empty. After giving the office a quick look over, Ronin opened his phone and called him. "Where are you?"

"Just leaving the parking lot. Why? What's up?"

"Bruce Tappet."

"Yeah, he met his maker a few days ago." Carmichael snorted. "His lifestyle finally caught up with him."

"Murdered?"

"Most likely. Waiting on the ME report. Why the interest?"

"He links to a smuggling deal I'm working on."

"Really." Carmichael snorted. "Well, he was the man for it. That man had his hands in damn near everything."

"So I've heard. What do you know about his dealings with rare animals?"

"Not much. Was he into that crap too? Then again, it's hardly a surprise." Carmichael added. "Anything anyone wanted, he could usually get. At least that's the word."

That was no help. "Okay. Good to know. Anyone handling his case? I wanted to check out his address, hoping for a lead." Ronin opened his notebook and double checked the address he had listed.

"I can take another look at the evidence." Carmichael coughed. "Let me know what you find. It's a mess. I figure some junkie tossed it first. The techs didn't find anything obvious so far. Then not all the tests are back yet."

"Will do." Ronin pulled the car keys from his pocket and headed to the parking lot. Finding the address where Tappet had lived was no problem. Ten minutes later, he was there.

Leaving his truck somewhere safe was the issue. The area was run down and poor. Old Bruce hadn't been doing all that well if this was his place. He double checked the number on the apartment building and walked to the ground-level corner apartment. The crime scene techs had been there and gone, so it should be empty. But in this neighborhood, there was no way to know for sure. He rapped on the door several times. Hard. There was no answer. He knocked again. When there was still no answer, he reached for the knob and gave it a twist. The door opened. Cautiously, he kicked it open with his foot and unbuckled his gun, calling out, "Hello. Anyone home?"

No answer. He entered slowly to find that he wasn't the first person to check out the apartment. Tossed was right. The single couch had been dumped on its back and the upholstery had been slashed. The cushions had received the same treatment. Newspapers and takeout-food containers were strewn across the floor. The coffee table and small kitchen table and chairs were tossed randomly across the floor. The single bedroom apartment was small and dirty, the smell so rank the odor leached into the walls. It had been in this condition for a while.

Ronin walked into the bedroom and it was in a similar state. Someone had gone through everything here very carefully. Had they been looking for something or were they just pissed that Bruce didn't have what they wanted?

Either way, there wasn't much left. There was no desk or laptop, tablet, or cell phone that he could find. He moved the mattress and kicked through much of what lay on the floor. The closet was full of dirty laundry and boxes and bags. But so much had been dumped in a heap. He picked through it, hoping for something useful. If Bruce had been smuggling tigers, there'd have been records somewhere.

But Ronin was too late.

He gave the room as close a go over as he could but found nothing. He shouldn't be surprised. If it had been important, the man would have kept it well hidden. Or...Tappet still had it on him when he died.

Ronin grabbed his phone and called Dr. Candace. "Did Bruce Tappet have a notebook on his person when he was brought in?"

"I have no idea. Let me look."

Ronin could hear sounds of her rustling with something in the background. "There was nothing in the clothing and nothing listed on his file."

Damn. "All right. Thanks for looking."

He hung up. With a last glance around, Ronin left the room.

As he closed the door behind him he realized he had just enough time to pick up some groceries and get back to Exotic Landscape on time.

He hadn't even made it to the car when his phone rang. Dr. Candace.

"It was in his boot."

Chapter 18

Monday afternoon

The animal smells hit her first. Acrid, wet woolliness and yeah, fear swamped her as she walked inside the office of her beloved reserve for the first time in days. She'd taken the long way around to say hi to many of the animals. Now inside, she could hear sounds from the medical rooms in the back. It was surgery day. She should have been in there taking care of business. The will was there but her strength was not. Still, she walked to the door and peered inside. Her new vet, Zane, was treating an injury on a dog.

"There you are." Sue's voice broke her concentration. Tabitha turned and was engulfed in a warm hug. Tears collected in the corners of her eyes.

"I'm glad to be back," Tabitha admitted, "even if it's only on a part-time basis for a day or two."

"You should be in bed." Sue led her to her office and pushed her gently into her seat. "I've been coming into the office to help out, so the workload shouldn't be that bad. Please don't overdo it. I'm going to grab you a cup of coffee." And she raced away.

Tabitha logged into her computer and settled in to get a few hours of paperwork done. She doubted Ronin would be late, so she set aside some work to take home.

First she needed to see the security feed. Bringing it up, she forwarded it to the right day and time. She watched in shock as the male dressed all in black walked to the lynx pen and cut the wires. There was something off about the figure. She didn't do people readings the same as she did animals and that was too bad right now. He carried himself like a young man with a spring in his step and he didn't appear to require much effort on his part to nip the wires. That interested her as that was heavy gauge steel. It shouldn't have been that easy. She wanted to groan at the ease with which he destroyed the barrier.

Interesting that he walked away without attempting to touch the animals. They were hidden in the back of the pen. She leaned forward. *There.* The man jerked around as if he heard something. Then he raced away. Interrupted most likely. She had security guards. Chances were good one was on his rounds at that hour. She needed to show this to Ronin.

Had this man acted alone? Or had there been there another man waiting by the vehicle, or worse, causing damage to another pen? She clicked through the different camera feeds looking – but no...there was no one else. She slumped back.

The man had just cut a chunk of fence then disappeared. If he'd intended to steal the animals, that would be a different story altogether. She'd have to wonder if he was connected to Trinity's smuggling. Speaking of which, she didn't have all that long before she'd have to go back and check on Trinity to reinforce the energy keeping her calm.

Sue came in with her coffee. Tabitha asked, "Did you watch the feed?"

Sue nodded. "Yes. I'm presuming it's someone still trying to make trouble for the Center."

Her mind puzzled over the video feed. There was something...almost familiar about the person she'd viewed. But she wasn't sure what it was about him that tweaked her memory.

As she mulled over the problem of who this man was, she buried herself in work. The door opened.

Ronin.

"Ready to go?"

Surprised to realize it had been more than three hours since he'd dropped her off, she nodded and stood up stiffly. "Take a look at this first."

"Your dad said not to be late." He sat down to watch the feed.

She paused. "He's still there? Maybe that's a good thing. I need to ask him about a box he took from my father's desk. Stefan said it was important."

That caught his attention. He raised his eyebrows. "In that case we need to know what's inside that box. Your father had an overnight bag in the front hall. I'm thinking he's planning on sticking around for a few days."

He returned his attention to studying the feed. "Damn little useful here. I'll call Roman see if he hasn't anything clear enough to print a couple of images off for me." He stood up. "Let's go. Your father is cooking."

She shook her head at that. *Why would he stick around?* It had been years since she'd slept under the same roof as her father. Unless it had something to do with Grandpa's death? And the future of the place. Had her grandfather changed the paperwork? Would she lose the Center? Her heart squeezed tight. Her grandpa wouldn't have pulled a fast one on her. Surely not. He'd loved her. This was her place. But it had also been his. Worried, she hardly noticed when Ronin parked the truck in front of her house and hopped out.

She followed slowly, her mind worrying about her future and her animals.

Her stomach, now devoid of food, cramped tight, and a shakiness worked its way up her legs. Hating the fearful thoughts overwhelming her common sense, she entered the house to find wonderful smells coming from the kitchen. She had no idea when she'd last eaten, but the smells highlighted how empty she was.

She took a deep breath and walked into the kitchen. Tripod greeted her as always, his comforting yelps of welcome and his soothing, caring energy so happy to see her. She crouched down and hugged him. The love so freely given helped ease the rawness inside. After his boisterous greeting, she straightened and walked over to her father, who appeared to be making chilli. In spite of her worries, her stomach growled.

"Dad, why are you still here?" She hadn't meant it to sound like an accusation but it slipped out that way. There'd been a lot of that in their relationship. Accusations and miscommunication. With her grandfather gone, her father had lost the chance to mend fences with him. But for everything else it meant a whole new day.

Especially for her and her father.

His back stiffened, the only indication that he'd heard her. "The chilli is almost done. Start setting the table, please."

With a look at his blank face, she slowly complied, hating the sense of impending doom.

"Can I help?" Ronin asked. He stepped in front of her, taking the plates from her hands. "I'll put these down. Maybe you could get the rest of the stuff."

She nodded and rushed to the sideboard for the cutlery. She didn't know what was wrong, but something was bothering her father. She wanted to ask him but the words wouldn't come out.

Tripod was underfoot and she accidentally kicked him. He yelped and bounded out of the way. She stopped and leaned her head back. *Damn. Sorry, Tripod.* She sent him soft, loving, apologetic energy. *I didn't mean to hurt you.* His response as always was generous and accepting. He whimpered from the side.

She bent and hugged him. "Sorry baby." Tripod and Tango, like all animals, were sensitive to moods and tension, and she'd been the one he was responding to. To her fear, her emotional pit and her energy blocks. The animal in him could do no less than respond. He leaned into her hug, almost knocking her over. She laughed. He woofed and wagged his tail happily.

Feeling better, she stood up and turned around. The table was set and her father had already served dinner.

Ronin held her chair for her – a nice gesture.

She opened her mouth to ask her father about the estate when he said, "Your grandfather's will is a bit convoluted."

Her appetite drained away as he spoke.

"It shouldn't be," she said. "I saw it a couple of months ago." She paused, remembering Stefan's message. "I gave you a box from Grandpa's desk. Full of his papers. Have you been through it yet?"

"No. I took a brief look but it didn't appear to be legal documents, so I left it for later."

"I need to see it," she said abruptly, her gaze sliding to Ronin.

His gaze widened in understanding. "It would be good if we could see that box tonight, if possible. It might have a connection to the break-ins going on at the center."

"Connected to the break-ins? Her father stared at her, open-mouthed, then adding, "Tonight?"

Tabitha nodded. "As soon as possible. There could be something in there regarding the will, too. Maybe it will have the information you need to help out with the estate stuff."

"That would be good." Her father nodded. "He had some bequests for people, but not much in the way of contact information for them."

"And you can't find them?" Ronin asked as he lifted a spoonful of chilli to his mouth.

"Not so far."

"Like who?" Tabitha asked.

"Jumbo. Now a last name would help, for a start."

Tabitha laughed. "That's so Grandpa. I have Jumbo's contact information. If he's still alive." She shrugged. "I haven't seen him in a couple of years."

Her father frowned. "And Chester."

"Chester is another old carny buddy, but I'm pretty sure he died of cancer last summer."

"That's what I mean. How am I supposed to find these people?" her father complained.

"Is that why you're here?" she asked. "To find out about his friends?"

Her father's face lowered and he played with his food. So obviously not. She put her spoon down and looked at him. "What's wrong? Is there something in the will that I'm not going to like?"

His eyes opened wide in shock. "No. Not at all. The house is yours. Exotic Landscape is yours. There's a little cash but..." He looked at her apologetically. "Not much."

She snorted. "That's nothing new." She smirked. Inside she smiled with relief. The place *was* hers. Thank God. "Grandpa never had much."

Leaning back, she closed her eyes briefly. The panic started to unknot, the band around her chest loosening, and she opened her eyes. "Thanks, I needed to hear that."

With a shake of his head, he smiled reassuringly. "Sorry, I should have made that clear right from the beginning. He had more than you think. I've been trying to get him to invest for years. We'll need to talk about what you want to do with it, but you aren't destitute."

Removing her hand from her heart, she sighed happily. "I have a roof over my head and the animals are safe, so we're good."

"This house needs some work," he said. "A new paint job inside and out. New furniture. I bet the plumbing needs to be updated."

She snorted. "As you said, there isn't much money." She swallowed her mouthful. "Besides I'm, not ready to make changes."

"Don't wait too long. I know you loved him, but it's time to make this space yours and not just live in his house."

She tilted her head. Interesting choice of words. "Is that what you felt, Dad? That it was never your home? That is was always his?"

"It *was* always his house. I didn't live here long enough to change that."

His words rang true, but there was something more going on here. But what? She knew little about her father's friends, his likes, his dislikes. Except for his business associates like Eric and Germaine. She'd heard a lot about those two. Then her father had a talent for business. He was good at making money, but not at relating to her.

Or she to him.

"You never really felt at home with him," she said intuitively. "The house had nothing to do with it."

His face set and he refused to meet her eyes.

"Why was that? What was so wrong between you two? I get that you don't like animals in the same way as I do, but there's got to be something else there. Something that drove a wedge between you two."

He gave a mocking laugh. "Everything was black and white with him. Right or wrong. His way or the highway." He stabbed the contents of his bowl viciously. "I chose the highway."

Tabitha stared, shocked. She knew the two hadn't been close but hadn't realized the level of animosity. It saddened her. Her grandfather had been everything to her. Her father almost nothing. *Why was that?*

"Was it me?" If it was, that would make her feel worse, but she'd rather know now. She'd lost her grandfather. She didn't want to lose her father as well.

"What?" He shook his head. "No. Not at all." For the first time since they sat down, he smiled at her warmly. "He was very happy to have you."

"Well, whatever your problem with grandpa was, it's over. He's gone." And damn if she didn't feel the tears collecting in the corner of her eyes again. She sniffled them back. "It's time to make peace with whatever it is and move on."

"That's what I'm hoping to do here and now," her father said without looking up.

She looked at him in surprise, her full spoon halted in midair. "*With me?* What do I have to do with it?"

She glanced over a Ronin who sat eating quietly across from her. He listened but stayed out of the conversation. That was probably wise. She turned her attention back to her father.

"In a way, everything." He put his spoon down and dabbed his mouth clean. Then he put the napkin down. Tabitha slowly put her spoon back and waited Whatever this was, it was big. And difficult.

She studied him closely for a long moment. Unable to handle the suspense much longer, she asked, "What's wrong, Dad?"

He took a deep breath, raised his eyes to stare at her and said, "The real reason my father and I never got along..." He gave a short laugh. "We had a huge fight about it. Once he knew the truth...well...I think he honestly hated me." He stopped, glanced at Ronin, then back at her. "I told him..."

She prodded. "Told him what?"

With his gaze locked on her face, he said, "I told him I was gay."

***

As bombshells went, this one was big. Like over the top, completely re-evaluate your life type of big. Ronin kept quiet, but he watched the shock dawn on Tabitha's face. Only it didn't appear to be as big a shock as he might have expected. *Had she known? Had she any inkling?*

He couldn't image hearing that himself. From a close friend, sure. Even a sibling. But from a parent? Wow. Having no parents himself, he didn't have an understanding of how that relationship would work.

Both Tabitha and Ronin had been raised by their grandfathers. But for different reasons.

The silence at the table grew and he realized that perhaps he should leave. Give them privacy. No one said anything to him. In fact, they were oblivious to his presence, but he felt as if he was in the way. He polished off his chilli and damn, it had been good. He realized he had a perfect excuse.

He stood up and said into the shocked silence, "You cooked, so I'll do the dishes. Tabitha, eat up."

"Don't worry about it, Ronin. I'll do them," Tabitha said, her eyes never leaving her father's face.

He walked over to her side and nudged her plate closer. "No, you won't. One, you should be in bed, and two, you have more important things to work on right now."

Ronin walked to her father's side and collected his empty plate. "Thank you. It was excellent, by the way." Loaded with dishes and silverware, Ronin headed to the kitchen.

Whew. There were some times when people really should be alone.

This was that time for them. And he'd be happy to clean up. He'd seen the kitchen earlier, enough to know that Dennis was a decent cook and cleaned as he went, so whatever washing up that was left would be minimal.

Maybe by the time he was done, they'd have worked through their differences, and they could put their heads together to solve at least some of the problems facing them.

In fact, he wanted action. Not this damn waiting for something to happen. He'd found many leads, but there was nothing concrete. His mind went back to the mess at Tappet's house.

What had the person been looking for? The coroner had the book she'd found in Tappet's boot, but it was in code. She'd sent it to the lab. It would be analyzed, and if there was time, someone would try to decipher the code. All she'd added was that she'd seen a lot of WC listed. That meant nothing to anyone he'd asked. He'd already requested to have the pages scanned and sent to him. With any luck, they would be waiting for him when he logged onto his email.

That wasn't all. This was a busy and frustrating day. He'd already run Fez's name through the databases and come up with nothing.

So far the search for a Timothy, vet or pre-med student, was resulting in a huge list. He needed something to narrow it down. There were just too many to contact personally.

There were so many elements at play. The tiger on the black market connected to Tabitha. The break-ins at Exotic Landscape. The man on the video cameras. If he'd been wanting to release the lynx, why hadn't he taken them?

If he hadn't wanted them, then why did he bother to cut the pen open?

"Maybe he put something into the pen?" he murmured to himself. Considering that idea, Ronin thought about all the things that could have been slipped into the pen without showing up on the surveillance camera. And dismissed the idea. The staff had searched the pens for the animals, and would have noticed anything majorly different.

He checked the time then called his brother.

"How's Tabitha doing?" Roman asked.

"She can't keep this up. Hell, she was slim before but now she's one step away from being gaunt."

"I can imagine." Through the phone, Ronin could hear his brother sigh. "Okay brother, what do you need?"

"Did you get the security system checked out on Exotic Landscape?"

"I did. There are some uncompleted sections, but that's all part of the new office expansion happening in the back of the building."

Had he heard anything about that? Ronin wasn't sure. "I don't think she wanted everything monitored. She's operating this as a reserve, not a zoo."

"Except she needs to bring in donations to keep the place running, and live web cams bring an audience. That brings in money." Roman continued. "But they also bring in the bottom feeders. These camera feeds clearly show where the animals are located."

Ronin ran his fingers through his hair. "There is decent security, strong fences and as much as most people might want to keep these animals, to go and stealing them is a much bigger step than most of the general public is willing to take."

"And that other level of the world already has suppliers for these animals." Roman's voice deepened. "I'm getting the feeling that the two incidents aren't related."

"So do I. And that just pisses me off. I'm not making any headway on finding Fez or figuring out how Tappet was connected to Tabitha's tiger."

"Black market specialist, Bruce Tappet? What's going on with him?"

Ronin brought his brother up to speed.

"So someone offed Bruce. No surprise there. He was working for Colby."

Ronin's gaze widened. "Winston Colby? Jesus, I forgot about him."

"You don't want to do that. Turn your back on that guy and you'll get you head cut off. "

That's when he remembered Tappet's code book and the multiple WC entries.

Chapter 19

Monday late afternoon

Tabitha stared at her father, shocked, confused...and yes...she felt betrayed. How long had he kept this bottled up inside? Telling her years ago would have helped them both?

She'd been very close to her grandfather, but she'd turned to him because she had no one else. In her heart, she'd wanted her father. But he hadn't wanted her. That had been her belief.

With his disclosure, she felt her whole childhood being flipped. Her surety disintegrating.

He sat across from her, staring at her steadily. Those soft gray eyes willing to accept whatever judgement she'd placed on him.

What he must have gone through.

Her grandfather hadn't been an easy man. In fact he'd been damn hard. Unyielding. And no way in hell would he have accepted his son's sexual orientation.

But times had changed. At least for other people. For her grandfather, his best days had been while he was in the circus. He'd loved the life. Loved the people. When he left the circus community, he'd changed. Or maybe it had happened after Tabitha's grandmother passed away. In recent years the animals were the only things he'd continued to love and he'd forever reminisced about the good old days.

If her father had grown up in today's world, he'd likely have found acceptance amongst his peers. Forty years ago, the phenomenon hadn't quite started.

"I'm sorry."

His gaze widened. That was obviously not what he'd expected to hear.

Then again, it was not what she'd expected to say.

She took a deep breath and clarified. "I'm sorry that grandfather felt so threatened that he couldn't accept the truth. I'm sorry you felt so threatened you couldn't share the truth with me. And...I'm sorry for me."

Then she added in a soft voice, "I spent a lot of my childhood wondering what was wrong with me that you didn't care enough to be around. What was wrong with me that I was so unlovable? I turned to animals, like Grandpa, because they loved me back. Unlike you."

A horrified sound ripped from his mouth. He leaned forward and covered Tabitha's hands with his and said, "There's nothing wrong with you. You're perfect. You always have been."

"And yet Grandfather raised me. You were never here," she accused, pain rising to the surface. "Ever."

"I couldn't." So concise, so clean, so cold.

She sat back and closed her eyes. "Tell me."

In a halting voice, this man who ran million-dollar corporations shared how hard it was when he told his father. How he'd been kicked out. How he'd been forced to leave the animals he'd loved and never come back. How he'd tried to be straight. How he'd wanted to be normal. And for a little while, he succeeded. With her mother...

"Then your mother and I broke up. She left and I tried to go out with other girls." He traced the wood grain in the tabletop. "I drank a lot. Experimented with anything and everything. I'm not proud of what I did, but I was hurting, and I did everything that would dull the pain and make me forget what I was." He took a deep breath. "And finally I realized I was lying to myself. I was never going to be normal. And my sexual orientation was never going to be 'normal' as per my father's standards."

He turned to look back at her. "When your mother arrived with you, the long and short of it is she came to me with a three-month-old baby and said that you were my responsibility."

"She walked out of your life and my life that day, and I knew I was no more equipped to raise you than she was. I was a mess," he admitted. "And my lifestyle was not safe for a baby."

He settled back in his chair to stare out the window moodily. He let out a broken laugh, but there was no humor in it. "Can you imagine? And my life back then...I was living in a house with four other party animals. There was booze and girls and guys and drugs everywhere." He turned to glance over at her. "I planned to get my life together, but it would take time and I knew here was the one place where you'd be safe. Where you'd have someone to love you. And where I could still be in your life. So here you are." He waved an arm around the room. "And the place still looks the same today as it did back then."

Tabitha had let him talk uninterrupted. She didn't know what to say or what to think. So much of her history needed to be rewritten. She had no problems with her father's sexuality. His explanation made sense and answered a lot of questions.

But not all of them. "Why didn't you take me home with you later when you started sorting your life out?" She tried to keep the hurt out, but a lifetime of holding it all in was hard and now that the dam was breaking, she needed to hear the answers.

"That was your grandfather. He said I was unfit to raise you and now that you were under his care, you'd stay here. I could visit, but I'd never again have custody." He traced a knot in the wooden table, his face twisting with old memories. "Unfortunately, my uncle, your grandfather's brother, was there at the time. He'd been a major part of our lives when I was growing up. But at that time, they were having some kind of major disagreement. Maybe he wouldn't have been such a hardass then if his brother wasn't around all the time feeding him venom. The thing is, once your grandfather set down rules, he never would reverse them." He shrugged as if shaking off the memories. As if he didn't care.

And she'd bet he'd cared a lot back then.

She didn't want to think about the legalities involved. Her grandfather had been a very interesting person. She had no memories of his brother. As far as she knew, he'd died when she was little. Her grandfather hadn't always been easy to live with, but there'd been one thing she'd never doubted. He'd loved her.

Maybe he'd needed her as much as she'd needed him. And maybe he'd felt as guilty over his son as his son felt over his own daughter.

Her grandfather had often spoken of his life in the circus, but never of his life with his son or any extended family. She'd had no idea if her father traveled with him or stayed elsewhere. Or had he come along later? She dredged through her memory banks, trying to figure out what she knew about her grandmother, and realized she was coming up blank. Just bits and pieces from her grandfather's stories.

"You aren't saying much."

Startled, she pulled herself back to the conversation. And him. She studied the uncertainty in his gaze, the tension around his mouth. This had to be hard for him. And liberating. For that she was glad. But she could do so much more. "For the record...I don't have a problem with you being gay. I want you to be happy." She smiled tentatively. "I just want you to be in my life."

His gaze warmed as she spoke. He tilted his head. "You can't possibly think I don't love you?"

She snorted. "As much as you're capable of, maybe. But from my perspective, there hasn't been very much of your love thrown my way. If you'd told me this a long time ago, it would have been much easier for both of us." She sighed. "I could have told you a long time ago that it didn't matter to me. That I loved you as you were."

"I couldn't," he admitted softly. "That was a promise I was forced to give my father. To never tell you. To never poison you with my twisted, perverted lifestyle."

"Ouch," she murmured. "He was very strong in what he believed was right and wrong."

"His version of it."

"And is that why you are finally telling me? He's dead and gone and can't judge you anymore?"

"I no longer need his permission." He smiled. "But I made a promise to him and I couldn't break it while he lived."

"That had to have been difficult," she murmured.

"The hardest thing was he wouldn't let you stay with me when you were younger because you might be influenced by me and my 'sordid' lifestyle."

She shook her head, her heart sad. "He missed out on so much."

"And so did I." Her father's voice thickened suspiciously. "And I have to ask: Has this happened too late?"

There was sheen to his eyes and she felt the answering moisture in her own eyes. God, what he had been through. What she'd been through. Because of a judgmental old man who couldn't handle his own fears. She'd loved her grandpa and that would never change, but he'd done his son wrong. She strongly believed there was plenty of love to go around. It was so sad that these two strong men hadn't believed in themselves or in each other.

And it was well past time for this to be cleared up. And laid to rest.

There was an uprising of emotion. A welling of pain bubbling up and over...to dissipate under the gift of acceptance. An ache from an old wound she'd barely recognized, having lived with it so long...began to ease.

And a freedom she hadn't recognized before as having been denied...opening.

She smiled. "Hello, Dad. Welcome to our new life together."

She reached out a hand.

He stood up, grabbed her hand and pulled her into his arms.

She burrowed in close, reveling in such a simple thing she'd missed all her life – her father's hug.

***

Later that night Tabitha curled up in Ronin's arms. At Ronin's quiet insistence, her dad had left to get Grandfather's box. He had keys and when he returned would let himself back in, so they'd gone to bed.

To enjoy each other. She hoped. Her mind couldn't stop tossing and turning on her father's words. His life. Her life. How one thing had impacted so many? So not fair.

"You're thinking too loud," Ronin murmured. "Go to sleep. You need rest."

She turned her smile to his shoulder and kissed his hard muscled skin. "Not my fault," she murmured. "My mind's got a lot to work on."

Looking into his deep brown eyes, she shifted enough to let her hand glide down his hips and then up between their entwined legs. "But maybe I can think of something else."

Fire smoldered as he shifted restlessly under her touch. He slid his hand up her smooth long lean body, stopping to explore her ribs, before sliding higher to cup her breasts. Stoking the fire within, soothing, caring, promising. Finally he reached to tilt her chin up and lowered his mouth. He brushed her lips once, twice. Then followed with a deep melting kiss that left her wanting so much more.

He rolled onto his back, pulling her gently on top.

Smiling, she sat up, gently guided him into her. "Nice." She sighed. When she began to move, it was gentle. Easy. She loved that about Ronin, the big strong, take-charge cop had the ability to lie back and let her – take charge. It took a strong man to surrender. It took trust. And she hoped – love.

Needing more, he tugged her down for a long drugging kiss. She sighed, a low thrumming sound as pleasure slid through her. All thoughts left her mind. There were no more questions. No doubts. No insecurities. There was just now. Just him. Just them.

She surrendered to it. To him. To the moment. And let herself ride. Head back, eyes closed, she let the heat set the pace. When need pulsed through her, demanding action, she leaned over and framed his face, wanting to see the dark depths of his eyes.

And found them full of love. Her system overloaded with joy.

She cried out, arching her back.

His hands clenched her hips, holding her in place as he drove up inside her…once, twice. He twisted beneath her and shuddered with his own release.

God she loved that. Knowing she'd brought him this, that she accepted what he'd so freely offered… She leaned over and kissed him gently, before sliding down to lie beside him.

"So good," he murmured, lazy satisfaction in his voice. He tugged her up against him, his fingers drawing slow circles on her shoulders.

"Mmmm." She nuzzled his shoulder, happy and calm for the first time in… Since…? She had no idea since when.

Peaceful silence stretched between them. She yawned sleepily. Tired, but not tired enough to sleep, she wanted to enjoy the moment. The closeness.

"That was a good thing you did tonight," he said quietly, "for your father.

What? For a moment there, she'd wondered what he was talking about. She twisted her head so she could see his face. "I didn't do anything."

"And that makes it even more special."

She stared up at him, puzzled.

"Your acceptance. Not many people would have given it so quickly or so easily."

She smiled and nestled closer. "It was awkward but it explains so much. I truly am happy for him. To live one life but desperately want another for yourself... That would be hard."

"Sounds like his early life was tough."

"His teen years," she correctly gently. "As a child, he'd have been fine. My grandfather loved him. It would have started once he understood he was different."

His heart beat a steady tempo under her ear, his body heat was warm and cozy. She yawned. "I desperately need a good night's sleep."

"Then sleep."

"I will, but..." She winced, knowing he'd have a hard time with this. "But I need to check on Trinity. Reinforce her energy so she stays calm."

He'd stiffened at her initial words, his arm tightening around her.

"Is that safe?"

"Yes," she answered honestly. "We have to find her. This connection I have with her… It could be very dangerous if she dies and I'm still in her heart line."

"Heart line?"

"A bond that could take me with her," she added softly.

"Then I'd better get back to work."

He started to rise.

She pushed him back. "You need rest too."

"I need to find this tiger. I have several leads, but nothing concrete."

"I'll go reinforce the tiger's energy. You get some sleep. Then I'll sleep and you work."

At that suggestion, he lay back down. She hoped he'd sleep – they both needed it, but she had things she had to do. She'd left it too long. The feeling came over her suddenly. That inner knowing that she'd cut her time short. Possibly too short.

Shuddering, she closed her eyes and opened her inner vision. She knew the pathway now. She jumped free and raced to Tango. He slept soundly. His energy rippled and shifted like quicksand, absorbing her into his own. The acceptance warmed her heart all the way to her soul. She grounded herself mentally and emotionally before returning to the energy highway that would lead back to her aging female tiger. Tabitha closed the gap faster and faster, and then slowed down as she reached Trinity. She dropped into the huge cat.

She sighed and stretched, feeling so feline and graceful inside. That she was truly one with a tiger was a wondrous thing. It produced a feeling like no other. She opened her eyes and smiled.

The tiger lay calm and peaceful in a corner of the cage. Her stomach gurgled loudly. "At least you've eaten, milady," Tabitha murmured gently, easing the energy to the meridian relating to the stomach region. The noises eased. The tiger stretched out with a contented sigh. Tabitha loved the feel of the power in the long legs, the big toes that stretched, then curled gently.

Such a different body. Such a different experience. Murmuring softly, she stroked and soothed, reinforced and calmed the tiger's meridians along with her aura. The tiger was doing so well.

In the background, she heard noises. There'd been something earlier, but it was low key so she hadn't recognized it. Now the noise level had risen. Men. Arguing.

And coming closer.

Tabitha poured out soothing energy for her sake as well as for the tiger's. She didn't recognize the voices. *No. Wait.* One of the men was Fez. So he was fine after all. Too bad. She'd have liked him to suffer for his part in this.

"I want to move her because of the change in plans. I didn't go to all this trouble to lose her at this stage." A cold chilling voice slipped through the air. Hushed but authoritative…

Tabitha knew she'd have no trouble recognizing it again. She tried to search through the darkness. Trinity's vision was excellent at night time, but the cover on the cage was absolute. Almost. She managed to coax Trinity to stand up and walk over to stare out between the slight parting of the covering. She could hear Fez talking. "Maybe beef up the security?"

"You are the security. Why would I add more than you and Keeper?"

"Because we can't always be together. Because they know we're here. And because I was attacked."

"You're the idiot who allowed someone to sneak up on you." The boss snorted. "Maybe you're the problem."

Silence.

Tabitha grinned to herself. A falling out among thieves.

"If you'd seen your attacker, at least we'd have some idea of who was after her. The question is why?" This last bit was added thoughtfully.

Tabitha watched as Fez walked into view. He winced involuntarily with every step he took. It was obvious he needed to lie down. Or go see a doctor, at least. His head was covered in dried blood.

"You're thinking the buyer might have been checking her out on his own?" Fez shrugged. "Why? Because he probably didn't believe your story."

There was an uncomfortable emptiness in the air. Tabitha could only hope these two would do or say something that would help her out.

"No one," the boss said in a silky voice – a spider to a fly, "is going to screw this up."

Tabitha held her breath. Now that man scared the crap out of her.

"No one will," Fez stepped into her line of vision again. He was holding his head. "I don't feel good."

"A bashing over the head will do that." As if making a sudden decision, the boss said, "Stay here."

Clip. Clip. Clip. "I'll be back in a few minutes." And a door shut. Quietly. Too quietly.

Tabitha wondered if Fez knew his days were numbered. She didn't think anyone screwed up twice with this boss.

And apparently getting hit over the head was akin to screwing up.

***

Ronin swore he could tell when she left her body. And didn't that stretch his sense of reality? What part of her had she left? And what part of her had left? These were questions that he couldn't answer, but they reverberated in his mind. Her body, still draped over his, had become...boneless. It was weird because it was more than as if she were asleep. It's as if she had died except her chest still rose and fell in a relaxed manner. Her color looked normal; her breathing sounded normal; but she didn't *feel* normal.

He wanted to get up and go to work. Sleep was the furthest thing from his mind now.

Tabitha needed to get back fast. That something could go wrong and he'd never know... He didn't want to dwell on that.

He couldn't believe what he'd seen and done these last few days. But there was one person who could possibly help him deal with his cat problem. If he would.

Reaching out gently so as to not disturb Tabitha, he snagged up his phone and called Stefan.

"Hey, I'm hoping you can help me." He stopped, not really sure how to start. Should he even ask? At least Stefan might be able to give him answers no one else could. And he needed to deal with this fast – if he could. He tried again. "I have a little problem."

"Really?" Stefan murmured, humor in his voice. "I'm not a counselor."

"Damn. Not that kind of problem," he growled. "Another problem. A problem from my past. At least Tabitha suggested it might be from there...if such a thing is possible."

"What type of problem?"

"Cats. I get a weird reaction when I'm around cats..." He winced, took a deep breath and explained what happened when he came close to them. He groaned. "Most of the time it's no big deal, but around Tabitha..." He gave a bitter laugh. "And if I tell myself that often enough, I might believe it."

"And what do you want from me?" Stefan asked.

"I wondered…" Ronin paused and stared moodily at the ceiling of Tabitha's bedroom. "If you can see inside my mind...my history, my energy... Is there anything in there that would explain this?"

"Interesting problem." Stefan's voice grew distant, thick in an odd way. Ronin wasn't sure what to make of it.

"What does that mean?" he joked. Even admitting there was a problem was hard.

But necessary.

Whoa. Stefan was in his head again. Ronin stared nonplussed at the phone in his hand. Should he just hang up?

Give me a moment, murmured the whisper in his ear.

"Yeah, sure. Take your time." Yet...he couldn't help but hold his breath. It was such a weird feeling. He could sense Stefan's progress through his mind. Like a cat creeping up on a mouse to trap it. A shudder rippled down his spine.

Thanks. Can't say I've ever been called a cat before.

Ronin winced. Shit. "Sorry, but having you move around in my head, it's a similar feeling to a spider on my arm. Raises the hairs on the back of my neck too."

Hmmm. Interesting.

"What? What's interesting?" he asked cautiously. "As in the stuff about the cats is interesting or something else?" He waited, but no more was forthcoming. "Stefan? Is something wrong?"

No, there isn't. At least not the way you are suddenly concerned. You don't have a cancer eating away at your physical body, but a kind of fear has been eating away at your psyche. Interesting. You play music, huh?

Ronin frowned. "Yeah. Both my brother and I do. How did you know that?"

I can see it in your energy. It's how you soothe your soul. And... He gasped. A gasp so loud that Ronin sat up, accidentally shifting Tabitha's position beside him. "What?"

Then Stefan chuckled. It started as a simple light laugh and transformed into a full-on belly laugh. The waves of laughter rolled through Ronin's mind. It was contagious. He grinned. "Well, I'm not sure what you're doing in there, but I'm thinking it can't be all bad."

Oh, it's not bad at all, Stefan gasped when he could finally talk. *In fact, it's bloody perfect. And it confirms that just like your brother and regardless of how you feel about it – you are psychic. And the reason you are terrified of cats...is you're being haunted by one!*

***

Fez watched the boss walk away. For several moments, it had appeared there were two men standing, his vision had been so blurry. It had been all he could do to speak clearly. He knew he wasn't thinking clearly or he'd have disappeared already.

Damn. He took several shaky steps to sit down on a nearby crate. If his days were numbered before, now he figured he could count his life in hours if that tiger died. If he could just hold on for a week.

He shuddered. This was not how he'd planned to get the hell out of here.

He stared at the cage and its contents. What had seemed like a simple transport job had gone sour. Why? Why couldn't she just be handed off to the buyer? Greed, of course. All because the tiger was pregnant. So a bigger payday. It was one thing to sell her for that price when she was old and ailing, but now... Yeah, the boss had gotten greedy.

Determined to take a closer look, he stood up slowly, bracing himself on the wall, and made his way to the cage.

He pulled back the drape and let light into the cage. A growl started, but it came out without any heat.

"Have you given up, girl?" Fez said painfully. "I don't blame you. I'm almost there myself."

He tried to study her, but she kept wavering in and out of focus. He swore he saw a woman in the cage with her.

He leaned closer and blinked several times.

Chapter 20

Monday evening

Tabitha stared into the injured man's eyes. Could Fez see her? No. Not possible. She gave herself a good shake. There was no way. But of course there was a way. So often psychic powers lay dormant for decades until some trauma woke them up. She didn't know what the reason could be in this guy's case, but it sure seemed as if he was seeing her inside Trinity.

His next words proved it.

"Hey, lady. Are you all right?"

What a question. Was she all right? *No.* But how could she make him understand that?

And could he hear her? If he could see her...

"No. I'm not all right, you asshole," she finally said in exasperation. He reared back and slapped a hand over his mouth.

She wanted to do the same. *Holy shit.* He could hear her. Stunned, she stared back into his shocked eyes.

Fez swung his head in a slow bullish manner. "No. No. This can't be so. I musta had a bigger knock on my noggin' than I thought."

"Oh, you heard me all right. What's the matter, have you never seen a woman trapped inside a tiger before?"

He backed up in a panic, shaking his head like a crazy man. She could see the whites of his eyes as they darted from side to side, searching for an exit. He swallowed heavily before opening his mouth. No sound came out.

He shuddered. A visible movement rippled down his body.

She knew how he felt.

At the same time, she recognized the gift. If he could see and hear her, he could help them.

If he didn't run screaming from her, never to return.

"Hey, what city are we in?"

His mouth worked. "Portland."

She brightened. First piece of good news she'd heard in a long time.

"Where in Portland?"

"The Olde Riverside Shipyard area."

"Do you have an address?" she prodded.

Of course her luck ran out. His phone rang and he fumbled, trying to pull it out. "Yeah." He turned his back on the cage and ran his hand over the back of his head. "Yeah. Yeah. I'm fine. Just a conker of a headache."

He moved further out of hearing distance. Tabitha watched, her ear tuned in. She realized she was separating mentally from the tiger in an effort to hear better. Feline hearing was incredibly acute. She pulled back inside and mentally spread her energy outward, connecting, blending and becoming one with the tiger, pouring energy into the tiger's hearing. She listened in on Fez's phone call.

She heard little bits about a buyer, moving, vets.

And nothing else.

Suddenly she heard the phone click closed and the sound of Fez muttering, "Shit, shit. Shit."

"What's the matter? What happened?"

Fez's spine stiffened at the same time his neck almost disappeared into his hunched shoulders. "I don't need this. I just wanted to get paid and get the hell out of here."

"And I can help."

She was taking a chance, but it's not as if she had anything to lose. And from the sound of it, neither did he.

He walked closer.

"I have got to be concussed if I'm seeing you. There's no way you're for real."

She laughed. "Hey, this isn't the way I expected to spend my last couple of days either. But I need help and you need help. Between us, we can do this."

He looked toward the front door. "Do what? I'm so screwed here..."

"And I'm what? Do you think being caught inside a tiger is fun?"

He frowned. "You're inside the tiger. You're not the soul of the tiger?"

That question surprised her. But then again, for anyone not into the psychic stuff, maybe that was as reasonable an explanation as anything.

"No. I'm psychic. The tiger, in her panic caused by you assholes, reached out and nabbed me. Now I'm connected to her. She's dying and I need to help her in order to escape." She knew that would sound crazy to him, but there wasn't a better way to say it.

He just stared. Then laughed, but that turned to a groan quickly. He held his head in his hands. "Don't do that. It hurts."

That wasn't good. She needed his help. "You should get that injury looked at."

"Ha. I got no money, and if I leave here and the boss finds out, I'm dead."

"Let me help. Tell me where we are so I can get someone here to help the tiger. We'll pay you so you can move away and start over again."

He stared at her.

"Hurry. Before someone comes. What can it hurt? You get to live, I get to live, and the tiger... Well, she'll be able to live out the rest of her life in a better place than this."

"He'll kill me if he finds out. There's no place I could hide without having to look over my shoulder for the rest of my life."

"My friend is a cop. He'll help us."

Fez laughed, a grainy coarse sound of despair.

"No, he won't. He'll get killed just like the rest of us."

"Why?" Tabitha didn't understand.

But it was bad. Fez's face twisted with despair. "Because the boss is a cop, too."

✳✳✳

Ronin couldn't process Stefan's words. He'd had one cat in his lifetime. Mr. Boots, a tuxedo cat he'd lost when he was nine. It had to be the death of Mr. Boots that had brought this on.

"Haunted?" That was unbelievable.

Not in the sense many people would interpret that word. Stefan said. But he'd refused to elaborate any further.

So much for clarity. He'd left with a disturbing final comment. *You'll find out the details soon, I'm sure.*

What? And how?

He wasn't sure he wanted to find out anymore. Not now that the memories were flooding back. Losing his beloved pet had devastated him. His parents had tried to comfort him, Roman had tried to share his beloved dog at the time – and that had helped some. But watching Mr. Boots get squished under the tires of that damn car... Yeah, that was something he hadn't forgotten – or gotten over apparently. At least according to Stefan.

Ronin could understand now that it had been pointed out to him.

Especially now that his chest tightened and his throat constricted just thinking about it. The same reaction he had whenever he saw a cat.

He'd been having the reaction to the loss of Mr. Boots over and over again.

God, the mind was a tricky bugger. It was scary to think that Mr. Boots had been sitting in his psyche this entire time. Then he remembered what Stefan had said about the cat haunting him. Did that mean Mr. Boots was still here?

The death of his pet had been his first experience with death, and he'd learned a harsh lesson that day.

He'd been learning to play the piano around the same time. It had been his way of dealing with the pain. He still played. A lot. Usually to calm down or to reconnect with the better things in life. His brother had learned to play at the same time. And Roman had also excelled at art.

Ronin couldn't draw a straight line. And he'd tried, oh how he'd tried.

Being twins, there'd been a certain competitiveness between them. One that had grown over time. They'd fought like little bastards when they were small, had even grown up with different groups of friends. The loss of their parents had pulled them together.

He had no idea what to think. Or who to talk to. *A ghost cat.* And yet why did that sound familiar? Hadn't Shay had a similar experience? It wasn't too late to call, and he needed to know. Moments later, he had Shay on the phone. She listened for a moment then chuckled.

"No, Ronin, not a similar experience – that experience. Morris is with me still."

"Explain," he said tersely.

With a laugh, she said, "Morris was around me but in a free floating energy. During my return to my body through Roman's painting, he painted Morris and through that process pulled Morris back to his original ghost form. As he still is today."

Silence. He shook his head. "I had no idea. Sure, I'd heard a little about this, but I didn't really understand. "*Who could?*"

"I know. I wasn't sure if Roman would have told you about the blue in his paintings or not."

"So in a way, he was picking up Morris's presence as well."

"That's because at the time he was painting me, Roman was actually walking in his dreams to visit me. Morris was always around, but spread far and wide. Roman sensed a presence around me and painted blue, representing this presence, into every painting. He didn't realize it was Morris."

"You do understand how far from normal you're sounding right now?"

A light tinkling laugh swept through the phone. "You don't sound much better nowadays, do you?" she teased.

"I know," he grumbled.

"Maybe you should talk to Mr. Boots the same way you talked to Tripod when Tabitha was hurt. Let Mr. Boots show you the way." And she hung up.

He snorted. *Like hell.*

Chapter 21

Tuesday, just before dawn

Tabitha's mind refused to function. The litany of prayer reverberated in her head. *Please God, let it not be. Please God, don't let a bad cop be involved.*

How could she save this tiger if those who were supposed to help were the ones doing the hurting?

And if Ronin tried to investigate, wouldn't that put him in danger? A bad cop would do what was necessary to keep his activities secret. If cornered, he'd have nothing left to lose by killing another cop.

Her heart pounded inside her chest as the implications grew.

She had to tell Ronin. Before he walked into something he wasn't prepared for.

She needed to leave Trinity again to tell Ronin, but she had to get Fez to help her, too. Help them all.

"You could call my friend."

He stared at her, a bit of fire starting to come back to his eyes. "Call a cop? Are you kidding? I'd get murdered over something like that."

"Apparently you're likely to get killed over this anyway," she reminded him. "Or have you forgotten that?"

He shook his head. "I'm not a snitch."

She groaned softly. "Remember that part about being dead? How much of it didn't you understand?"

She knew prodding him wasn't the best idea, but she was out of time. And so was Trinity. She needed antibiotics and maybe surgery. She was fading badly. If it wasn't for the energy Tabitha was pouring into her...she'd look so much worse If she died...

Well, this whole mess would get really bad for everyone. Her. Fez. Ronin. The reserve. All the animals in her care.

"No," Fez said. "Big difference getting killed on the job or turning snitch."

She stared at him. "Really? This is a job to you? A job worth dying over?"

"I'm good. I ain't gonna die." But he kept glancing nervously at the front door and tugging on the completely destroyed front of his sweatshirt.

His fear was palpable. But it was his fear, not Trinity's, and not hers. He had some reason to be afraid. Something he knew that made him afraid.

"Has anyone else died on this job?"

He jumped back. *"Whaat?"* A shudder swept through his frame, taking the last bit of color from his ruddy complexion.

Bulls-eye. And she remembered Stefan's sketch of the floater.

"Did your partner die? Did your boss take him out back and shoot him? Or was it your predecessor? Are you replacing a man they deep-sixed in the river?"

That did it.

He bolted for the front door and ran outside. She did not hear a sound from him, but his silent scream of terror echoed on the energy waves around her.

Shit.

* * *

Ronin walked back into the bedroom and checked on Tabitha. She was still in a comatose state. He hated to leave her, but he had to find the asshole who was hunting tigers.

Tabitha's father, Dennis, walked up to him as he stood by the doorway.

"It's early. What's going on?"

Ronin didn't have a clue what to say. Did Tabitha's father have any idea what his daughter could do? Or had she gotten her skills from her father?

Dennis frowned at Ronin, who was still working out what to say. He looked past him toward the still form on the bed.

If Ronin hadn't shifted to cast yet another glance at Tabitha, he'd have missed it.

A look of horror and...recognition on Dennis's face.

Then he turned a bleak look toward Ronin and said, "It's gotten worse, hasn't it?"

Oh boy. "Worse?" he asked cautiously.

"Don't play games." Dennis snapped. "You couldn't be in her life and not know she goes off into these weird catatonic episodes."

"So she did this as a child?"

"My father told me about them. He laughed. Said he'd seen it before. Said his brother used to get them too. Said I should ignore them." Dennis shrugged. "I was so out of my element at the time, I did try to ignore them. He said she was getting better years ago." His face hardened. "But that was obviously just another lie."

And there was that bitterness again.

Genetics. What were the chances that Tabitha's great-uncle or grandfather had been psychic and hadn't shared that information with her? *Or had one of them?* He glanced back at the bed. They hadn't discussed her grandfather much. It seemed as if the old man had held a lot back from his son, and vise versa. That had to have been tough. Dennis would have grown up feeling as if he was always on the outside.

Which would have made for a difficult life.

And would have created an angry man.

As he stared at the clouds blistering Dennis's face, he had to wonder what extent an angry man would go to, to get his revenge on his father.

That made him ask, "How did your father die?"

Dennis's eyebrows shot up. "Damned if I know. Poisoned by his own personality for all I care. I assumed it was old age. I got a report from the medical examiner, but I can't say I read it."

He didn't say it, but Ronin got the impression that Dennis might have danced for joy on the old man's grave.

Definitely no love lost there.

But as Ronin watched the worry shadow Dennis's face as he studied his daughter, he realized the man loved her. He might have done something to hurt his old man, but he'd never have done anything to hurt Tabitha.

"Let's go take a look at that box."

***

Tabitha returned from this trip shaky and feeling, shocky. Trinity was fading. Her unborn cub was suffering, Fez was panicking and this situation was sliding into the sewer fast.

She slammed back into her body so quickly, it hurt, damn it. But there'd been no time to slow down. Or inclination. She needed to contact Ronin immediately.

The hard landing forced a groan from her lips. She wanted to hop up and run from her bed, but her body moved similar to molasses on a frosty day. Getting this flesh-and-blood cage to do anything was almost impossible. *Shit.* She should have slowed down for the re-entry. Damn. She knew better.

"Rnnn?" The garbled message slipped from her numb lips. She tried again. "Ronin." Better, much better. Only it was barely a whisper.

"Tabitha? Are you okay?"

She couldn't open her eyes yet, but her mouth worked, trying to answer him.

Her father asked, "What's wrong with her?"

She groaned, a sound this time that would have been better kept silent. *But her father? Really?* She so didn't have time for this.

He knew nothing of her abilities and this night's weirdness went way beyond that level of basic comprehension.

Finally, she could open her eyes. She was lying in bed with both men looking at her.

First things first.

"Trinity is in the Olde Riverside Shipyard area of Portland. Fez is alive, but he has a bad head injury. The floater Stefan found might be his old partner...or predecessor. I can't be sure."

"Finally!" Ronin narrowed his eyes as he grabbed for his phone. He opened his mouth to say something else. She didn't give him a chance to speak. "And his boss is a cop. You're dealing with a bad cop, Ronin."

"And how do you know that?" he demanded. "Did you see him?"

"Fez told me."

She struggled to sit upright. Her bones were rubber and her muscles had a mind of their own with no interest in obeying her commands. "I mean Fez saw me. As in he *saw* me."

She shot a warning glance her father's way.

And realized he'd caught it. Not understood it, but...

"What the hell is going on here?"

She'd have laughed then, only her nerves decided to come back to life right that moment and sent liquid fire up her veins. She cried out as all her biological systems came alive. Finally.

Or you could do things the right way and not cause all of us to panic. Stefan's voice rippled through her mind.

She'd have laughed if she could, but everything hurt too much. "Right. I could do that too."

Ronin stared down at her and she realized she'd spoken out loud instead of inside her head where Stefan was. "Sorry," she said apologetically, "I was thinking of a conversation with Stefan from before."

From the sudden widening of Ronin's eyes, she knew he'd understood.

Her father was also here and getting more upset and impatient. Not good.

"Dad, there's lots to explain, I just don't know how to explain all this, or even if this is a good time."

"You explain. I have phone calls to make and a search of the Olde Riverside Shipyard area to organize." Ronin stepped outside the bedroom.

"Are you having more blackouts?" her father asked. "Talking to imaginary friends again? Seeing things that aren't there?"

She swung her legs to the floor and stared up at him. "Did I have problems like that as a kid?"

He glared at her. "All the time!"

She shrugged. "Then chances are I am having lots more of them. Because they aren't bad things, Dad. I'm psychic. That means I see things you don't. Talk to people you can't. Among other things." She waved a lofty hand in his direction. "And it's way too late for you to try to do anything about it."

She looked over at her father, wondering how to get rid of him so she could talk to Ronin openly.

"Oh, I know that expression," he said. "Forget it. I've been cut out of your life way too long. I'm in now and I'm staying."

She raised an eyebrow and wondered if he'd still want in once he understood. She decided to give him a chance. He hadn't been there for her until now, but perhaps, as he claimed, that hadn't been entirely his fault. This was way out of normal, but she'd really love to be honest, to have no secrets from him. He'd shared his history and orientation and now she wanted to share hers.

Or rather, she wanted a relationship with her father, one where she didn't need to keep a part of herself separate from him. The actual sharing part wasn't something she was too keen to do at the moment.

She pushed herself upright, happy to see her legs were working again. She walked the short distance to stand in front of her father. "There are lots of things you don't know about me. About what I can do. I'm happy to include you, but..." She narrowed her eyes at him. "I don't want to hear any talk about getting help of any kind. No doctors, no shrinks, no carny witch doctors."

He gasped at the last one. "Did he used to threaten you with those, too?"

She smiled. "He might have tried when I was younger, but not once I was old enough to understand."

"Understand what? I really don't know what you're talking about. When you say you're psychic, surely you're not talking about carny palm readers or crystal ball readers?"

She sighed. His history could really impinge on his ability to understand. "No, Dad. I'm not." She watched some of lines on his face smooth out, then added, "What I do is much more than that."

He paled. "What do you mean?"

Well, it was now or never. With a long look at him, she said, "I'll give you the short and fast version. You can ask questions later."

In as clear and concise an accounting as she could – considering that time had become a huge element – she explained her abilities and what was currently going on in her world.

Her father kept looking toward the hallway as if searching for Ronin to get confirmation, then back to Tabitha. He had to have felt as if he'd fallen down a rabbit hole, lost forever in someone's horrific fantasy.

She fell silent, studying him to see how he was taking it.

He stared at her but never made a sound. She gave him a moment to process, as he didn't appear ready to ask questions.

She twisted as Ronin returned, saying, "I tried to get Fez to help get me and Trinity out. He's terrified of getting killed though. He's got some weird sense of honor that getting killed on the job is okay but being a snitch isn't. Even if it saves his life."

Ronin nodded. "Not the first time I've heard of that." His phone rang again and he left to answer it.

***

Dennis stared at the daughter he'd never gotten to know, and wondered how she could be so different from him. Not for the first time, he wondered if she really was his daughter.

Now if only he could find something solid in her story to latch on to. *Psychic. Yanked by a tiger out of her body? Floating in the energy highway?*

He shook his head. Did he even want to know more?

And how much of this could be laid at his father's feet and all that carny bullshit?

"Wondering if you can walk out of my life as fast as you walked back in?" she asked him. No – she challenged him. As if to say, *Hey old man. If this is too much for you...*

But he'd faced tougher foes than her across many a boardroom. "Is that what you're wondering?"

"What? Wondering if you're ready to disappear or are you wondering if I am?"

The words she flung at him reminded him of how gracefully she'd taken his news. Was it because the younger generation had been raised in a more open era? Or was it just her? His daughter.

"Look, Dad," she said defensively, "I know this isn't your thing. Feel free to leave."

He laughed. "That is not going to happen. Do you really think I'm going to walk out after it took so much to walk in?" But now she looked as insecure as he'd felt when he'd arrived.

"Oh, Father, the problems you created." He didn't realize he'd said it out loud until Tabitha's gaze narrowed. He smiled. "I did love him. But I buried it under all the hate."

She tilted her head and studied him. Then with gentle sarcasm, came back with, "I really do love you too. I just forgot under all that hate."

He blanched and took a shaky breath. "Jesus. You don't pull your punches, do you?"

She looked away as if in shame, bright flags of color on her cheeks.

"That was a little harsh," she admitted. "Grandpa loved me. But he wasn't you. I never had a father to show up during parent-teacher meetings, or to see me in a concert, to watch as I graduated." She shrugged. "Those things didn't mean anything to Grandpa."

"I know. I never had them either."

Her gaze flew up to meet his, seeing the truth in them.

"Sorry," she said.

"Sorry," he responded gently.

She gave him a sad smile. "He missed out on so much."

"So did we."

"And yet here we are."

Standing across from each other. Both closer than they'd ever been before, but not to where either would like them to be just yet. Too much had happened. Or rather not happened.

Now it was just awkward.

But they'd come so far already. It didn't have to stop at this point.

"I'd like you to meet Eric, my live-in partner."

Her eyebrows flew up at the mention of his assistant whom she'd spoken to many times but had never met. Dennis hadn't been able to take that step - until now.

"Okay," she said. "Better make it quick in case I'm not here next weekend."

Shock slammed into him, making his heart pound deep inside. "What? You were really serious about this tiger stuff?"

"Very," she said, her voice thinning. "If Tabitha dies, there's a good chance I will too. For all I'm standing and looking normal to you, my heart chakra, my cord, is connected to her."

"And if you survive this time? We all die eventually. What happens when her time comes? You said she wasn't in good health to begin with. So what happens then?"

Soberly, she stared at him. "I don't know."

Chapter 22

Tuesday at dawn

Tabitha left her father to stew on her words and headed out to find Ronin. It was still the middle of the night for many people. There was so little he could do right now.

Only she couldn't find him. In the kitchen, she turned around slowly, wondering if he'd really left. Wouldn't he have said something first? Wouldn't she have heard him close the door or something? Hear his truck start up at least?

Her father came in behind her. For the first time, she realized he was fully dressed. "Did you not go to bed?"

He waved in the direction of the living room. "I was working."

She glanced at the clock. "So late?"

He hesitated. "I couldn't sleep."

Him too. She certainly had enough nights like that herself. Especially lately.

"Did Ronin drive away?"

"No. I didn't hear any vehicles."

"Neither did I." She frowned and walked out the back door. The stars were bright in the sky, adding to the glow of a waxing moon. Another couple of nights and the moon would be full.

She studied the long pathway into the trees. Tripod barked at her. He stood at the end of the glow of light from her backdoor and stared at her. "Did he go down there, honey?"

Tripod barked again. She glanced down at her slippers and robe, wondering when she'd put that much on. Tripod barked again.

She started down the path toward him.

"Tabitha? Where are you going?" her father called from inside the house.

RARE FIND

"Tripod is upset. I'm going to check it out."

"Wait a sec!" her father said. "Let me grab my shoes. I'm going with you."

She could hear a mad scramble behind her.

"You shouldn't be walking around out here on your own."

"Really? And who else is going to check out the place? It's mine, remember?"

His exasperation wove through his voice. "Yeah, I do know. I hate that you live out here all alone."

"That's not going to change."

"It was one thing when your grandfather lived here, but now that you're alone..."

"What, you think I can't handle it?" she asked incredulously. "Dad, I've run this reserve on my own for well over a decade. Grandpa couldn't get around much anymore. Not for a long time. Living here alone is no hardship."

Tripod barked louder from somewhere in the trees. Tabitha raced after him. Then she heard sounds of someone running off. She raced off after them. If there'd been someone on the grounds...

***

Ronin swore as his fourth attempt to raise anyone on the phone failed. It was five in the morning. This night was done for him.

He heard barking then a shout. He spun around. *Damn.* He'd automatically come out the front door of Tabitha's house instead of out back door where that damn cat was.

He wasn't ready to face that yet. And neither had he shared Stefan's insights with Tabitha.

He heard Dennis shout. Ronin raced back inside and out through the back door. "Tabitha?" he roared, "Damn it. Where are you?"

"Back here!"

Her shout came from the path heading toward the office of Exotic Landscape.

He reached her side in seconds, almost knocking Dennis over in the process. "What the hell is going on?"

"Someone was here." She held her hand to her chest and gasped for breath. "Jesus, I almost caught him."

"Are you crazy?" He caught her by her shoulders. "You actually went after the intruder?"

"Of course I did. This is my home. My place. My animals. I will do everything I can to keep them safe," she snapped.

He gave her a good shake. "Oh, of all the dumb-ass stunts."

She gasped and opened her mouth to blast him when he tugged her forward and kissed her. Hard.

She was still spluttering when he set her back. A snicker had him turning to see Dennis trying to hold back his laughter.

"Love is a many splendored thing," Dennis murmured.

"Ha. Tell your daughter that."

This time Dennis guffawed. "As if that will help."

"Hey, guys. I'm right here." She stuck her face in Ronin's face. "And what was that comment all about?"

He sighed, tugged her forward and led her back to her house. "Stay here with your father while I go and check out the place."

Once back in the circle of the outside patio lights, he gave her a gentle push and sent her back toward the house. "I'll be back in a few minutes."

"I'll come with you," Dennis offered.

Ronin nodded toward Tabitha. "I'd rather you stayed with her. She's might bolt."

Dennis sighed and followed Tabitha inside.

With a backward glance, Ronin headed down the path to the office of Exotic Landscape.

***

"If he thinks for one minute that I'm going to stay home like a 'good little woman,' he's sorely mistaken," she muttered to herself as she stormed into her house and up to her room. Her movements were sharp and jerky but efficient as she stripped off her nightclothes and changed into jeans and a t-shirt. This night was over, and the thought of more sleep had become a distant dream.

Some asshole was messing with her place. With her animals.

She reached for her phone and called security. The phone rang and rang.

"Crap." She pocketed her phone and went in search of her shoes.

"Where are you going?" her father asked, standing in front of the doorway. From the wide stance and crossed arms, she deduced he had thoughts about stopping her.

"My security men aren't answering. I have to make sure they haven't been knocked out, that they're awake and on the job."

He frowned. "Isn't that a job for the police?"

"Ah, the police is here, remember?"

"I don't think he wants you out there."

"No, he doesn't. But those are my men. One of them should have answered. Neither did. That could mean trouble."

Her phone rang just then. She pulled it out and checked the number. "It's Ronin."

She answered it. "What's up?"

"I've called for paramedics. Your security guard has been knocked out."

Her gaze flew up to meet her father's somber look. "I'm on my way. There should be a second guard there. Neither answered their phones."

"I'm on it." She could hear the sounds of doors opening and closing. *Was he inside the center?*

"Where is the guard?" she said sharply. "I'll come look after him."

"He's outside the back door of the clinic."

"Have you checked inside? We were wondering because of the earlier break-ins if maybe junkies were after the drugs there."

"Do you keep many?" Ronin sounded distracted.

"Hell no. But the junkies might not know or care."

"Right. Bring your father."

"Will do. Be there in five." She put away her phone and slipped into her shoes. "He wants you to come with me. One of my guards has been attacked. Ronin has called for the paramedics, but I need to go and see what I can do."

Her father was already pulling the door open and said, "Does this happen often?"

"First time. Some other problems started a few months ago." Outside, she led the way back along the path to the office.

"Was your grandfather worried about anything?" Dennis asked. "Did the break-ins upset him?"

"Yes. He'd gone very quiet these last few months. As if something bugged him, but he never talked about it."

"No autopsy was done – did that bother you?"

"No." She shrugged. "I didn't see the sense. He was old, his health failing." From the pathway, she could see the lights were on inside the center. She frowned and picked up the pace.

She entered the front door and found the lights on throughout the building. She walked through the office, her heart sinking as she took in the mess. The desk drawers had been pulled out and dumped, the chairs had been overturned, the pictures tossed.

Damn. What about the animals that just had surgery over the last couple days? They shouldn't be disturbed. She hurried through to the clinic side and found the animals untouched. They were nervous, stressed and hurting from their various procedures, but as far as she could see, their energies were solid. No additional injuries or damage.

Immediately, she poured waves of calm energy over the pens and animals, stretching it out, letting it float to the far corners of the reserve.

It's okay. Everything is fine. Relax.

As she turned her attention to the rest of the center, she heard Ronin call her.

She raced to the surgery to find Thomas, her long-time security guard, stretched out on the table.

"What on earth...?"

"My thoughts exactly." He motioned to the door at the far end of the room. "This is the second guard. The first one is outside."

She studied the man's face. There was no apparent injury, but he was definitely out cold. As if sleeping. Or drugged. Her heart sank.

She pulled his sleeve back to see a red injection site. She closed her eyes. "Ah hell. He's been drugged."

✳✳✳

Ronin left Tabitha and her father at the center and did a quick look around. He was pretty sure that the intruder was gone, but this was no longer a simple case of mischief. Now two guards had been attacked, which said something about the seriousness of the intruder's intentions.

He headed for the security system, wondering if the intruders knew about the upgrades. He knew his brother's company received a copy of the feed. Had they received an alert of an intruder?

His phone rang, and he knew it was Roman before he picked it up. This happened sometimes, as if Roman could hear his thoughts.

"Are you at Exotic?" Roman asked.

"Yeah," Ronin said. "Two guards were attacked and we disturbed an intruder heading for Tabitha's house."

"Professional job?"

"Quite possibly. The guards were knocked out with drugs. The offices have been tossed." Ronin stared out into the early morning light. Inside, his stomach knotted. "What the hell is going on?"

"There were no alarms set off on our end."

"Well, that answers that. The system's new; it has to be an inside job." Ronin paused. "Who installed it?"

Roman's tone turned thin and hard. "I'll be checking into that. You check on her the staff at Exotic?"

Ronin snorted. "Working on it. She doubled her staff after her extended hospital stay. She had to. She's still not back to full strength. At this rate, Exotic will need a new owner, too."

Silence.

"Is that a possibility?" Roman asked seriously, "because that's motive right there."

Ronin thought about it. "It's possible," he answered slowly. "There's no one else in her life at the moment except her father. And those that work at the center."

"Who inherited everything when the grandfather passed away recently?"

Running a hand across his forehead, Ronin told himself to think. To see this for what it likely was – a money grab. Trust his business-minded brother to cut through the distraction and get to the root of the problem.

"Tabitha did, supposedly. Is there any money in this place? It's run by donations and the sweat off Tabitha's back."

"And a large amount of donation money from Shay's Lassiter Foundation."

So true. "I'll look into the inheritance issue and who the beneficiaries were and who stands to benefit if Tabitha can't."

"Although, I doubt anyone could make the tiger do what the caged tiger's done to Tabitha," Roman said, "that doesn't mean the intruder you disturbed tonight wasn't after something else."

"Shit." Ronin hung up the phone.

While he worked his way back to the offices he heard the sounds of the ambulance in the distance. He pulled out his phone again and keyed in Tabitha's number. "Hey, I'm on my way back. I didn't see anything, but that doesn't mean he's not arou—"

Ronin's head screamed in agony. He dropped his phone, both hands going to his head as he fell to his knees.

"Jesus. Tough bugger, aren't you?"

A second blow dropped Ronin face first into the dirt.

Then he knew no more.

Chapter 23

Tuesday early morning

Tabitha screamed, "Ronin. Ronin!"

No answer. She stared at her father in shock. "He stopped talking mid-sentence. I heard another voice. Something about *'Jesus, a tough bugger, aren't you.'*"

Her father stiffened an odd look coming over his face. He shook his head. But his voice was calm – maybe too calm. "That could be anything. Try him again."

Already opening her phone, she sent her father a suspicious look. Hating that because she didn't truly *know* her father, his words were sending off internal alarms. Wondering if she could trust him.

She walked to the far side of the surgical room where she could look out the window and keep an eye on the still-unconscious guard and her father.

There was no response to the call. She knew there wouldn't be. Something had happened to Ronin. Talk about being in an ugly spot. What could she do? *Roman.* She called him on her phone.

"What?" growled Roman.

"I think something has happened to your brother," she answered quickly, "but I can't check because I'm standing guard over the other two men who've been attacked. The ambulance is just coming up the road."

"I was just speaking with him. He was fine." Now Roman was all business. "What's happened."

She quickly explained.

"Stay inside. Don't let anyone in or out, do you hear me?"

"I hear you, but I can't do that. One guard is on the ground outside and I have to deal with the paramedics. After that I can go look for Roni—"

"No. I'm on my way and I'll call for backup. You stay put."
He paused for a second. "Are you alone?"

"No, my father is here." She turned to stare at her father...
only to realize he'd left. "Shit."

"What?"

"My father was just here." She walked into the other room
looking for him, loathe to leave the guard alone. "But he's
disappeared."

She swallowed. "Maybe he went out to direct the
paramedics. Just get here fast."

"Already in the car."

He hung up, and she walked to the window. Sure enough,
there was her father, directing the ambulance. She heard him yell,
"They are over there. One outside, the other in."

He pointed to where Tabitha and the guards were.

As the paramedics ran inside, Dennis bolted in the other
direction. She lost sight of him as she raced to her patients. What
was he up too? Then she didn't have a chance to worry.

Thankfully, the paramedics were in and out in minutes. The
injured men were safely on the way to the hospital. She'd wanted
them to wait for her to find Ronin, afraid he might need their
services more than her guards, but they only had room for two.
They'd promised to come back, if needed.

She shuddered.

By then, it might be too late.

She locked the front door and raced out the back. Tripod's
panicked bark pulled her up short. She sent a hard wave of
soothing energy his way. Immediately, she was slammed with his
panicked response and pictures from his mind.

Ronin on the ground. Blood in the dirt. The smell bothered
Tripod, Ronin's limp body bothering him. She could see even as
she ran to his side that Tripod was nudging Ronin's body and
whimpering. She soothed Tripod's energy, and forced her body
to move faster.

Tripod, easy boy. Take it easy.

The dog whined deep in the back of his throat. He calmed, knowing she was close, but it still wasn't enough.

She took a quick glance around, but there was no sign of animal or human energy that she could see. Stefan would say that the only thing stopping her from seeing other people's auras as well as she did animals was that she did not *want* to see them.

Humans had layers that were less than nice to see, and the more they tried to hide the layers, the more the deception showed in the disruption to their energy. Who'd want to know that level of information about their fellow man?

Up ahead, she could see Tripod standing guard over a crumpled form.

She knelt beside Ronin and checked for a pulse. His color was paler than normal but his pulse was still strong. He looked fine. Except he was out cold. She started to key in Roman's number again but heard his shout before she finished. She yelled, "Over here!"

Tripod barked as Roman's footsteps came closer. "Easy Tripod. He's a friend."

"How is he?" Roman asked, dropping to his brother's side. He immediately started to check his brother over.

"He's out cold but I can't see any injuries."

As Roman ran gentle fingers over his head, Ronin groaned.

"Easy, Ronin. You've been knocked on the side of your head."

Ronin's eyelids fluttered open. "What the hell happened?" he said, but the words came out more as a snarl.

Tabitha smiled. "I was hoping you could tell me that. We were talking on the phone and all of a sudden you stopped – mid-sentence."

His stared at her, a distant look in his eye before everything suddenly seemed to snap into focus.

"I was talking to you and then...nothing." He grabbed hold of his brother's shoulder and pulled himself into a sitting position. He reached a tentative hand to the back of his head. "Ouch... Did you see anything?"

Tabitha shook her head. "No. But I heard another voice saying 'Jesus, tough bugger aren't you' right before we got disconnected. That's when I called Roman. The paramedics left with my injured guards and I followed Tripod here."

He looked at her then shook his head. "Thanks, Tripod. Glad you found me." He reached out a hand. "Help me up." With Roman's assistance Ronin stood. He took two steps in the direction of the offices and stopped.

Tabitha watched him reach an arm out wondering what it would cost him to ask for help?

"Not as much as you might think," he muttered when she put an arm around his ribs.

"I didn't say anything." She stared at him carefully as they walked slowly back to the office. "And you need to get that injury checked."

"Right." *So not going to happen.*

"What?" She stopped in outrage. "Yes, it is going to happen. Injuries like yours kill people."

Stop reading my mind.

"I'm not reading your mind. Now stop arguing. You're getting checked out."

Roman laughed. "You two sound like an old married couple."

Tabitha snorted. "As if that would happen."

Ronin murmured. "Sure it could." *If he could deal with his cat shit and she could deal with him.*

Tabitha stopped. "That works for me."

What was going on? Was he speaking telepathically or was she just tuning into his thoughts. And how did that work? She heard him think, *How much further? My head is killing me.*

"Not much," she answered. "Just a few more minutes."

He leaned heavily on her shoulder.

Roman spoke quietly behind her, "Do you want me to take him?"

No, she doesn't. I'm fine. Or I will be as soon as I can sit down.

Tabitha shook her head. "He said he's fine."

There was no doubt now. Somehow Ronin had suddenly started talking telepathically to Tabitha in his head. At first he assumed he was speaking out loud. *Damn.*

She couldn't stop her instinctive call to Stefan for help. This was definitely his specialty not hers.

She motioned to the open back door as they approached. Roman rushed forward and opened the door wide. Ronin grabbed the doorframe and pulled himself past the doorway. He stumbled into her office and collapsed into the visitor's chair. "I just need a minute."

Roman snorted. "You'll need more than a minute."

"I'll be fine. A drink of water would be good."

Tabitha rushed to get it, as she returned she heard Ronin say, "Dennis, Tabitha's father brought over a box of papers he'd taken from her grandfather's office last night. We were thinking there might be something in there to explain the current situation."

As Tabitha watched and worried, Ronin closed his eyes as a wave of pain crossed his face. After a moment, he added, "A few hours ago, while we waited for Tabitha to return from..." He shrugged as if the right word failed to appear. "Whatever she was doing, we took a look inside."

She gasped. "Really? You didn't tell me. What was in there?"

"We haven't had a chance to sort out everything as many of the papers are really old. But there was a bundle of hate mail that went way back. No name or identification on any of them and each was signed, 'You know who I am.'" He straightened, tentatively at first then with more confidence. "The last one was particularly nasty."

She narrowed her gaze. "Then what are you not saying?"

Roman reached out and grabbed her hand. "Tabitha? Where's your father?"

***

Dennis had no idea where Ronin could be, but he had a horrible feeling he understood how Ronin came to be attacked. And God damn him if he was responsible...

Surely not. Damned well better not. But that voice on the phone...and the language...

He knew this acreage well after years of being involved, even if only on a periphery level. He'd supplied much of the money that had gone into building this place. It was his way to ease his guilt for ignoring his daughter and for letting his father dominate him. Damnation. He should have done something about reconnecting with her a long time ago. Now with his father's death, the bonds that had held him back had suddenly dissolved, setting him free.

He'd built himself a life without his daughter and his father. A decent life. At least he'd thought so. But that voice he'd heard through Tabitha's phone – God, it sounded like someone he knew. And knew all too well.

He barreled down the back path heading to the large feed barn.

Please let him be wrong.

Please. Now that he'd lost his father and regained his daughter, he didn't want to lose another person in his life. *Please, let me be wrong.*

He whipped along the pathway searching for the back gate. He was probably too late. But he could hope...

The morning light shone clear. There were a few animals stirring, but as he ran past he could see them shy away from him.

Probably just as well. If he found what he was afraid he would find, he might just do some violence himself.

***

Tabitha stared. Then she spun around to stare out the open door. "He directed the paramedics then took off to the back of the reserve. I figured he was looking for Ronin. But I haven't seen him since. *Shit.*"

She ran to the back door.

"Tabitha, wait. Don't go out there alone."

She stopped at the doorway. "Then someone come with me. He could be lying injured anywhere. I'm not leaving him out there alone." She spun around to look at Roman. "You said you'd call for backup. Where are they?"

Ronin said gently, "He called a couple of my guys. Figured as they'd been handling the break-ins, it made sense to get them in on this. They are on the way."

She threw up her hands. "Fine, I don't care who you bring in. Just, please, let's figure this out and stop it."

"We don't know who is involved and how far this goes." Roman added, "Or how long this has been going on."

That stopped her in her tracks. "What are you talking about?"

"You said your grandfather went real quiet the last few months before he died. How do you know that something nasty wasn't going on? Maybe he was being blackmailed? Or threatened?"

"My grandfather? This has something to do with my grandfather?" She hated the rising panic in her voice. She stared at them. "Or are you suggesting he might have had something to do this nightmare? Because there's no way he'd be involved with anything illegal."

They just stared at her. Her stomach roiled at the thought. "No. No. Oh no." She walked backwards several steps, shaking her head. "I'm not going to stand here and listen to something so ridiculous. I'm going to find my father."

She turned and dashed outside, but after several feet, she stopped and bent over, breathing hard. Desperately trying to make sense of this. Of what they were saying. Of what they weren't saying.

She wanted to throw up. But at the same time, she wanted to rant and scream at them.

And that just brought her father back to mind. He was the one she needed to ask some of these questions. He might have the answers.

Or he might not. She didn't know him enough to tell. What she had learned – the important things about him – had come these last few days. After her grandfather's death.

Each new calamity sent her body reeling and her mind grappling for a solid ground to stand on. And none of what was going on right now seemed related to the bigger issue in her life. Trinity.

Or was it?

Or rather, how was it not? What were the chances that Trinity and the problems at the reserve were *not* related?

Zero to none, she'd say. She was also assuming the problems at Exotic Landscape had something to do with black market animals – when it might have no connection at all.

Or was someone trying to make her look incompetent? Make her look as if she couldn't handle the responsibility?

And there was only person who'd benefit from that. Her father. The reserve and everything to do with it would belong to him.

Her heart squeezed tight, clogging up her blood flow and sending pain radiating outward. She took a deep shuddering breath as she forced herself to contemplate such a betrayal. It couldn't be. Her father didn't want Exotic. He'd never wanted it.

No, there had to be another explanation.

She turned slowly to face the brothers who were standing beside her now. Ronin looked better, but his color was still off. Then again, she was sure hers was way off too.

"We can't answer these questions until we find my father." She ran her fingers through her hair. "I need help to do that."

"We're here."

She shook her head. "Ronin, you can stay here until the staff arrive." She glanced down at her watch. "Which should be in the next half hour. Explain about the guards and that the reserve is locked down to the public today. Wendy might have to field calls if the media finds out." She glanced at Roman, who stared back at her steadily. "Will you come with me? Help me search for my father?"

"Like hell," Ronin snapped. "I'm going with you. He can stay here."

Roman turned to glare at him. "You're not one hundred percent and you're needed here. You can be the hero next time."

Ronin stood firm, glaring at his brother. Then he shook his head like an angry grizzly bear. "I'm doing fine. I'm going with her."

"Damn it." Roman glared at his brother, then as if realizing there'd be no reasoning with Ronin, he said, "Then tell me where you're going. I'll be following as soon as I can."

A few minutes later, she led the way through the maze of pathways. As she walked, she dialed her father yet again. Still no answer.

"What do you think happened to him?" asked Ronin.

A shudder of denial whispered through her. "I hate to say that I hope he's lying unconscious somewhere, but that is preferable to finding out he had something to do with this mess."

Ronin stayed quiet after that. She was no fool and she hadn't had a relationship with her father. But she'd hoped – and after yesterday's revelation – she'd believed, if only for an hour, that they had a basis for one.

And that made his possible betrayal that much worse.

***

Dennis's panic increased with every step. He had to be wrong. He'd spent many hours bitching about this place. About the money he was constantly forking over, first blackmailed into it by his own father to help with Tabitha's care and then by his guilt. He'd thought he would be free after his father's death, but instead the bonds holding him here had been reinforced. He didn't object to helping out the reserve. It was all tax deductible and he could use that. He made money. A lot of it. But he'd also invested much of it into his father's pet project.

He hadn't thought it was an issue. But now little things came back to haunt him.

Comments that meant nothing at the time, but in the greater scheme of what he knew now he had to wonder about. To question. If he was right, his whole life was about to be brutalized by yet another betrayal. He'd thought he'd been through the worst and now he knew there was a possibility everything he'd been through so far was a prelude to this.

"Dennis? Is that you?"

Dennis spun around to see Germaine, his long-term friend, business partner and the financial head of his company, standing in front of him. A big smile on his face.

With a big gun in his hand.

Chapter 24

Tuesday morning

Tabitha sent a wave of questing energy out to her animals. Surely one of them was bothered by something. If there was anything going on, intruders or other predators, the animals always sounded the alarm. Except she'd already sent out a layer of suppression energy to calm them all down. Crap.

She would have to do a systematic search for her father. There were acres of land here. If her father was around, he could be just about anywhere.

Then she heard panic in the lions' corner. Something was wrong. She bolted in their direction, calling back, "Over here."

"Did you hear something?" Ronin called behind her.

"The animals in this left corner are disturbed by intruders. They've gone into hiding but I can sense their panic...and fear."

She veered left, then right, her feet flying over the gravel path.

Just as she was about to turn the last corner, her shoulder was grabbed from behind. "Wha—?"

A hand slapped over her mouth. Ronin whispered against her ear. *"Shhh.* There are voices up ahead."

She stiffened. She'd been listening for the animals, not for people.

"Let's see if we can hear what they are saying."

She craned an ear, closing her eyes to hear better. The sounds were muffled.

Her father's voice. "What's going on here, Germaine? And what's with the gun?"

Tabitha shot a horrified look at Ronin, then watched with equal shock as he unclipped a weapon of his own.

She didn't have time to adjust when she heard the response.

"What's to figure out? God, you're slow. A brilliant money man for sure, but your instincts are just about non-existent when it comes to people."

Her father's pained voice answered, "Obviously, when I trusted you all these years. Maybe you could explain. What are you even doing here?"

A coarse laugh disrupted the serene air around them.

"This place is a gold mine. See, getting my hands on it is a bit of a problem."

"A big problem, I'd say. You won't get it by killing me. Even if you do, it's still not going to be yours by killing my daughter."

"Ah, but I like to think long term and killing your father was just the first step."

Tabitha gasped in shock. Her grandfather had been murdered? And she hadn't known?

Ronin squeezed her arm in warning. She stared at him in pain as she listened to her father scream in outrage. "You killed the old man? Why, for God's sake? What did he ever do to you?"

"He wasn't...shall we say...cooperative."

Dennis spoke, his voice vibrating in anger, "So you killed him? Over this place. Why? It's a money sink. That's what it is. I pour thousands into it every month."

Germaine said, "And that's why I had help doing this. There is someone who doesn't appreciate all the money being funnelled in this direction. He seems to feel it could be better spent on him."

Tabitha strained to hear her father's shocked whisper, "Please, no."

That coarse laugh again. But Tabitha was already vibrating with outrage. Her poor grandfather, and although she didn't understand who the accomplice was, it was someone else close to her father.

More betrayal.

"Of course it's true. You should know that power, sex and money are really the only motivators in the world. And we have them all here." The disgust in Germaine's voice confused Tabitha.

"I would have never done this. But then you brought that pretty boy into your life. A second wind, a midlife crisis. A fucking joke is what it is."

"My relationship? That's what this is all about?"

"No. But that's what cut the bonds of loyalty for me. We were best friends. Until you decided to come out of the closet. I kinda knew all along but I just didn't want to confirm it. The status quo was working, so why mess it up? Then you started with the pretty boy. What is he, fifteen to twenty years your junior? And now that you are openly gay, people started looking at me. We'd been such close friends for so long, they assumed we must have been lovers. That you'd taint me and my family with your perversion was disgusting. It wasn't so bad in the beginning until you and pretty boy started living together a couple of years ago. I wouldn't have done anything about it, although I was trying to figure out how to get out of the company without losing everything. If I'd known before this recession, I could have cut and run. It was really bad timing when stocks plummeted. We're barely back on our feet as it is."

"And this makes sense, how? Why?"

"God, you're dense. See, I want the whole company." Germaine laughed. "And once I realized what you *could* control, if you so chose, well, then I wanted that too."

"Could control?"

Tabitha's thoughts mirrored her father's question.

"Your grandfather always made the provision that you were to look after Exotic Landscape if your daughter Tabitha was incapable. After being in a coma several times in the last month, the break-ins and the vandalism problems, it's obvious that she isn't mentally or physically stable, and that means she isn't capable of managing Exotic Landscape. So this property should fall nicely into your hands."

"Hell," her father said in disgust, "I don't want it. I don't want anything to do with it."

"Too bad, because the paperwork has already been taken care of. After your pretty boy, Eric, got a hold of your father's will, a handmade one... He really didn't trust anyone...did he?"

"*Paperwork?* Eric?"

Tabitha was too angry to speak. This was all about taking Exotic Landscape? It wasn't even her grandfather's property. It was hers. She'd made sure of that a while ago. At least she thought she had.

"No, that's not true," Dennis protested. "We have the official will."

"Well, hand-written ones are official too. Not when written under duress of course, but as we've already filed this one, giving Eric the right to manage it and you the ownership of the property, it's all good."

Ronin's arms were the only thing keeping Tabitha from racing into the middle of the mess and decking the asshole flat to the ground.

"And how is that going to help?" Her father's bewildered voice made Tabitha hurt. He didn't understand because he didn't want to see the level of betrayal in his world. She couldn't blame him. She didn't even know these assholes, and look at how she felt.

"Then, as you've been living common-law with pretty boy for several years, he stands to inherit everything."

"No, my daughter does," Dennis protested.

"And that was the final straw that brought pretty boy to me in the first place." Germaine laughed. "He found out you made out a will that left everything to your daughter and not to your lover."

"He's in my will. I left him a half million dollars." Her father's voice cracked in shock.

"And no one wants half a million when you give millions to a daughter you can't even stand. A daughter you hate."

Even after everything, that statement hurt.

"I have *never* hated my daughter," Dennis said. "I hated my *father*." He groaned. A sound so full of despair, Tabitha hurt for him too.

"What do we do?" she whispered.

But Ronin didn't have a chance to answer.

"I don't think that's going to be a decision you will have to make," said a rich voice from behind her. "No, don't bother turning around."

She stiffened.

"Shit." Ronin swore under his breath.

"Don't turn around, just keep moving forward and join your father." There was a rustling beside her. She caught the new arrival sliding Ronin's gun out of its holder. Damn.

"Who are you?" Tabitha asked as she walked ahead of Ronin.

Her father came into view. "No," he cried out. "Leave her alone."

The asshole Germaine asked, "Dennis, what part about the inheritance didn't you understand?"

Tabitha groaned. "The dead part, of course."

She was shoved toward her father. She stepped over to his side. "Hey, Dad. You really shouldn't have taken off like that."

"I didn't want to. But I thought I heard *his* voice through your phone talking to Ronin before he was knocked out."

"And you did." Germaine smiled. "And now we have the whole family here, including the security specialist. Except you really don't want to assume that those in an office know nothing about security themselves. It's so easy to fix things with inside people."

Security specialist? He was assuming that Ronin was Roman. Good. Then he couldn't know that Roman would be on his way in minutes. To delay their plans, in order to give Roman more time, she said, "You haven't fixed anything. I had the deed transferred into my name before he died."

"Ah, yes. You certainly filled out the paperwork and left it with your father to take care of. Of course, he gave it to Eric to handle. Only he made sure the papers were never sent off. But then...you haven't been capable of handling things around here in a while." And he smiled, a nasty smile that made her cringe. She looked at the second man also holding a gun. He was maybe in his mid to late thirties. "Dad, who is the second asshole?"

He glared at the younger man. "Eric, my assistant. Also known as pretty boy, apparently."

She gasped. "Your partner – the one you live with? The one you wanted me to meet?"

"Not this way." He sighed, a sadness on his face that broke her heart. "Not at all now."

"Sorry, Dennis. But if you think I'm going to wait around while you rekindle a relationship with her..." Eric shook his head, long black curls flying around his attractive head.

"Dad, we're going to have to talk." She snorted. "Pretty boy is all about glitz and short-term gain. He's not going to go the distance."

Eric gasped. "That is not true. I've been there for him all these years. Where the hell have you been?"

She didn't have much to say to that. But he looked like a disgruntled boy who'd been denied his toys. "Somehow I doubt my father has treated you badly." She sensed Ronin's shift from one foot to the other. She took several steps forward. "My father's a very generous man."

"Generous is not the same as having it all yourself. My looks aren't going to last forever. I decided I didn't want to wait for him. I'm still young. I don't want to tie myself down. But I need money to live as I want to. And between the two of you, there is a hell of a lot of it."

"See, I don't get that." And she didn't. She spent everything trying to pull enough pennies together to keep the reserve functioning.

Eric smiled. "Your father never told you, huh? Your grandfather left you a nice little trust fund. And then there's the value of all this land. So close to town. It's worth thirty million, easy. And as the manager of the reserve is incompetent, your father will be forced to shut the doors or hand the reins over to another manager while the animals can be moved elsewhere. It'll be easy to sell them off to private investors. The land will be sold to recoup costs and pay off the massive debts."

She gasped in anger. "I don't have any debts."

"Well, as there's no more money coming your way from Dennis." The gun wavered toward her father. "You will start accumulating them now."

"No." She shook her head. "There's no way you can do this."

"And, about your office manager?" Eric laughed. "Wendy is my sister. I'm sure this will turn out just the way I want it to."

Tabitha couldn't even begin to think of the type of damage that Wendy could have done while Tabitha had been out of commission. Wendy had been referred to her by one of her regular suppliers. *Had they known? Were they in on it?* It could take months to sort out the damage. Just the thought of losing Exotic Landscape to this slime in some land grab made her physically ill.

"She's going to heave."

She bent over, gasping. Ronin gently rubbed her back. Dying now would likely kill Trinity as well. She couldn't let that happen.

"Easy, honey."

"What are we going to do with them? We can't just shoot them," Eric whined. "That would leave all kinds of unanswered questions and evidence we don't want."

"She's got lions here. Tigers. All manner of animals that are looking for fresh meat. And Wendy will make sure they aren't found for a long time."

Tabitha froze. Ronin growled. For him, this would be a nightmare come true but inside, Tabitha's heart leapt with joy. Now this would be the first positive break as far as she was concerned.

Eric smiled. "Perfect."

"The early morning feeding time is soon. The cats will be hungry and they should finish them off quickly. We need them to kill them before anyone comes."

"Or we can shoot them to draw the animals. The scent of blood will speed up the process."

The men were busy talking, but Ronin had a strong grip on Tabitha's arm.

"Don't worry. They'll never touch us."

Her father snorted. "They'll take us down in minutes and go after the soft tissue first."

She sighed. The men in her life had so little idea of her world. "No, they won't," she reassured the two men in her life.

"Put them in with the lions." Germaine motioned to the gates behind them. "Wendy said lately the lions have been more aggressive than any of the others."

Ronin's grip tightened.

She winced but didn't bother trying to reassure him. She was more afraid of the bullets.

"The lions are one path over. Get moving."

✳✳✳

Ronin tensed looking for a break. He'd take a bullet over a lion any day. But it sounded as if he might be getting both.

The two men motioned him toward the other two. He'd easily take on one guy. Two on most days. But two men with guns was asking for a death sentence. Or he could trust Tabitha. She appeared to be unconcerned.

That's because I am.

He quaked at the thought of her reading his mind. There were a lot of things in life he could handle, but he wasn't so sure that was one of them.

And I didn't read your mind. You're speaking telepathically.

He snorted. "You're crazy."

Dennis turned to look at them.

Eric said, "Hey, no talking."

Ronin shrugged. They were standing in front of the lions' pen. Tabitha walked up to the computerized lock and entered the passcode.

She opened the door and motioned her father and Ronin inside. As they stepped past her, she whispered. "Run for the trees on the left."

"And you?" Ronin asked as she stepped inside. "I'm staying right behind you."

Her father bolted. With one last look at the two men holding guns on them, she zigzagged for the trees herself, Ronin beside her.

Shots fired behind her, but they were either shooting into the air or they were lousy shots. Either way they reached the trees safely.

Her father was already there, looking around anxiously. "We have to get out of here," he cried, "before the lions find us."

"They already have." Tabitha spun around. "Nothing happens in their space without them knowing about it."

"Shit." Dennis spun around, terrified.

"Calm down. It's your fear that will set them off. Stay calm and let me handle them." He nodded and she turned to face Ronin, making sure he understood. She saw his face. "Are you hit?"

"Yeah, but it's just a scratch. I'll be fine." He lifted his arm to show her a long red streak under the tear in his shirt.

It looked raw but wasn't bad. It would sting for a while but wouldn't slow them down. Still, it had to hurt. She gave him a quick kiss. "Sorry."

He shrugged philosophically. "It could have been so much worse."

"Yeah." She gave a short hard laugh. "They could have done some target practice."

Dennis backed away from him. "No way that's nothing. That's fresh blood. That's a dinner bell to a lion." He kept backing up. "Nothing personal, Ronin, but Jesus."

Tabitha sighed. "Stop backing up, Dad. If you get too far away from me, I can't protect you."

He stopped in his tracks. "You? Protect me? How?"

"Because the lions are already here."

Her father jumped back toward her. "Where?" he snapped.

She hated to answer him. "Nisha is above you."

She watched sympathetically as the color completely drained from the faces of the two men beside her. Poor Ronin. He'd done well so far but this... yeah, this would push the strongest of men into full-on panic. And yet he was holding on better than her father.

Her father's reaction wasn't one she'd seen him have before. But it would also explain some of the reasons why her grandfather despised him. Her grandfather would consider his obvious fear to be a weakness. Moneymaking hadn't been important to her grandfather. Animals were. If her father couldn't stand to be around the animals, then he'd be nothing in her grandfather's eyes...although her dad appeared to handle Tango and Tripod just fine. Then again, he'd met them many times. They knew him – unlike the ones out here.

She called up to the tree and the lioness watching them with interest. "Nisha, do you want to come down and meet these two men?"

At the same time, she sent Nisha a warm loving greeting to boost the continuous wave she'd been blasting out since entering the compound. There was another female in here and one big old male. Captain was old and cranky. Salba was the second female, and she was young and hyper. Tabitha expected she was racing toward them right now. Nisha was the dominant female, the hunter of the pack. The one to keep an eye on. Automatically, Tabitha did a quick scan of Nisha's energy. She looked good. Happy and calm.

But hungry.

She glanced at her watch. Feeding time. Not that the lions would be a problem. They had a great relationship. But all animal trainers knew that any animal could be dangerous.

Nisha stood up and stretched, then jumped lightly to the ground.

She walked over to Tabitha first and jumped up, placing her big paws on Tabitha's shoulders in her usual greeting, then she rubbed her face against Tabitha's head.

"Hey, baby. How are you today?" Tabitha murmured, giving the loving tabby a big hug before stepping to the side so she'd jump down. "Nisha, this is Ronin and my father."

At Nisha's head shake and snort, Tabitha laughed. "She's not impressed."

"You know," Ronin said, "that's understandable. I'd be happy to leave anytime. How about now?"

"I'd have preferred leaving ten minutes ago." Her father went to take several steps backwards.

"Don't move, Dad," she cautioned. "All animals know how to sense fear in others."

He took a shuddering breath and nodded quickly.

"Same for you, Ronin." Tabitha could feel a bright energy racing toward her. "Here's Salba. That means Captain won't be far behind."

"Oh shit. You mean there are more of them?" her father groaned softly.

"Only three here. They get along famously."

"Uh uh."

She laughed at the stiff nod from Ronin. "Hey," she said gently, "you're holding up really well."

Beads of sweat formed on his forehead and he gave a short laugh. "Like hell. But I'm still standing."

Just then, a light brown streak came flying toward him. Ronin's eyes became wide and he opened his mouth to scream. And caught it at the last second.

"Stop, Salba." The lioness roared lightly and wrapped itself around Tabitha's legs. Tabitha laughed and bent over to hug her. "Good girl." The lioness gave her a rambunctious greeting then twined her long lithe body around the men's stiff legs.

Neither moved. Neither bent to touch her. Neither breathed.

She grinned. "Doing good, guys. But there's one more."

"Hello, Captain." And she sent out a wide loving wave of cool soothing energy toward the big old male that strode toward them, his nose lifted, checking out the air. Picking up the scent of the males. The scent of the blood.

Easy, boy. We're just here to visit. All is well. She tweaked his aura, laying down a light suppression energy wave on his system. He roared, but it was a happy one. He walked up and rubbed his huge head against her ribs.

She smiled and gave the big teddy bear a scratch under his chin.

"Hey, big guy. Life is treating you pretty good, isn't it?"

He started to purr. His big diesel engine rippled outward across the countryside. Tabitha laughed and looked up at Ronin. He was staring at her in bemusement.

"He's not dangerous?"

"Oh, in the right circumstances, he's very dangerous. But with me...? No." She shook her head. "As he doesn't know you two, I laid a layer of energy to keep his hunting instincts suppressed."

"Thanks, I think."

Ronin glanced over in the direction of the road. "Nothing personal, but any chance we can get the hell out of here now?"

***

"Where the hell is Dennis and the others?" Germaine scanned the pen. Rocks, brush, trees. And no sign of the rest of them. "And why is there no screaming? Yelling? Hell, the damn lions should be roaring...shouldn't they?"

The two men stared at each other.

"I'm more worried about them getting away," Eric said. "There's no way they can be allowed to live at this point. We have to make sure they can't tell anyone."

Germaine groaned. "We can't go in there. We should have shot them dead and then thrown their bodies over the damn fence."

A cold hard voice spoke from behind. "A little too late for that."

Eric stiffened. "Shit."

"Don't say a fucking word," warned Germaine.

"Hey, I'm not going down for this," Eric cried. "I haven't done anything."

"Don't. Just don't. Keep your mouth shut," Germaine snapped. "They don't know anything."

"I wouldn't say that exactly. Hands out of your pockets and turn around slowly."

They turned slowly. Eric gasped. "We put you in the lions' pen!"

Roman smiled a little grimly. "Actually, you put my twin brother in there. But he's fine. No thanks to you. At least one of you, if not both of you, is a lousy shot. Not that it matters. There are cops coming up behind me."

The two men looked at each other. Then bolted into the closest field. The fence wasn't high enough to slow them down.

They heard shouting behind them, but neither of them slowed enough to make the words out. Big mistake.

Coming from the side and ripping forward at an incredible speed in their direction was another cat.

"Oh shit. That's a fucking tiger."

Chapter 25

Tuesday 8 am

Tabitha heard the shouting. "Sounds as if help has arrived."
She scanned the paths to see which would take them to the new
arrivals. "The sounds are coming from over there."

"And what's over there?"

She sighed. "Tigers."

"Dangerous?"

"Remember the part about all wild animals in captivity still
being wild creatures in the right circumstances?"

Then a horrific scream made her pull in her shoulders. She
lay down on the gravel in front of the astonished men and
jumped free of her body. In spirit form, she raced down the path
toward the chaos. She could hear Boran, a big male. He was
running, chasing prey, his blood pumping with the hunt.

Shit.

She slammed into him. He never faltered. Up ahead, Eric
peeled across the ground at a breakneck speed. He saw the fence
in front of him and flew up as high as he could go. She watched
as he made it almost to the top before Boran jumped and clawed
at him.

The male cat caught him by the foot. Eric screamed again
and scampered up higher. Boran couldn't go any higher.

He was pissed. The man struggled at the top of the fence
but it didn't have a bar to support him. He had to get over or
climb back down again. He chose over.

She watched and wondered what she should do. She'd have
loved to seen Boran eat him for breakfast, but that was hardly
fair. Plus it might make Boran sick.

She gave Boran several good loving strokes of sympathy as
he paced below the prey. *Sorry, buddy.*

Sighing, she slipped back to her body. She groaned at the harsh landing but managed to sit up fast and face the other two. "Eric is sitting at the top of the fence between the tigers."

"Between the tigers?"

"Yeah, there are two females on the other side. And Tango's pen joins in at the far end."

"He goes out with the other tigers?"

"Of course," she said. "Socializing with other tigers is important to his well being."

"Can we leave now, please?" Her father's voice quivered. "As much as I hate what Eric has done, I don't want to see him as tiger bait."

"Too late," said Ronin cheerfully. He went to take a step forward when Nisha twined around his legs. "Is it safe to leave?"

"Yes, but they are happy with the company." She bent to scratch the sides and belly of the biggest lion in her family. Captain sucked it up.

"Amazing."

She studied Ronin's face, a fat grin on her own. "You do realize you're barely reacting?"

***

Once back on the path and feeling as if he'd been given a second chance at life, Ronin turned to see his brother approaching.

Roman called out, "Hey, you survived the lions?"

"Yeah, can't say I'm as bothered anymore." Ronin slapped Roman on the shoulder. "Amazing what a little hands-on experience will do for a guy."

The two brothers grinned. "If you're ready," Tabitha said, "let's get Eric down and you guys can take him away. My place is a mess and I have a lot of animals looking for food."

"Yeah, I presume you've picked up Germaine already?" Ronin asked.

"No. We think he's hiding in the one of the pens. We're looking for him now."

"Not the smartest place to hide."

"And yet you're fine."

Ronin motioned to Tabitha, who'd entered the pen where Eric hung, suspended, just out of the cat's reach. "She's the reason. I can't say for sure how these guys would act without her, but in there with her, the damn things were pussycats." Ronin shook his head. "I had no idea such a thing was possible."

"Like that?" Roman pointed out Tabitha's progress toward the tiger.

In the distance, Tabitha called, "Boran, come here, boy."

And the damn tiger barreled toward her, his big body jumping and twisting with joy.

"Jesus."

Roman stood beside his brother, watching as Boran knocked her to the ground, lay on top of her and proceeded to clean her face with long slow licks.

Eric chose that moment to sneak down the fence and bolt for the gate. Roman let him out and Ronin cuffed him. Dennis left with the police and their prisoner. Germaine had been picked up on the other side.

"Tabitha, we got Eric." Ronin called out.

She waved a hand in the air but didn't appear to be in any hurry. After a moment, she stood up and walked to a gate on the far side. From where the men stood, Ronin could see that Tango and a large golden-colored tiger were pacing on the far side. She pinned in the code at the gate and walked through to Tango.

"Boran isn't too happy to be left behind."

Ronin watched the golden tiger pace and whine at the closed gate. "Neither is the golden one," Ronin said. "She's magic with them."

"It's an energy thing."

"Can you see it? The energy stuff?" Roman asked.

"No," Ronin said, "but weird stuff is definitely happening."

"Like?" His brother slid him a long sideways look.

"I can't say exactly. It happened after the knock to my head." He shrugged. "I'll ask Stefan about it."

"It seems he's always around."

A contemplative silence fell between them.

Roman nudged him. "Is she the right one?"

Ronin didn't have to guess at his brother's meaning. "Hell, yes."

With a grin, Roman asked, "Does she know?"

"She should. It seems as if she knows everything else." Ronin laughed. "It's an odd feeling."

"You'll get used to it."

***

Tabitha bent and gave Tango a big hug. "It's been a long day, hasn't it, big guy?"

He rubbed himself all over her, hard enough to make her stumble against the fence. Boran's cold nose poked at her from the other side. Feeling better about life than she had in a long time, she reached through and scratched his nose. "We got the guys. Somehow, we'll fix the rest of this mess."

She had to. That so many people had been involved in the damn conspiracy scared her. She'd been so unaware. It had happened under her nose and she never knew. Then her father had also been totally taken in. That had to be tough for him.

Her poor grandfather. She had avoided going through his papers, not being in great shape herself. She'd been happy to leave everything to the others. The pain had been too sharp for her to delve in any deeper until she could handle it better. Now, there was no choice. She needed to find out if anything else had gone wrong and to make sure her house was in order.

She'd spent her life helping these animals. She would make sure they were taken care of.

She glanced through the fence to see Ronin standing on the path with his brother, watching her. She waved at him. She had a mess to clean up, but with Ronin at her side and her father back in her life, she was confident she could handle it.

She opened the gate to return to Ronin's side through Boran's pen when her knees buckled.

She cried out. "Ronin!"

"Tabitha, what wrong?" Ronin cried.

The cries inside and outside overwhelmed what little clarity she had left. A roar, loud and panicked, ripped through her mind. Ripped into her body and soul.

Trinity was in trouble.

With all the chaos here, she'd forgotten about Trinity. And her own fate that was so connected to the captive tiger.

Now it was too late.

"It's Trinity!" she screamed. Through the long distance of energetic time, she heard the sound of gunshots.

Her body jerked. Once. Twice.

She looked down at her body.

Blood welled from her side, with more coming from her left hip.

"Noooo!" she screamed. *Stefan, help.*

And she collapsed.

✳✳✳

Ronin raced to the fence. "Tabitha? Tabitha!"

No answer. Roman was at his side, studying the locks. "I can open this gate," he said, "but I do not know what to do about the tiger."

Ronin stared through the fence at Boran. The Bengal tiger roared fury. The gate was open between Tango and Boran, but they were more concerned with Tabitha, who'd fallen face first on the ground. They circled her, nudged her. Tabitha never moved.

"What do we do about him?"

Just then Boran roared at the top of his lungs. Then Tango answered.

"Ah shit," Ronin cried. "There's no way we can get in there."

"What about the other staff?"

"Which ones?" Ronin searched for Sue. "The ones that double crossed her to steal the damn place or the ones that worked here before that?"

"We need Stefan." Ronin was already keying in his number.

Roman looked at him quickly. "Can't you call him telepathically?"

"No idea." Ronin lifted the ringing phone to his ear. "Can you?"

"Sometimes." Roman stared back at Tabitha and the milling tigers. "I expect he's already over there with her."

"Well, he's not answering his phone."

I'm busy. Stefan's exasperated voice slipped through Ronin's head. *I can only help one of you at a time, and right now that's Tabitha.*

"What can I do to help?" Ronin rolled his eyes at his brother as he put away his phone.

Get in there and keep her safe.

"And the tigers?"

Remember that personal problem about cats you asked me to look into?

Damn, he didn't want to go in there. He'd survived because Tabitha had taken care of the lions. Now it was his turn to take care of her...and he could barely function.

You have to. Someone has to keep her safe.

***

Stefan left Ronin to make a decision about the cats. He had bigger issues. Tabitha had disappeared quickly. She'd had no warning. That meant the layers of calming energy she'd left surrounding Trinity had been cut through by something major. Something drastic. And there were injuries showing on Tabitha's body. Which meant, as he assumed it had something to do with the tiger, that Trinity had been the one injured.

That was no good. They had to separate Tabitha from Trinity before the tiger died. Yet Tabitha would give everything to keep that tiger alive. She invested herself a hundred percent in her animals. If she failed in this case, it could kill her too.

As he looked down at her prone body, he realized she might already be past the point of saving. Except...he could see her cord, faint and thin...and that was a first. He zipped down the path. Flying as fast as he could travel, he whipped through the ethers, desperate to keep an eye on the tricky cord as it wove in and out of the clouds. He'd never been able to see it before. He could only assume that whatever method she'd been using to return to her body had helped to strengthen it.

Animal energy surrounded it, protecting it. Tango's. Tripod's. And another one's... He'd sensed the same extra energy inside Tabitha's house – Tobias! Stefan smiled in wonder as he searched through the rest. There was a lot of Ronin's energy, but as if it wasn't sure – as if he wanted to help out but did not know how. Stefan couldn't waste any time offering suggestions.

This was it. He knew it in his heart. This was the last chance to find the tiger and save Tabitha.

Just then he saw the cord lead into a warehouse.

And could see the address.

***

Tabitha slammed back into Trinity's sinewy body. And screamed. Her body twisted in agony. So much heat. So much panic. Her leg refused to work and blood dripped steadily onto the floor of the cage. And her mind was so afraid that she couldn't function. It sent her emotions immediately back into victim status.

She opened her eyes, adjusting to Trinity's sight.

Instantly, she slammed her eyes closed and opened her hearing.

"Well, she's dead. See what price you can get for her now." Footsteps strode away, angry, clipped.

"Damn it. The boss is going to get you for this," Fez blustered to the stranger's retreating form.

She re-opened her eyes as she lay down a mess of healing energy, trying to keep Tabitha alive. Trying to stop her from bleeding to death. They had to hang on. Ronin would save them.

Somehow.

She poured healing energy into the wound, into Tabitha's aging heart. She needed her to keep the faith. To keep trying. Once an animal gave up, it was almost impossible to bring them back.

The smell of blood, of fear, of death, surrounded her.

Stefan, I could really use some help.

No answer.

Crap. *Ronin, where are you?*

***

Ronin stared at the gate Roman had managed to open. He took one step forward when Stefan spoke.

3346 Calder St.

And just as fast, Stefan was gone. Ronin quickly relayed the message to Roman then took a deep breath. "You go to that end and help her there. Save the tiger."

"I'm on it. I'll take a few men from here." Roman turned away then stopped and looked back at Ronin. "What about you?"

Ronin smiled grimly. "It's time to face my past." And he turned to walk into Boran's pen.

The tiger raced toward him, his roar deafening...and freaking scary. The huge cat was going to defend Tabitha, and as far as he was concerned, Ronin was an intruder.

When Ronin approached cautiously, he heard Stefan say, *Talk to him. He's an animal. He's a feline. You have an affinity for them or else your pet wouldn't have been there in the back of your psyche all this time.*

"Haunting me, I believe you said. How is that having an affinity?"

Oh, it is. You loved him and that love is what attracts him. He needs it as much as everyone else.

"Except he's dead."

Energy never dies. Remember that rule of physics.

"And that applies now – how and why?"

Because he can help you deal with Boran.

"What?" And then he had no time to ask any more questions. Boran was on him.

Never show fear.

Ronin snorted. He took a deep breath, closed his eyes against the rush of tiger teeth.

And waited.

Nothing.

He peeked under his lashes to see Boran sniffing around his legs.

With a second deep breath, he murmured, "Hey, Boran. Let's help Tabitha, okay?" He took several steps toward Tabitha.

Boran roared again, but he seemed confused. He milled around Ronin's legs and got in the way but didn't attack. In truth, he seemed not to know what to do with Ronin.

Ronin took another step forward and Boran swatted at him. Not in anger or hunger. It was playful. Maybe. Ronin didn't want to count on that. And if the next swat was any worse, Boran would draw blood. "Boran, we have to help Tabitha. She's in a bad way."

He took another step. Boran roared. Ronin felt his throat close up. *Shit. Shit.* No time for a panic attack. Feeling like an absolute idiot but willing to try anything, he murmured, "Mr. Boots, if you're here, please tell Boran I mean Tabitha no harm."

There was a weird whooshing energy, as if a bird darted past so close to his face that he could feel the movement of the air.

Boran whined.

"It's not a good time for any of us, is it?" Ronin offered.

He had no idea if Mr. Boots was here or if he'd spoken to Boran – if he even could be, for that matter. However, Boran walked back over to Tabitha. He glanced up at Ronin as if to say, *What's taking you so long?*

Stiffening his spine and expecting to feel claws raking his side open at any moment, Ronin dropped to his knees beside Tabitha. He knew one shouldn't touch a psychic when they were deep in a session. But he had many times and so had the animals... Surely that didn't apply in Tabitha's case? She wasn't even in her body, was she?

He lifted the corner of her shirt and sucked in his breath. Bullet holes. One on the hip and one on the top of her thigh on the opposite side. Blood was slowly dripping from the wound and sliding down to pool in her flat belly.

There was no smell of gunpowder, but the blood was real.

Except there had been no shots fired. There'd been no gunfire, but the gunshot wounds were unmistakable. The smell of fresh blood was something he would never forget. The small entrance wound was clean and too damn real to ignore. He ripped off his shirt and used it to staunch the flow of blood. That it was sluggish and dark scared him. He was afraid the worst of the bleeding would be internal. He slipped a hand underneath but found no exit hole. Shit. That was so not good. He reached for his phone to call for a paramedic.

And heard Stefan's voice. *They can't help her.*

"Then who can?" he called out, grateful he was alone in the field. "There has to be someone or something that can."

Dr. Maddy. But I can't reach her.

"Where is she? We have to find her."

No. The problem is the tiger is dying. Tabitha appears to be showing the same injuries as the tiger. You need to find the tiger and try to save it.

"Roman is on his way, but what can I do from here? I can hardly leave her. Not bleeding and in the middle of two damn tigers."

Both tigers are essentially her pets.

"Yes, but she said something about laying down a level of suppression energy to keep the aggression levels of the animals down. If she's out like this, what happens to that? Will these animals turn on her?"

Interesting, murmured Stefan. *That's very clever of her. The energy stays for a long time and these animals know her.*

"Animals in captivity attack their owners and trainers all the time."

This is a very different situation.

Ronin stared down at Tabitha. Sue, one of the workers from the reserve, called out to him. "Is she okay? Have you called for an ambulance?"

Ronin shouted back, "Yes." Although it was a lie. He'd yet to call anyone. He looked down at Boran, now lying beside Tabitha.

"Do you think you can move Boran to another pen?"

Sue snorted. "If he's not hurting anything, then maybe he's better in there with you. He's very protective of Tabitha. If we try to move him he's likely to be difficult."

Ronin blew out his breath hard. *Shit.* He could feel the sweat dripping down his back, but at the same time there was this voice inside saying these reactions were what he'd expect to see. Because these were the reactions he'd always had to cats. That didn't make them real.

"So, assess," he said aloud to himself. "You're in here with two tigers. Two tigers that appear to be uninterested in your presence. You made it across the field to Tabitha. You managed to speak with Boran and now you are squatting between the two of them. Not only that, your stomach isn't attempting to empty itself. All in all, this is major progress."

Maybe Stefan was right.

I usually am.

"And always irritating," Ronin said absently as he stroked Tabitha's arms. "Are you sure there's nothing I can do from here?"

There's always something you can do. You can fill her with love, cover her with adoration and make her want to come home to you. She's using her animals to ground herself. And in a weird way, she uses lots of them. As if she doesn't believe that one will be enough. Or if one betrays her – dies, so to speak – then she'll have backup.

"Yes, that would be Tabitha," Ronin added thoughtfully. "Her grandfather. Her mother. Her father."

Exactly. Dennis was right. Her grandfather had no time or energy for humans. If you walked on four legs he'd bend over backwards to help, but in his world the two-legged animals were the ones you couldn't trust. He'd made sure she learned that.

"And he treated Tabitha that way?" Ronin asked incredulously.

Her less than the others, but his distrust encompassed everyone else. She lived with that prejudice. Was raised with it. Breathed it on a daily basis. And don't forget she was her father's daughter. Her grandfather could never reconcile himself with the parts of her father that she inherited.

"She said they were close."

He's the closest role model she had to formulate her values. There was her father, but he left. She had a fiancé and he bolted. All of this reinforcing her grandfather's views. Leaving her with only one lesson – that animals were the ones you could trust. But animals die too – and at a much younger age than humans. So she made sure she had many so that there were always some of them around to love her.

"Wow. She's really messed up because of her childhood."

And yet she's still strong, relatively sane and a good person. And most of that she learned through her relationships with animals. She learned to work with energy to help them. She could use it to help people, but she doesn't really believe they deserve it.

"Ouch. That's a little harsh, isn't it?"

Not for energy work. Look at yourself and how your relationship with animals was impacted by the death of your pet.

"That just means I was a neurotic kid who never quite grew up."

No. You're missing the other life event that happened at the time. I'd hoped you'd make the connection but...

"Now what are you talking about?"

You spent days weeping over your cat. And you blamed your father. He was the driver of the vehicle that killed Mr. Boots, wasn't he?

Ronin winced. He'd deliberately buried that fact. "Thanks for that reminder."

And do you remember what came afterward?

"No. I obviously don't want to either."

Yet it's time. You can't sit on these time bombs forever.

Ronin stared down at Tabitha. "So tell me then. We're out of time."

You told your father how much you hated him. That he was a killer and you were going to spend the rest of your life making him pay. Making killer's pay...

Horrible images flooded Ronin's mind. Him screaming at his father, who stood staring down at the still body of Mr. Boots. His mother trying to shush him. He sat back on his heels and realized this was his reason he became a cop. He wanted to make sure that others paid for what they'd done wrong.

"How can such a small incident be the driving force, a passion for a specific career?"

Because at the time, it wasn't a small incident. Your father, accident or not, had taken someone you loved.

"All my life, I was driven to be a cop..." he murmured.

And then in a nasty karmic twist, both your parents were killed and you lost them too.

Jesus.

Think about why you don't do art like your brother does.

"Because I suck at it," Ronin snorted. "Like that's hard to work out."

Because you were drawing on the sidewalk when Mr. Boots got hit.

Chapter 26

Tuesday mid-morning

Lassitude overtook Tabitha. The blood loss made her weak. And angry. With the added injuries, Trinity was likely to die. And the baby with her. Tabitha poured love and healing and caring into Trinity, trying to help her to deal with the shock, the pain and the blood loss. Trinity's heart was pumping steadily, which meant blood continued to leak from the double bullet holes. But neither were in vital spots. Neither would kill Trinity if she'd arrived in time.

Unless Trinity gave up. Damn, she needed Ronin to find them. Where was he?

And she couldn't shake the nagging suspicion that she might need to have Trinity close to her body to save her. How that would work, she didn't know. But Trinity was injured and Tabitha could help heal her. It would be much easier if she was physically there to help her. But her body was with Boran and her spirit was here with Trinity.

Stefan, I need to have my body here.

That's a little hard to do.

I know. But I think it's the only way.

I'll tell Ronin.

"You want me to what?" Ronin sat back on his heels in shock.

Take her to Trinity.

Ronin gave a broken cry. "Isn't that going to cause more damage?"

Roman is almost at The Olde Riverside Shipyard. I'll direct you when you get closer. Grab her and go. There was a pause, then Stefan shouted, *Now!*

Shit.

Ronin hopped to his feet. His sudden action caused both tigers to rise, growling in the back of their throats.

"I don't have time for this. I have to take her somewhere and I have to take her now."

He bent down and scooped Tabitha up. Her head lolled to one side. He tried to shift her weight so he could carry her comfortably and he needed to move fast.

Boran growled.

"Damn it, you have to let me take her. Mr. Boots, tell him, for Christ's sake."

And damned if Boran didn't narrow his gaze as if he was listening to someone. The fur on the back on his spine relaxed. Not having time to waste. Ronin called back, "Thanks, Boran...and Mr. Boots." He hadn't said anything to Tango. He cast a long glance back to Tabitha's pet and said, "You know I'm helping her – right?" He kept walking forward, and damn if he didn't catch a glimpse of something...someone...inside Tango. He stopped and stared. The image disappeared. He shook his head and all but ran to the gate where Sue waited to unlock it.

"How is she?" Sue asked.

"Not good. I'm taking her to get help. I don't have time to explain. Make sure the cats are okay, please."

"They're fine. Tabitha has always been able to connect in an unearthly way with her felines."

Ronin groaned. "You don't know the half of it."

Holding Tabitha tightly, his muscles straining, he raced to his truck then struggled to get Tabitha on the front seat and buckled up safely before anyone saw what he was doing. No one would agree to him taking an injured woman into town and to a deserted warehouse.

Christ, Ronin hoped he was doing the right thing.

Roman checked the area. He had only three other cops here. Geoff and Carmichael were here with him and there was more spread out to cover the back of the place. Inside, the warehouse was silent. And that was unusual in itself. Either they'd been found out, or the place was deserted. According to Stefan, the tiger was here.

Somewhere. According to Tabitha, there were two men looking after her.

Apparently Ronin was on his way. With an unconscious Tabitha. This shit was freaky. He struggled to understand Ronin's decision to bring her here and not take her directly to the hospital. Perhaps she wasn't badly injured.

She is, Stefan said. *This needs to happen.*

Roman leaned up against the wall, his gun out and ready. Thankfully Ronin's men were here. He wouldn't want to deal with this without any backup.

As it was, they could be shorthanded, depending on what they found inside. Carmichael and Geoff were in front of him framing the front door. Carmichael pushed it open.

The door moved silently.

Immediately a nasty smell leaked outward.

"Oh gross," Carmichael whispered.

Roman leaned forward to see inside. The place appeared to be a huge open cavern. But it looked as if he might be in the right place. There were cages of all sizes stacked along one side and several big cages down at the far end. The smell was rank. Was anyone hosing this place down?

Down the way, they heard someone talking.

"See, I don't know if you are really in there or not, but to believe I'm talking to a lady in a tiger... That makes me crazy."

Roman almost laughed. He was definitely in the right place.

"What the hell is he talking about?" asked Carmichael in a harsh whisper.

Geoff shrugged.

274

Roman shook his head. There was no way to explain. And this job did make people crazy. Jesus, could this guy actually see Tabitha?

"Hell, it doesn't matter. You're not a cop anymore, Roman. Stay here with Geoff. I'll scope it out and come back."

And Carmichael disappeared inside.

***

Tabitha's strength was waning. Trinity sucked up everything Tabitha threw at her to keep her calm and to help ease her pain. She didn't have a lot of energy left to heal the bullet holes. And the less energy Tabitha had to heal, the more agitated Trinity became and the harder it became for Tabitha to work.

And then there was Fez.

He was on guard duty. He didn't have a gun, so Tabitha was still unclear about who shot Trinity.

And then she didn't have time to wonder as Trinity growled and tried to bite her injury. Tabitha was exhausting herself trying to stop Trinity from doing more harm.

"See, if you're in there, then that's my beliefs about life and death blown right out of the water. I don't know what to do with that. I want to help you, but there's a part of me that thinks you are my meal ticket out of here. You're incredibly rare and if I find the right buyer for you... Wow, I could make a fortune. But I got to convince them you are in there. So how do I do that?"

The damn idiot didn't seem to realize that soon there was only going to be a dead carcass to sell. "You realize I'm dying in here. That you shot me and now I will not survive without medical attention."

His face lit up. "There you are! And how do you know about medical attention. Is that something animals think about?"

Oh Lord. He thought she was the animal. "Why did you shoot me?"

"Oh hey, that wasn't me. That was the buyer when he realized he'd been double crossed. And if he couldn't have you, he figured no one would." He leaned in close. "Although I'm thinking he's got a vet here right now. He could have killed the tiger but instead placed those shots so she wasn't really badly hurt by them."

Wasn't really hurt? Jesus. Maybe Fez should get shot in the same damn places and then he could decide what hurt. With great difficulty, she reined in her emotions.

"Where did he go?" She was sorry she missed seeing the asshole shooter. He's the one she really wanted. Anyone who put orders for these animals were just as culpable in her mind. She wanted to nail his ass.

"They heard something outside and disappeared." He looked around as if afraid they'd snuck up on him. "Between you and me, my boss won't tolerate this. He'll take care of that asshole – permanently."

"Take care of them?" she asked cautiously. "Like kill them?"

"Oh yeah, he'll kill them. He's killed a lot of people."

Tabitha paused her energy work long enough to study Fez's face. Because he thought she was a tiger and wouldn't be able to tell anyone, he appeared to be treating her as a confidante.

"What's your boss's name?"

"Ha. He insists I call him 'boss.' He doesn't like real names to be used." Morosely, he added, "But everyone knows my name. If anyone goes down for this, it's going to be me."

"Unless you help me."

"What can I do? I'm no vet."

"No, but men are looking for me. They are coming to help me."

He looked around fearfully. "Here?"

"I hope so," she muttered, pushing more healing energy into the injury. She had almost stopped the bleeding, but the damn bullet was still in Trinity and that was a lot harder to deal with.

Trinity would pull through if Tabitha could get her out of here. Captivity, particularly in bad situations like this, did something to the psyche of an animal. They fought it and fought it and fought it then they gave up. That was dangerous. Animals had been known to lie down and die even when nothing was physically wrong. In this case, Trinity was hurting and injured and needed to keep her spirits up.

To that end, Tabitha gently pushed a little more energy into her heart chakra. Brightening and softening, bringing light into all her dark places.

"When?" Fez cleared his throat, reminding Tabitha he was still there. She hadn't exactly forgotten, but she was struggling to keep her focus as it was. Her connection to Trinity was draining her life force at the same time as Trinity's. So the dying Trinity was trying to be saved by the dying Tabitha. She'd have laughed at that mind-bend if she could have. Instead, she just wanted to cry.

Fez cleared his throat.

She struggled to answer. It all seemed so pointless. But Tabitha knew that was Trinity's energy expressing Trinity's thoughts…her negativity. Tabitha pushed them back, fighting the depression with love. It took several minutes for the despair to leave and for her to remember that Ronin and Stefan were fighting for them. And they had friends who were coming to help.

Damn right. Stefan's voice rippled through her mind.

Oh God, Stefan. This is so hard.

Her feelings are dominating. It's a difficult thing to fight the onset of negative emotions of another soul at the same time you are absorbing her feelings.

And how, she murmured in her mind. Just his presence was light, healing, soulful. She immediately felt soothed, blessed.

And could see where she'd gotten sucked into confusion again. She had to think without her body and the experience of the physical – to be one of pure energy, pure love. To distance herself from the injured body, the pain. She could feel her spirits rising yet again. Healing energy poured into her, through her and into Trinity.

The cycle continued, each lap stronger, more powerful, more energetic. Trinity started to heal even as Tabitha watched. Trinity grabbed the energy and used it herself. Intuitively, her body knew and understood what to do. Tabitha watched as torn muscles struggled to push out the bullet, struggled to stitch the muscles together, to fill the flesh behind it. It would take time, but Trinity had turned a corner. Trinity's earthly experience wasn't over yet. Shaky but gaining strength by the minute, Trinity stood up. And roared.

Fez screamed. "Holy shit."

Footsteps sounded behind him. Fez turned and Tabitha watched as his face became respectful. "Sorry bos—"

The boss stepped back with a smile and yelled, "Police, hands up."

Fez stared in confusion.

"Put the gun down and get your hands up." When Fess stood in shock, his hands automatically going up, the boss yelled, "Now!"

Fez's arms shot straight up.

The boss brought out a second gun and fired. Then fired his police issue gun sending a second popping sound echoing throughout the vast warehouse.

Stunned, Tabitha watched Fez collapse, a red stain spreading across his chest. The boss had just shot an unarmed man. *What just happened?*

Stay quiet. Stefan whispered. *The balance of power just shifted.*

Ya think, she murmured. She stared out of the cage at the boss. Casually dressed, he held a gun as if he was used to handling one. He walked over to Fez and said in a low voice, "Fucking idiot. Do you think I was going to let you ruin things for me? Hell, I wasn't even planning to pay you."

He looked around, then carefully placed the second gun in the downed man's hand, giving the appearance the man had been armed and dangerous. Then he called out behind him, "All clear."

***

Roman heard the call and came in through the back. He'd been peering through a grimy window and had seen the man go down. Until he walked closer, he hadn't seen a gun in the slain man's hand.

Then he saw the tiger and everything else went out of his mind. Jesus, she was big. Even hurt and in pain, she was a majestic animal. He walked closer to the cage slowly, trying not to set the animal off.

How could he tell if it was Tabitha?

"Tabitha?" he whispered.

The tiger turned those huge unblinking eyes on him. But there was no sign of Tabitha in them.

"Do you know this animal?" Carmichael asked.

"Maybe." Roman studied the tiger. "And maybe not." He motioned to the rest of the warehouse. "You should probably check to make sure no one else is in here."

Carmichael nodded. "Search is in progress. Although I doubt anyone is still here. I thought you were looking for a woman or something. And the tiger. But wasn't this op to find a woman?"

"Sorta." Roman walked around the tiger's cage, hoping the cop would take off and leave him alone to figure out the Tabitha-tiger thing.

He heard the other cops as they searched the area. Keeping his back to the tiger and a wary eye on the men, he called his brother on his cell phone.

"I'm pulling up outside," Ronin said. "Did you find her?"

"I think so. But there's a problem..."

Chapter 27

Tuesday late morning

Tabitha watched the events unfold around her. She hadn't been able to help too, by slipping a fine strand of energy out of the cage and down to Fez. He lay still, but there wasn't a massive pool of blood.

She'd never worked on a human. Hadn't planned on doing so either, but when the need was upon her, she'd found herself wondering what a guy like Fez would do with a second chance. Besides, he'd be a perfect informant against the cop that shot him.

Unable to help herself, she slipped another stroke of energy over his body. He wasn't dead and heat pumped off his chest. She slipped her energy into the injury and down into the pool of sluggish blood pumping from the torn veins and damaged muscle. The bullet had gone in high and had gotten lodged in the shoulder blade. Therapy was going to be a bitch.

Still, if she could, she'd see to it that he stayed alive long enough to make it there. He'd do jail time unless he could cut a deal. She lifted her gaze. And stopped.

Roman.

Yes. She was saved.

He stared at her. There was no recognition in his gaze. He narrowed his gaze as if trying to see inside Trinity.

Roman? Can you see me?

No answer. No sign he was aware of her in any way. Though Fez could see her, obviously Roman couldn't.

Roman walked up behind the cage and pulled out his phone.

Please let him be calling Ronin.

***

Ronin walked silently into the vast warehouse, his gaze quickly scanning the room. He headed for the cage at the far end and tried to avoid jostling Tabitha.

"Jesus, is she dead?" Carmichael said, standing in front of him, a complete look of shock on his face at the sight of him carrying the unconscious Tabitha. "What the hell happened, Ronin? What's wrong with her? And why is she here and not at the hospital?"

"You wouldn't believe it even if I could explain." Ronin said as he laid Tabitha down on the dirty floor parallel to the cage. He straightened and turned to stare into it. A lean, mean wild looking gray – or was that blue? – furred tiger stared at him, with haunting light-green eyes. Tabitha's eyes. "Jesus. Tabitha? Are you in there?"

"Hey, Ronin. Talk to me. What is going on?" Carmichael stood over Tabitha, a worried look on his face. "And what does this have to do with Tabitha Stoddard? She's hurt bad, man. Like, really bad."

No, she wasn't, but he wasn't going to be able to explain the problem to Carmichael. Not to mention it would put everyone at risk.

"Ronin?" Roman walked over, his worried gaze on Tabitha. "How's she doing, brother?"

"The same."

"The same as what?" demanded Carmichael.

"She's somehow connected to the tiger," Ronin said shortly. What was he supposed to say?

"Connected?" Suspicion threaded through Carmichael's voice. "How?"

"Yeah, it's a little hard to explain. But she sees what it sees. Hears what it hears and is in fact," he took a deep breath, knowing how bizarre this was going to sound, "inside its body. I don't get it myself."

"What? That's crazy." Carmichael's face was a study of shock, disbelief and mockery. Slowly, uneasy suspicion filtered across his face.

"And yet it's the truth." Ronin he didn't know what to do with her now. "Any time, Tabitha. If there is something else you need from me, now would be a good time to let me know."

"Did Stefan tell you what to do when you got her here?" Roman asked, standing beside his brother. "These are hardly sterile conditions."

"No." Ronin glanced up. "As always, his orders come with no explanation and of course he's not here now."

Yes, I am. And I'm monitoring the situation.

"Monitoring?"

Roman looked at him, one eyebrow raised. Ronin rolled his eyes and mouthed Stefan.

His brother gave him a hard half laugh. He knew that weird sensation of speaking out loud in answer to a conversation in his head.

"So now what?" Ronin said quietly.

The energy is...off. As if she's waiting for someone to do something.

"Hey, Ronin, you're really starting to scare me," Carmichael said. "You're talking about crazy stuff here. It's like you're in your own world and talking to no one."

"We found this guy skulking around outside." A cop pushed another man in front of them. Ronin gave him a quick perusal and recognized him as the man who'd exchanged a phone number for his cup of coffee. So he'd been involved in this mess, too.

The cop nudged the informant another few steps forward, saying. "Says his name is Keeper. And he doesn't know anything. Of course."

Typical.

Ronin turned his attention back to Carmichael.

"Actually, I am talking to someone you just can't hear." Ronin understood. He walked over to the tiger's cage and studied the big padlock. He could pick the lock if needed.

Tabitha says the key is in Fez's pocket, Stefan murmured.

Ronin walked over to the downed man and checked for a pulse. "Roman, make sure the paramedics are coming for this guy. He's still alive."

"Alive?" Carmichael spoke up. "No way. I checked."

"Well, he is." Ronin rummaged for the key and found it in Fez's right pocket. He straightened and held the key up. "Glad to see this."

But Carmichael was staring from Fez to Ronin, a calculating look on his face. Then he said, "You know Fez?"

Ronin spun on Carmichael. "Do you?"

Red washed over Carmichael's face. He blustered, "Not really."

Ronin glared at his long-time friend and co-worker while he asked his brother,. "Roman, did you make the call?"

Silence.

Ronin turned to see a stranger had somehow entered from the warehouse behind the tiger's cage, and was now holding a gun on his brother. Anger lined Roman's face as he said, "Sorry, Ronin."

Shit.

Ronin took a deep breath and said, "Who the hell are you?"

"The owner of the tiger."

Ronin felt Carmichael start, as if that was news to him.

"Really? And you of course have papers saying so."

"I can produce any and all paper anyone wants," the stranger said smoothly. "Of course."

"And who did you buy the tiger from?"

The man laughed. "From the asshole holding a gun on you, of course."

Ronin turned slowly to see Carmichael standing behind him, with his police-issue revolver pointed at Ronin's chest. He wondered where Geoff and the other cop were. They should be holding Keeper in place behind him somewhere, but...

He stared into the eyes of the betrayer. "Black market animals? Where's the money in that?"

Carmichael shrugged. "I 'procure' things for people. This was the first time for a tiger." He smiled at Ronin. "And I wouldn't worry about the other two helping you out. Isn't that right, Geoff."

Geoff laughed. "True enough."

Ronin slid a gaze to his younger friend, to find him holding a gun on Keeper and the poor cop. "Both of you? You're both in on it?"

"I tried to warn you," Geoff said. "With the damn pictures."

"How is that warning me? The pictures were of Jacob not Carmichael?" Ronin couldn't believe what he was seeing. His mind raced for ideas.

And fast, please, whispered Stefan.

"Yeah, they used to be partners, remember."

Then Ronin got it. "You were hoping to have Jacob blamed if something went wrong."

"Something always goes wrong." Geoff called back, a humorous note in his voice. "Figured I'd start laying the groundwork."

"Kid's got balls," said Carmichael. "We had a good thing going for a few years. Then we heard about Jacob and some hush-hush undercover stuff. Figured we'd need to spread the suspicion a little." He chuckled. "He was a perfect patsy. Besides, he has been in trouble with Internal Affairs a couple of times. Figured they'd look real hard this time."

Carmichael glared at the stranger. "And it's not your tiger, it's mine. That deal is off. I gave you your money back."

The stranger laughed. "Like hell she's yours. You are nobody. Just one more bad cop. Big deal. There are dozens just like you. But this tiger..." He waved the gun in Trinity's direction. "I shot her." He laughed. "But look at her now. She's not only alive and well, she's stronger than ever."

The stranger's too shiny smile made Ronin stiffen. He'd seen many similar men. Guys without a conscience. Ones that would do whatever they wanted with no concern for others.

Then the stranger added, "And that makes her worth a bloody fortune. Add in the cub..."

Not good.

"Who are you?" Ronin took a few cautious steps toward Tabitha, who lay as still as ever on the floor.

The man chuckled and then laughed. "Oh, that's rich. Winston Colby, at your service. You're trying to protect someone I'm trying to destroy. An excellent parting shot to someone else who died a week ago. But now...now everything's perfect."

Roman frowned at Ronin, a warning look his eyes.

Colby? This was the black market dealer cops had been trying to bring down for years? Ronin was confused. "I'm sorry, *what*? I'm trying to protect the tiger and Tabitha here. Who are you trying to destroy – Carmichael?"

"Not him," he corrected. "Her."

Ronin struggled to understand. "Tabitha? What has she done to you?"

"Everything. Absolutely everything." His face twisted in hate, which made Ronin take several more quick steps to stand over her protectively.

The stranger laughed. "That won't help her. I'll tell you why – she's taken everything that should have been mine. My animals, my reserve, my house...my fucking place!" He glared at Tabitha, fury shining in his gaze. "My grandfather started that place with her grandfather. They were brothers, partners. Until her grandfather cheated mine out of his half."

✳✳✳

Tabitha wanted to hide. There was no where to go. Her grandfather and his brother started Exotic? She had a cousin? *This man?*

She paced the cage, the pain of betrayal firing up a horrible inner knowing that there had to be something wrong with her for all the men in her life to treat her so badly.

Trinity roared.

Shit. She shuddered, desperate to shut down the emotional pain shattering her world...before it affected Trinity and made everything worse.

Her cousin continued to speak. "My grandfather left me a letter telling me all about his cheating bastard of a brother and how he'd tricked him out of his portion of the property. My dad told me to forget about it, that there was nothing we could do." Winston laughed. "But he was wrong." He motioned the gun toward Tabitha. "I kept tabs on the family, especially Tabitha. Watched her grow up with animals that should have been mine. I sent her grandfather letters every year once I was established. Telling him about the animals I dealt in. The money I was making. And that one day...one day I'd get what was coming to me."

He shook his head. "Then the bastard up and died. I already had this tiger on order once I heard about its existence. I was going to show the old bastard what I had."

He smiled. "But this... This is even better."

Tabitha listened in horror.

✳✳✳

"Why the hell is she crying?" Winston snapped motioning to Tabitha's still form.

Ronin looked down. Sure enough, there were tears streaming down Tabitha's face. No change in her expression but for the eerie tears sliding slowly and steadily down her pale skin.

"She's crying because she didn't know. About her grandfather's actions. About her uncle or you. About the hate, distrust and fear that has tainted her family." Ronin lifted his head to stare at Winston.

Winston stared at him, his gaze narrow with suspicion, emotions flickering rapidly across his face. "How do you know that?"

Ronin kept his gaze and voice steady as he answered. "Because I know her."

That made Winston laugh. "Too damn bad. See, I heard you earlier. I figure I can have the tiger and I can have her captive inside. And isn't that some freaky shit? Is she psychic? Because that's just going to piss me off more."

"Well, if she is, then maybe you are, too," Ronin suggested. Stefan had said the same thing to him about Roman.

"Then having her as my pet tiger while I figure it out is even better." Winston peered into the cage where the tiger paced back and forth, its big head moving from side to side. "She's really in there, huh?"

He laughed, turned and shot Tabitha in the back leg.

Trinity roared, her back leg going out from under her. She twisted and snarled.

Carmichael gasped. "Holy shit. Is that for real?" He took a step closer to Tabitha staring in shock at the new wound on Tabitha's leg.

At the same time Tabitha began to bleed, blood also slipped down Trinity's fur and an eerie sound came from the back of her throat. She locked her gaze on Winston as if waiting for her chance.

Ronin dropped to Tabitha's side and clamped his hand over her wound. "You'd shoot your cousin while she's helpless? What kind of man are you?"

And immediately realized his mistake.

Winston went berserk. "I'm the man in control. And I'll fucking shoot her as many times as I want to." He fired again and the shot ricocheted off the cage. Tabitha's body jerked as the bullet grazed her arm this time. Trinity's front leg buckled. And she howled, the sounds sending ice down Ronin's back.

A gun went off, but it whistled past Ronin from behind and hit Tabitha's cousin in the shoulder. Winston screamed.

Everyone scattered for cover.

Shit. The game shifted – again. Who had fired that shot?

"Roman." He threw the key to his brother while shots fired behind them. Ronin grabbed Tabitha's arms and dragged her back around the edge of the cage to safety.

He searched the warehouse, but there was no sign of anyone else. Ronin watched as his brother raced to the cage and undid the padlock. He pulled open the bars and backed away.

Trinity jumped awkwardly. She was in obvious pain but did her best to hobble over to Tabitha.

He tried to keep Tabitha covered with his body, his own gun out in case. This was critical timing. He'd seen Winston slip around the corner of another cage. Who knew where the others had disappeared to? The poor unsuspecting cop that had been caught up in this trouble would have called for backup if he could.

But who'd shot Winston? And why did he have such poor aim?

Winston screamed from the far side, hidden in the darkness. "Stop or I'll shoot her. I'll kill my fucking cousin *and* the damn tiger. See if I care if they both die."

"Damn it, Roman," Ronin whispered. "Who shot Winston?"

"I didn't see." Roman stared down at Tabitha. "She's really connected to the tiger, isn't she?"

"Yes. And I don't know how to separate them. At this rate, she could die no matter what we do."

"What the hell?" Roman backed up slightly.

Trinity was glowing. Blue lights surrounded her large body giving her an eerie shimmering look.

"Holy crap." Geoff approached Tabitha slowly. "This is too damn bizarre."

Hearing something, Geoff spun and crouched, his gun pointed out in front of him. A gun fired. Geoff dropped in place, screaming and holding his knee to his chest.

Winston shouted, "Shut the hell up or I'll put one through your heart."

Instantly, Geoff's voice dropped to agonized sobs.

The sound of yet a different gun cocking resounded in the huge warehouse. And a strange voice said, hard, determined and very cold, "You won't be shooting anyone again. Now get those hands up."

Ronin peered out from behind the cage. "Holy shit."

Keeper, the informant he'd met, was pushing Winston toward Ronin. Keeper called out, "Ronin, you there?"

And then Ronin understood. "Hey, Jacob. Nice disguise."

Carmichael stepped out from behind the tiger's cage and walked forward, a gun in his hand. "Keeper?"

New cops poured into the place, all with guns trained on Carmichael and Winston. Geoff continued to sob from the floor in the middle.

"Drop the gun Carmichael," Keeper said. "This is over."

"What the heck?" cried out a voice from the crowd. "What is happening to *her?*"

Everyone turned to watch the tiger. Trinity stood, weak and bleeding, with a deep vibrating blue glow surrounded her. A clearly visible, luminescent light surrounded her for all to see.

And her gaze was on Carmichael. That same unholy howl from deep in the back of her throat filled the warehouse.

Carmichael backed up, his gun pointed at her. In a trembling voice, he screamed, "What the hell is she?"

"It doesn't matter to you," Keeper said, his voice hard. "Now drop the fucking gun."

Carmichael squeezed the trigger.

Trinity's body jerked once, then twice.

In a split second, Keeper dropped Carmichael where he stood.

Ronin raced forward, arms out protectively, screaming at the other cops, "Don't shoot the tiger."

Not that it mattered, Trinity had crumpled to the ground. Cops quickly raced to secure Winston.

"Jesus, Ronin," Jacob asked. "What the hell is going on here?"

Ronin shushed everyone and walked quietly, slowly toward Trinity. She lay on her side, howls and whimpers sliding out of her mouth.

"Take it easy, Trinity," Ronin soothed. "Please calm down."

Trinity struggled to her feet, her head hanging. Then gathering her strength, but obviously hurt, she staggered backwards a step before limping to Tabitha's side. Ronin whispered, "Oh Jesus. Please, sweetheart, stop. Let us help you."

Trinity collapsed beside Tabitha. Close but not touching.

Someone in the growing crowd around them asked in a prayer-like whisper, "What is happening to the woman?"

In a bizarre movement, Trinity's spirit shifted to appear to be Tabitha's spirit. Then it switched to have Tabitha's spirit change places to be Trinity's spirit. Then they switched places.

And again.

Then again.

As if some kind of electrical short was happening. The two bright-blue lights kept switching from one body to the other.

"Christ." Whispers, swear words and prayers erupted from the observers. No one had ever seen anything like this. Not even Ronin.

"Jesus," Ronin cried out. "Stop this. Stefan, help."

You're the one that's going to have to help.

"Me?"

You. You have to reach out. One hand to Tabitha and the other to Trinity. You need to ground them both. The problem is Tabitha uses her animals as a ground. Since she's connected to Trinity, Trinity used her as a ground as well. It caused an electrical loop that has shorted. You have to complete the circuit.

Ronin reached out a hand to both Tabitha and Trinity.

Roman pulled his brother's hand back. "Are you sure?" he asked urgently. "This looks incredibly dangerous."

"No choice." And there wasn't. He had to do this. Ronin closed his eyes. Reached out both hands again and....

...closed the circle.

Instantly, a thousand pins and needles pricked his hands. As if an electrical current was hitting him – but not traveling through him.

In his mind, he said, *Tabitha, I have no idea what to do but if you do, please use me as you need to. I don't want to see you in pain any longer. Let me help you.*

No, I don't want to bring you into this, Tabitha cried. *You won't survive. Let me go.*

No, Ronin whispered, *I don't accept that.*

He refused to back off. Closing his eyes, he realized there was one other element he might be able to bring into play. *Mr. Boots. If you're there. If there is anything you can do. If there is anything I can do. Please help.* Then he sent his plea out wider. *If there is any other animal out there that can help...please... Tabitha needs us.*

And with that plea, a weird buzz filled his mind. His hands tingled, his spine straightened and he threw his head back as energy surged through him. And the last of his doubts crumbled. Acceptance that there might be something to Mr. Boots followed. And that there might be something to Stefan's words about his fears, about Tabitha's skills and this crazy-ass mess they were in right now.

He took a deep breath, desperate to save Tabitha. And as he thought it, his energy went outwards to heal her. Loving energy poured from his heart into hers.

And suddenly it was as if he'd stepped into a new world. A world of no sound. A world with no visuals. A foggy world. And he moved toward a voice calling his name. "Ronin?"

He turned. There Tabitha was, standing in front of him, a huge loving smile on her face.

"You're dead?" he asked starkly, his heart ready to cry.

"No," she rushed to reassure him, "I'm not. Not at all. Look." She pointed to the side, and there was Trinity resting peacefully on her back on the ground. Except there was no ground.

"She's okay now?"

"We're in the ethers. My favorite place to retreat."

Ethers? Him? No way. Still, Ronin looked around at the bizarre world. "We're not dead?"

"No." She laughed, her face beaming with love. "We're fine."

"How do we go back?"

"As soon as you think about it, we'll go back. But there's someone who wants to say good-bye." Her voice softened. "It's past his time to go."

He looked at her in surprise. "Who?"

And then he held a wiggling black and white tuxedo cat in his arms. *Mr. Boots.* Damn. He buried his face in his beloved cat's fur, tears coming to his eyes. Christ, he felt eight years old again, his heart stuffed full of emotion. "Does he *have* to leave?"

"No. He might stay if you can see and recognize him. He's been there for you all these years. I believe he's ready to go, but what he does now..." She shrugged.

A familiar voice cut in. "Hey, Ronin, you in there?"

And pain slapped across his face hard.

"That means it's time to leave." Tabitha laughed.

Then she disappeared. He blinked then blinked again to find Roman in front of him, his hand ready to slap him again.

"I'm here," Ronin croaked.

"Good thing," his brother said worriedly. "You've been out a long time."

Ronin shook his head, struggling to shake off the fog. He twisted to look at Tabitha. To find her still lying in front of him – only this time her eyes open and she smiled at him.

Oh thank God. Swallowing hard, he held out his hand and said, "Hey."

"Hey yourself." She reached up a hand to clasp his. "Thanks."

He snorted. "I didn't do anything."

She smiled and said with a knowing look, "Trinity and I both thank you."

That's when he realized Trinity lay beside him, her big head on his legs...alive. "Whoa."

Tabitha laughed. "Yeah, welcome to my world."

"Jesus."

Roman laughed. "Well, whatever you did brother, it worked."

Tabitha sat up. "That it did."

Chapter 28

One month later

Tabitha opened the cage wall and let both Tango and TJ into the living room. TJ tripped over his big paws in his eagerness to get to Tango. Tripod dropped his big nose and sniffed the cub hard enough to tumble TJ over on his back and keep him beside his mother. The cub yelped several times as Tripod licked his belly before letting him back on his feet.

The cub, TJ, turned around and waddled to where Trinity was resting. She'd survived against all odds, at least for a little longer. But as Tabitha had said to Ronin earlier that day, "Where there's a will, there's a way. And there is not always an explanation for miracles. You have to live with a little faith."

Well, Ronin figured he lived with a lot of faith these days. He watched little TJ get sidetracked by Ronin's scent and tumbled over toward him. His fat roly-poly body was shiny with a healthy gloss. And damn if there wasn't a slight slate gray-blue tinge to his fur.

Ronin scratched the cub under the chin then sent him back to his mother.

Trinity's engine started to rumble before he got halfway. He yelped at her then charged and barreled into her front paws. She grabbed him, flipped him over and proceeded to clean him.

"It all looks so normal, doesn't it?" he asked Tabitha as she walked back toward him. "Even Tango is okay with the new additions."

"Tango has taken to the two newcomers better than anyone could have expected," she murmured. "Then again, I explained to him what we've all been through."

Ronin grinned. "Like he'd understand that."

"You might be surprised."

He snorted. "I don't even understand everything, so how could he?"

"It's likely we'll never understand all the details," she said softly. "And you know something? I think I'm okay with that."

"Considering you gained and lost a cousin on the same day—"

"And learned more than I wanted to about my grandfather."

He sighed. "I didn't do well with betrayal either." In fact, the department was completing a full investigation to see what else Carmichael and Geoff had been involved in. Both were in jail and would do many years. Fez had survived and was yapping pretty loud. The DA's office had cut him a deal to roll over on the others and he'd do his time back East. He'd promised to be a different man from now on. Something about having seen a vision. The DA thought he was nuts, but as long as he held up in cross-examination during the trial, they didn't care.

Ronin understood that Fez's vision had been seeing Tabitha inside Trinity. If Tabitha had helped yet another person to have a better life, then it was all good.

Tabitha wrapped her arms around his waist and looked up at him, a loving smile on her face. He was never going to get tired of that look. He bent down and dropped a kiss on her forehead.

"And through it all, I found you," she said.

"I was always here," he protested. "Always."

"But a little reserved, a little on the sidelines. Interested but not involved."

"Yeah, that sure changed." He grinned. "I'm all in now." He'd even seen vestiges of other cats that had lived here before. Tobias for one. Ronin now realized Tobias's ghost was one of the energies he'd sensed early on, adding to his haunted feeling.

"And that's the way it should be."

"You're sure Mr. Boots is gone, huh?" He asked yet again.

Tabitha was healing, Trinity was healing, and he himself was healing. But damn it, it bugged the hell out of him that Mr. Boots had been there – waiting for him all his life – and he hadn't known. Now that he understood that, he thought it was unfair Mr. Boots was gone.

And then he heard it.

A tiny, faint meow.

Tabitha raised her head from his shoulder and laughed delightedly. She whispered in his mind, *Remember, energy never disappears. It only changes form.*

There on the floor was a black and white ball of energy beside TJ. Beside, around, over and on top of the sleeping cub.

Then the meow came again. The black and white energy shifted, a long ghostly paw stretching out over the cub before sinking back down to curl up and sleep.

"Mr. Boots!"

Epilogue

Several weeks later, a laughing group entered the large theater. Tonight was a special session with the Portland Symphony Orchestra featuring a series of visiting musicians. Stefan held the door open for several women, all special friends in his life. Dr. Maddy dropped a kiss on his cheek as she entered with her partner, Drew, at her side. This was the first time he'd had so many of his friends in one place.

Shay linked arms with Stefan. He smiled down at her. Stefan had always been reclusive, and he still had trouble understanding how his life had suddenly become so full.

You love it. Tabitha stood in front of him, and Ronin, tall and strong, stood relaxed at her side.

Ha, says who?

Tabitha laughed, mysteriously. *Your time will come.*

He rolled his eyes and followed the group to their seats.

The lights dimmed almost immediately. He settled back to listen.

He needed this relaxing time. They all did. There'd been so much pain and panic in all of their lives, it was important to take time to enjoy the good things about life when they could. And tonight was one of those times.

Stefan didn't have a musical bone in his body. But he adored listening to all different kinds of music. It called to him in the same way colors sent him running to his canvases. The urge to create surged through him as the notes swelled and filled the theatre. The house was packed tonight, and he could easily see why.

He closed his eyes and leaned his head back, letting the powerful notes roll over him.

When the song changed, he didn't bother opening his eyes; he just waited, suspended in joy and peace.

The delicate, haunting sounds of a harp filled the air, rolling in waves across his skin. Goosebumps rose and he shivered both in joy and fascination. Who could create such beauty? Who had such power, such talent?

Beside him, he heard Tabitha gasp. Then Ronin made a comment, followed by several others who murmured in delight.

Stefan frowned, but he opened his eyes to see what they were reacting to.

Colors floated on the ethers, wide lazy bands and narrow bouncing waves. One color, then several other colors danced and played throughout the theater. Filling it with life, with joy, with happiness.

He leaned forward, amazed. It was stunning.

Dr. Maddy murmured, "It's the harpist."

Stefan followed the ribbons of colored energy back to the source and turned to study the musician. And froze. He didn't need to see the details of her face. He knew them. He didn't need to see her energy; he knew it well.

It was *her*. His beloved. The other half of himself.

And a perfect stranger.

Shay, ever perceptive, said, "I believe Tabitha mentioned that now it was *your* time – your time for love."

About the author:

Dale Mayer is a prolific multi-published writer. She's best known for her Psychic Visions series. Besides her romantic suspense/thrillers, Dale also writes paranormal romance and crossover young adult books in several different genres. To go with her fiction, she also writes nonfiction in many different fields with books available on resume writing, companion gardening and the US mortgage system. She has recently published her Career Essentials Series. All her books are available in digital and print formats.

Published Young Adult books:

Vampire in Denial

Vampire in Distress

Vampire in Design

Vampire in Deceit

Vampire in Defiance

Dangerous Designs

Deadly Design

Deceptive Designs (fall 2013)

In Cassie's Corner

Gem Stone Mystery

Published Adult Books:

By Death Series

Touched by Death

Haunted by Death (fall 2013)

Psychic Vision Series:
Tuesday's Child

Hide'n Go Seek,

Maddy's Floor

Garden of Sorrow

Knock, knock…

Rare Find

Book 7 (tentatively titled The Wish List – Stefan's story)

Bound and Determined…to find love series
Unbound

Undone (winter 2013)

Other Adult novellas/short stories:
It's a Dog's Life

Riana's Revenge

Sian's Solution – part of Family Blood Ties

Non Fiction books
Career Essentials: The Resume

Career Essentials: The Cover Letter

Career Essentials: The Interview

Connect with Dale Mayer Online:
Dale's Website – www.dalemayer.com

Twitter – http://twitter.com/#!/DaleMayer

Facebook – http://www.facebook.com/DaleMayer.author

Made in the USA
Middletown, DE
17 August 2015